TEGAN AND THE FLAG OF FIRINN

THE SECOND BOOK IN THE CHRONICLES OF FELLNORE SERIES

JENNIFER WHIDDON

For Maddie:

I love you to the moon and back.

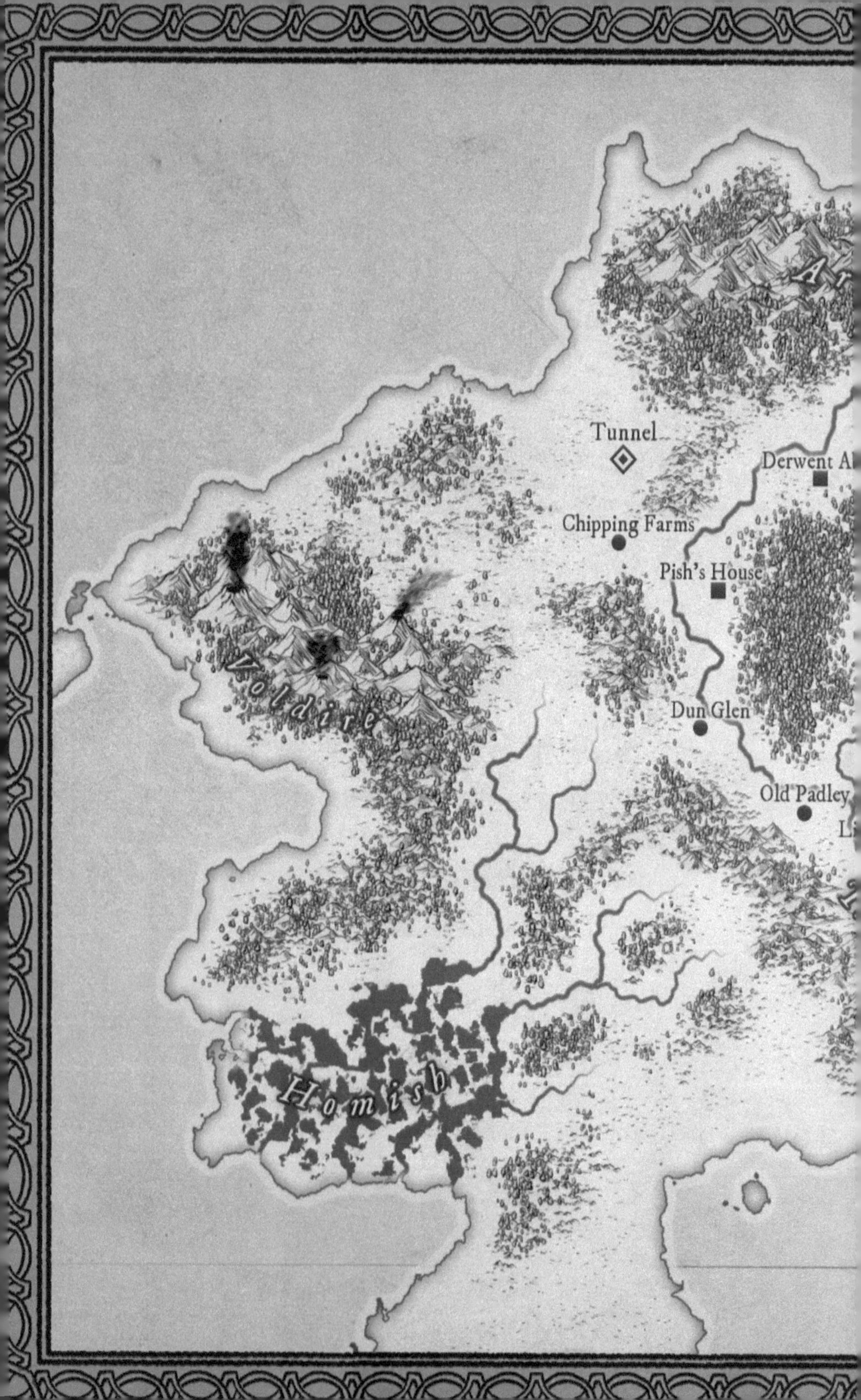

Tunnel
Derwent A...
Chipping Farms
Pish's House
Dun Glen
Old Padley
L...
Voldire
Homish
A...

Swynton
Mountains
Tunnel
Cave of Erasmus
Heads
Haven
's Landing
ver
FELLNORE

Derwent Abbey

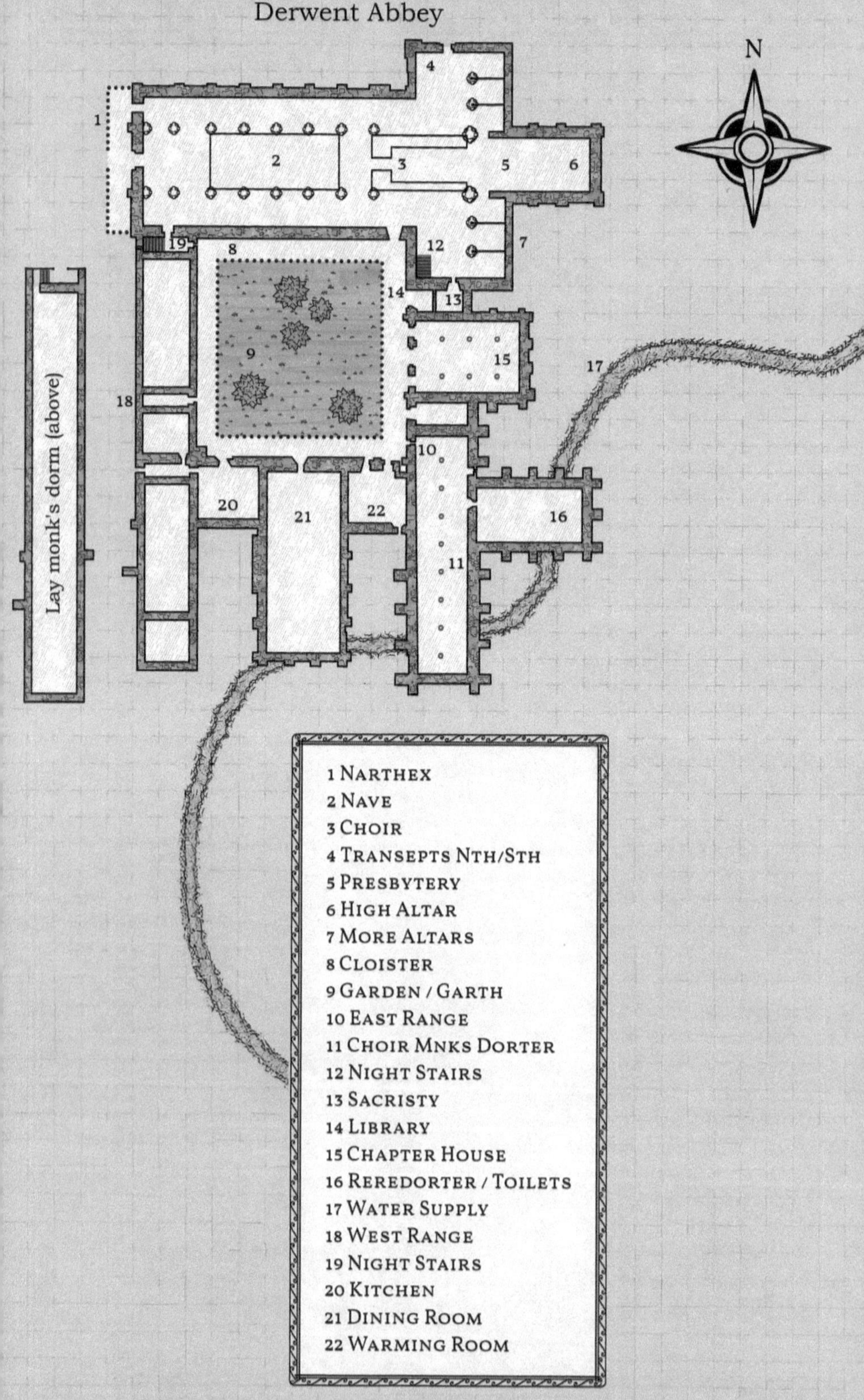

Character Index

- Tegan – main character, a sombel (cat-like creature)

- Beckett – Tegan's childhood friend, also a sombel

- Kenna –a fox scout and friend to Tegan and Beckett

- Bowen Whitethorne – Kenna's father and accountant under Edwin

- Rana – frog leader from Oren Plum

- Father Ennis – abbot of Derwent Abbey

- John Henry – monk at Derwent Abbey

- Edwin – former leader of Chipping Farms

- Wadsworth Bridger – former co-worker of Bowen

- Reginald – current leader of Chipping Farms who overthrew Edwin for control

- Adler – Kenna's cousin and Reginald's bodyguard

- Bin – Reginald's bodyguard

- Cormac – leader of the Moin clan of fairies

- Cu Sith – fairy hound

- Rolf – captain of Reginald's soldiers, also Adler's acquaintance

- Lucien – one of Reginald's soldiers

- Sabreena – raccoon tinker that lives in a caravan

CONTENTS

Introduction   1

Chapter 1   5

Chapter 2   15

Chapter 3   23

Chapter 4   32

Chapter 5   42

Chapter 6   50

Chapter 7   58

Chapter 8   68

Chapter 9   80

Chapter 10   91

Chapter 11   99

Chapter 12   106

Chapter 13   118

Chapter 14   128

Chapter 15	138
Chapter 16	146
Chapter 17	153
Chapter 18	162
Chapter 19	171
Chapter 20	181
Chapter 21	190
Chapter 22	198
Chapter 23	209
Chapter 24	217
Chapter 25	224
Chapter 26	233
Chapter 27	242
Chapter 28	251
Chapter 29	259
Chapter 30	269
Chapter 31	278
Chapter 32	288
Chapter 33	296
Epilogue	304

INTRODUCTION

To my lovely readers, thank you so much for supporting my endeavor by reading this story. The idea came about after a last-minute trip to Hobbiton in New Zealand in 2022 with my daughter. I never thought I'd actually finish writing the first book much less complete a second one, but here we are! And I'm thrilled to hear your comments on this story, "Tegan and the Flag of Firinn."

While this book is the second in the Chronicles of Fellnore series, it is not a requirement to read the first story, "Tegan and the Green Moonstone." However, the first book does provide depth of characters and an understanding of Tegan's world. I highly recommend submersing yourself in that adventure before settling in to enjoy this one.

If you've read the first story, thank you! Keep reading for the summary below so you can dive right into this book. If you haven't read the first story, spoilers ahead! Continue at your own risk.

Tegan, Beckett, and Kenna have just fought the black rats of Voldire and emerged victorious. In the process of delivering the terms to those rats for violating a peace treaty, Tegan wielded her sword with the green moonstone and rescued her uncle from capture as well as defeated the rat leader. The jubilant but weary travelers eventually make their way back to their little village of Haven. And this is where the second story picks up.

All my thanks to you, dear reader! Please sit back and enjoy the second adventure.

Jennifer

My daughter, Maddie, and me in Hobbiton, New Zealand. (July 25, 2022)

Chapter I

"A message arrived for you this morning," Sammy Fourpaws said to the petite fox standing across the bar from him.

Kenna, the little fox with dark brown fur, reached out her black paw and took the letter from the pub owner. She turned it over in her paws and cautiously unfolded the paper.

"Who is it from?" Tegan, a sombel or cat-like creature, asked. She stood next to the fox wearing a green, worn-out cloak over her shiny, brown fur and fiery red tail. Tegan glanced at Sammy who stood analyzing the fox visitor from top to bottom.

Here, in the village of Haven, most of the residents consisted of sombels, or cat-like creatures. Not only were sombels suspicious of foxes, but they hadn't seen one in their town for ages. So Kenna was a novel sight.

Sammy Fourpaws, the rotund pub owner, turned his attention to Tegan, "Congratulations on your victory in Old Padley. Your father must be very proud."

"Thanks, but I had plenty of help, you know," Tegan responded with a smile. She had only been away for a week; a quest to deliver a document to the leader of their enemy, the black rats of Voldire. And with a few friends and allies, Tegan succeeded in not only the delivery but also played a part in stopping the rats from expanding into her land. However, the struggles and hardships over the past few days had taken their toll on her. And while Tegan was relieved to be back home, breaking news of Kenna's missing father didn't sit well with her at all.

Kenna held one paw over her mouth as she read the letter.

"What is it?" Tegan asked and pulled her friend to the side of the pub for a little privacy. Kenna handed her the letter and she read:

> *Time to close your eyes and pray*
> *Save your tears for another day*
> *If I'm not here, please rest and know*
> *I'm never far away from home.*

Tegan looked up confused from the paper and asked Kenna, "What does this mean?"

Kenna was visibly upset, "It's from my father!" She walked a few steps away and then turned around, "He's somewhere close. I can feel it!"

Tegan flipped the paper to view the back. There was nothing else written down but Kenna's name and the message. "But how did he—"

"There's no time to waste," Kenna interrupted. She ran back to the bar and asked Sammy, "Who delivered this message, sir?"

Sammy wiped the countertop with a wet cloth, "Mr. Robinson dropped it off early this morning. Maybe an hour ago?"

"Who?" Kenna asked.

"The raven," Sammy replied. "The couriers bring messages here first thing in the morning."

Tegan trailed behind her fox friend, back to the counter where Sammy sat down and stacked drinking cups.

"Oh, and this was left here for you," Sammy reached a shelf beside him and handed Tegan a small soft package. No note, just a white linen wrap tied neatly with a blue ribbon. She nodded and took the bundle under one arm and grabbed Kenna with the other paw. They stepped through the pub door to the road out front so they could talk without an audience.

Once outside, the two sat on a log bench in the mid-morning sunlight. Soaking in the warmth on their fur helped these friends clear their minds of the early morning haze.

"Tell me, Kenna," Tegan started. "How do you know this message is from your father?"

"Oh," the little fox sighed dramatically, "It's part of a lullaby that my father used to sing to me when I was younger." She closed her big brown eyes and hummed a simple melody. "The song is *Little Red Bird*. We always sang the last lines together."

Tegan processed that information in silence. *Could it really be a message from Kenna's father? How did he know she would be here in Haven? Is there a possibility that someone is acting on his behalf; baiting her, perhaps?*

"Why did he write this lullaby instead of a more intimate message?" Tegan questioned out loud.

"This song has always been something like a secret code between our family members.....a way to confirm that we were safe. We used it during Reginald's coup to let each other know we were out of harm's way."

"Reginald's takeover of the Redlan fox clan," Tegan finished. "Is there a chance that someone outside of your family is familiar with this code? Anyone that might know why or where your father disappeared to?"

"I doubt it," Kenna responded. "Reginald is behind this; I'm sure of it."

"Tell me more about your father. How did he serve the previous leader (Edwin) before Reginald overthrew him?" Tegan asked.

"He was an accountant and served on the council Edwin formed to negotiate trading in distant lands. Because of his involvement in these negotiations, my father also kept up with the business accounts—past, present, and pending," Kenna stated. "That's all I know." She looked down at the paper again and breathed deep.

"If Reginald is indeed behind this, then we need to know more about what records your father kept. Is there anyone we can talk to that has more information? Maybe someone he worked with that is willing to meet with us?"

Kenna fixed her gaze on the mountains in the distance and said dryly, "I think I know who we can contact. He should know something or at least point us in the right direction."

"Where does he live?" Tegan asked.

"In a village near the river," Kenna turned her eyes back to Tegan. "Not far from here." She smiled and watched as Tegan's fingers played with the blue string on the wrapped bundle in her lap. "How rude of me!" she said excitedly. "What do you have there?"

Tegan held the package and examined it, "I'm not sure, there isn't a note attached to it." She flipped it over and then untied the ribbon. As the white linen opened up, Tegan noticed a dark green garment unfolding in the cloth wrapping. She held it up with her paws to get a good look. It was a gorgeous, hooded cloak with a small clasp on the front. Kenna and Tegan looked at each other with wide eyes.

"It's so beautiful!" Kenna exclaimed. Tegan nodded in amazement.

A piece of white cloth fell to the ground and Tegan picked it up. "There's a message on this," she said excitedly and read it out loud:

"From the pixie clan to Tegan:
We are grateful to you for a job well done.
In your debt, King Fallon."

"There's something on the back too," Kenna indicated with her paw.

Tegan flipped the cloth over and read:

"Please enjoy this handmade cloak
sewn from sioda silk.
I'm told you admired this in the market
when you first visited us."

The sombel pulled off her old cloak and slipped into the newly gifted one. The fabric felt like clouds as she rubbed her paws across the elegant garment. The dark green cloak was simply beautiful, and it fit like a glove! She couldn't wait to go home and show her ma and papa.

"Come on," Tegan said to the fox. "Let's go see what my parents think about this."

"Your cloak?" Kenna asked.

"Yes, and your message."

A brown fox with silvery whiskers and grayish paws stood at the edge of a small, murky pond. He adjusted his glasses and surveyed the area nervously around him. He was alone. Tucked under his right arm was a messenger bag closed tightly around its bulging contents. The fox stepped closer to the water's edge and poked at a lily pad floating on the surface. The waxy leaf bobbled a little on the water but maintained its sturdiness.

The older fox hopped precariously onto the pad, balancing his other leg and bag at the same time. The leaf dipped a bit and the cold pond water chilled his left foot. After steadying himself, the fox stepped onto another leaf with the same caution as before. Now he stood in front of a pink blossom centered between two other pads. He swung his bag around and jumped into the blossom, encircling himself with the soft petals over his body. As he sat camouflaged in the flower, he lowered his head to see out between the thickest of the petals. He held his breath and hoped he was fully hidden from the ones following him.

Then the older fox heard rustling in the grass near the edge of the pond. He bit his lip.

"Bowen!" one voice called out. "Bowen! Come out and give yourself up."

The fox trembled amongst the petals. *Can they see me?* He cowered in the flower bloom.

"Where are you?" another voice echoed. This one sounded deeper.

"Over there!" the first voice responded to his companion.

The fox closed his eyes and kept very still. If those scouts found him, they would force him back to the village; back to face the leader and he couldn't do that. Not now. He opened one eye to check on the scouts, but instead, noticed something on the lily pad next to him. He parted a few petals to get a better look and saw its sides moving in and out. It wasn't a scout...it was a giant frog.

The brown and black amphibian encompassed most of the pad and set its intimidating eyes on the smaller fox. The frog's tongue flicked out and snapped one of the pink petals that the fox was hiding behind. Then another flick, and another one. He put his paws over his head and laid down. *To be eaten or to be captured...which will it be?*

The scouts came closer to the pond and threw pebbles and stones at the frog. They laughed as the frog jumped from one lily pad to another to escape the stone assault. After a series of leaps from pad to log to leaf, the frog's leg became entangled in a water vine and it couldn't move anymore. The amphibian pulled and pulled, but the leg was stuck. It was useless. And just like that, the scouts immediately lost interest in their entertainment and walked on.

Bowen, the fox, waited in silence before poking his head above the petals for a view. On one side, he saw the struggling frog desperately trying to free itself of the vine. The water puddled around the amphibian as the skinny leg moved back and forth, creating ripples along the surface. On the other side where the scouts had been, the area was clear as the scouts had moved on. And hopefully, for good.

Turning his attention back to the frog, he wondered if he should help the amphibian get its leg free. *Or maybe leave it there since it tried to eat me.....?!* Bowen struggled with his conscious as he tiptoed over a few more lily pads. Once he neared the pond's edge, he could hear the frog croaking, a call to other frogs for help. A shiver ran down Bowen's back.

Instead of fleeing, he turned around and approached the frog from the side. The frog immediately whipped its head around and stared down the fox. Bowen held up his paws in surrender and said, "Whoa! I'm here to help." He pointed to the frog's leg. The frog let out a long *ribbet* sound and thrashed with its leg. Water soaked the fox, but he was determined to do what was right...and safest for himself. Facing one frog was scary, but if more showed up, he would be in serious danger!

Once the frog settled down, Bowen grabbed the end of the vine and pulled on it gently. It tightened to a point where the fox could hold the vine closest to the frog's pad. He looked into the frog's eyes and bit down on the vine. He noticed the amphibian relaxing and the leg holding still. Bowen bit through the vine with his sharpest teeth and the vine ripped in half. The frog's leg was free.

Bowen yanked on the unraveled vine and separated it from the frog's leg. The amphibian swam in a circle and hopped back onto a pad. It sat there and breathed heavily.

The frog finally broke her silence as she asked in an older, feminine voice, "What is your name?"

"Bowen," the fox responded.

"I haven't seen you before. Are you from around here?" she asked suspiciously.

"No, I'm just traveling through," Bowen replied. "What is your name?"

"Were those friends of yours?" she asked.

Bowen was silent. He didn't want to explain. He scratched his head and said, "I have something that those scouts want. I'm taking it to a safe place until I can decide what to do with it."

The frog squinted at the fox while she thought about his answer. "I can see you are in trouble," she finally said. "Be on your way."

Bowen nodded happily, ready to get away and find safety. He secured his bag around his arms and back and turned to jump. But before he leapt, the frog opened her mouth and spoke to him.

"By the way," she said. "I'm Rana, thanks for freeing me."

CHAPTER 2

Tegan's Ma made tea while her father looked over the message sent to Kenna.

"If what you believe is true," Papa said. "Then this message proves your father is in hiding somewhere close by." He studied the letter again with his glasses close to the end of his nose. Tegan's father, Arthur Wells, represented the little town of Haven where they lived. He had spent his early days in the military but soon found that serving as village chieftain suited him better. And he rather enjoyed his job.

"Cream? A little honey?" Ma asked.

Tegan and Kenna both nodded. As they prepared their tea, Papa asked, "What are your plans, Kenna?" He laid down his glasses on the table and picked up his teacup.

"I know someone that my father used to work with. He lives in Lansbury, close to Lake Headley," Kenna replied. "I plan to meet with him and see if he knows where my father might be hiding out."

"Hmmm, Lansbury. Yes, I know that area," Papa sipped his tea. "My unit trained there near the lake years ago. Lovely site."

"Well, it's also on the way to Chipping Farms, where my mother stays. I may need to sneak back into the village to speak with her," Kenna said.

Tegan choked on a sip of tea and coughed, putting one paw on the table and the other on her chest. When she caught her breath, she asked, "You want to go *back* into Chipping Farms?! I thought we were done with that place!"

"Indeed, it's a daunting task. Let's hope that it doesn't come to that," the little fox replied.

Tegan took a moment to compose herself and then asked, "What is your contact's name?"

"Mr. Bridger," Kenna said.

"What does Mr. Bridger do?" Papa asked.

"I'm not sure..." Kenna trailed off. "He used to drop by our house at night after work. But once Reginald took over as leader, I never saw him again."

"Sounds like he has the information you need," Papa responded.

"But how do you know that he's in Lansbury? I mean, he could've been captured during the uprising...or worse, killed," Tegan said gently.

"Well, the last time we were home in the village, my mother received a letter from Mr. Bridger addressed to my father," Kenna replied. "The return address indicated Lansbury."

"Was that at the same time we were held captive there?" Tegan asked.

"A day before that incident," Kenna said. "My father was acting paranoid, scared. The letter seemed to set him off."

Papa stood up and handed his empty cup to Ma. "So, when do you leave then?" he asked.

"As soon as we pack a few supplies," Tegan replied. "And find Beckett."

Her childhood friend, Beckett, was another sombel keen on adventure. He would surely join these two and help them locate Kenna's father. He had to.

"Very well," Papa sighed. "Off you go then." He hugged his daughter and smiled.

Ma handed Tegan a few oatcakes wrapped in a cloth for her journey. The sombel collected her messenger bag and stashed the snacks inside. She packed her sword, a bit of ale, and coins to make purchases down the road. Now she just needed her buddy, Beckett, and walked outside to call on him.

Reginald, leader of the Redlan clan of foxes, stood behind a makeshift desk in the middle of the room. With several lanterns glowing and a small fire in the pit, he shuffled papers around and mumbled to himself. The fox stood back and placed both paws on his hips to admire the plans he had before him. His blue tunic wrinkled around the waist and his glasses tilted to one side. He hadn't slept much lately.

But something about this plan struck his fancy. The door swung open and the military captain for the foxes let himself in. "Sir," he said. "We're ready for our orders."

"Come here," Reginald commanded. "Do you see this?" He pointed to a large area outlined on a map. "This is where we're going."

"Yes, sir," the captain replied.

"This will be our biggest score yet!" The fox scratched his scraggly chin. "It's time we had a proper place for our operations." He straightened his back and walked around the table towards the captain. "Tell me, any word from our bounty hunters?" His cold eyes stared callously into the eyes of the fox across from him.

"Not yet, sir," the captain replied. "But we know we're getting close."

The fox leader grunted. Another day and that runaway would be beyond their grasp.

Reginald crossed the room and opened the door. He needed fresh air. Outside, the leader adjusted his tunic and headed towards the pub, just down the alley and to the right. Two bodyguards followed closely behind him, selected specifically for their stocky and fairly muscular frames.

As he walked, Reginald played the scene over and over in his head. The bounty hunters he sent witnessed the escape; or so they claimed. For all he knew, they were all in it together. They were entirely out to get him! How could he maintain this if the fox with all the secrets went missing? This sensitive information could certainly topple his leadership--if the clan discovered what the runner knew. It simply cannot happen....this fox had plans.

Reginald pushed the front door of the pub wide open and entered the noisy establishment, the Boar's Nest. Patrons clamored as they drank their ale at small round tables and sat on toadstools at the bar. The smoky air smelled a bit like hay and hops, but he could also tell the kitchen was busy preparing the evening's specials: salted herring and brown bread.

He headed straight to the bar as customers backed away to let him through. Reginald called out to the barmaid, "Maeve!" The fox slammed his fist down on the bar top to get her attention. "Show me the room!" The two bodyguards standing on either side of Reginald looked at each other; one was puzzled, the other, scared.

Maeve, a petite framed fox, wiped her paws on her apron and timidly motioned for the leader to follow her. Around the side of the counter stood a huge cupboard with shelves full of bar utensils, cups, pitchers of ale, breads and cheeses, and clean aprons. She shuffled a few of the utensils around to reveal a small lever on the side of the structure. Maeve pushed it down as far as it would go and heard a release sound, a pop, from inside the shelving.

A modest-sized opening appeared between the wall and the shelving. Maeve leaned forward to look inside but Reginald pushed her out of his way. The room smelled of days old candle smoke. It was a dark, windowless, shallow cove hollowed out by hand. A small table and a petite bookshelf housed piles of neatly organized ledgers and business papers. Reginald walked around the table and fumbled through the documents on the desk. Nothing out of the ordinary: purchasing orders, deeds, bartering agreements.

He moved a pair of eyeglasses and a jar of ink out of the way, pulled out a small chair from under the table, and sat down. The fox rubbed his paws over the tabletop and down the side of the structure. He pulled on a drawer to his right, but it was locked. Reginald yanked on the handle a few more times in frustration.

"What?! Why would he lock...." He said angrily.

His paws rummaged through an open drawer on the left as he searched for something he could use to pry open the lock. Lots of candles, small pieces of wood, pieces of ribbon, wax for seals....oh! He found a letter opener and jammed it into the lock sealing the other drawer closed. He grunted as he wedged and fiddled with the lock. Finally, a 'clink' sound as a bolt hit the rocky floor, and the once secured drawer was now open. A sigh of relief overcame those standing at the doorway.

But that relief was short-lived. The drawer was nearly empty....except for one piece of paper. A letter. Reginald held it up in the meager light streaming in from the door opening and read over it. He growled in frustration, "He took the files with him!" Crumpling the letter in his hand, the fox leader threw it across the small room, hitting the earthen wall, and landing on a few ledgers stacked in the corner.

Reginald stood up and demanded, "Who found this room?"

The two bodyguards stood silent before him. The fox pushed his way through those two, turned around, and thrust his finger in their faces, "Who?!"

One of the bodyguards nervously glanced over at Maeve. Reginald followed his gaze and asked, "Maeve? Did you discover it?"

"No, no sir, I—" Maeve answered shakily.

"It was me," the bodyguard replied. "I found the room."

"You?" Reginald asked. The bodyguard nodded. "You found it, Adler?"

The bodyguard stood his ground, "I have been making inquiries on my own, sir."

The fox leader adjusted his glasses and took a deep breath, "When were you going to tell me? Were you keeping this a secret, Adler?!" He stepped into his bodyguard's personal space and breathed heavily. "What other secrets are you keeping from me?" he whispered through gritted teeth.

Adler cleared his throat and continued, "Sir, the fact that Bowen left suddenly, and put you in jeopardy....well, I...., uh, wanted to do what I could to protect you." Adler shifted his feet nervously.

Reginald took a step backwards and adjusted the blue robe around his shoulders. With his snout lifted high, he peered down his nose at Adler and asked inquisitively, "So you wish to protect me, huh?"

Adler stiffened, "Yes, sir!" he answered.

The fox leader grunted, "Mmmhh, I've got my eyes on you from now on. You hear me?"

Adler nodded as beads of sweat gathered on his brow.

Reginald eyed his bodyguard from top to bottom and then turned and headed to the door. Adler relaxed a little, his shoulders sagging, and whispered to Maeve, "Don't worry, I'll take care of this."

She scooted inside the hidden room and grabbed the paper that Reginald had crumpled earlier in anger.

"Here," she said and handed it to Adler. "Take this and see what you can make of it."

The guard glanced up and noticed the other bodyguard watching his movements. Adler panicked and stuffed the paper into his pocket. He turned to Maeve and said, "If you come across anything else, send me a message." Maeve smiled.

Adler then made his way through the customers and caught up with Reginald and the other bodyguard, Bin. Shaggy and disheveled, Bin had been observing his counterpart in the pub, quietly questioning his movements...and his loyalty.

"What are you doing, Adler?" Bin asked in a hushed tone.

"What are you talking about?" Adler responded.

"You know exactly what I mean!" Bin looked around and then continued. "The room? The barmaid? And I saw you pocket that paper...."

"I am loyal to the leader, Bin." Adler staunchly stated. Then he lowered his voice and spoke to Bin in a whisper, "But something isn't right. This disappearance is not what it seems."

CHAPTER 3

Bowen followed an old peddler's footpath beneath the tall, meadow grass. Towering beech trees dotted the fields before him. As he stopped to stretch his back, he recognized a stone structure in the distance, behind what looked like a crop of cherry trees. The building itself contrasted the blue sky with its dark gray façade and stone fencing around the property. It sat alone, with no signs of life around the perimeter, except for a few ducks swimming in a stream along the winding wall. Bowen knew this place well, but hadn't stepped inside in many years. And based on his boyhood connection, Bowen hoped to find refuge here.

Derwent Abbey, a monastic community settlement, rested along the Tana River. As Bowen crossed the green field, he remembered playing along these tree lines as a young kit. He and his brothers and sister grew up not too far from this very abbey in a small village located further down the trail. When the sun came out in the mornings, the siblings ran to this open meadow to play ball with other pups from town. The smell of fresh grass reminded Bowen of how much fun he had during these youthful summer days—hours spent playing ball and swimming in the river.

As Bowen neared the stone wall, he noticed several piles of stones where parts of the fence had fallen. He shifted his bag around his shoulders and carefully climbed on top of one of the piles, hopping down on the other side to enter the premises. From there, he viewed the structure itself. Its mighty curved arches and precisely hewn stone walls still left an impression on his humble soul. Mild disrepair and missing chunks of bricks dotted the structure; however, the kitchen, dining room, and choir monks' dormitories seemed fairly intact (at least from his point of view).

To his right, Bowen heard the faint trickling of a sizeable stream flowing just behind the abbey's east range. He turned and skipped up to the window, standing on his tiptoes to get a look inside. Along the dining room walls stood two long wooden refectory tables, stained from years of steady use: community luncheons, monks' dinners, celebratory feasts, and simple meals with visitors.

And it appeared to be a special occasion today. Silver candle sticks with half melted candles sat on top of the oak tables, along with small chalices, fresh lilies, and various ceremonial platters. Bowen searched the room for inhabitants, but it was empty. He heard the faint droning sound of singing down the hall and stepped away from the window to investigate further.

Around the visibly aged exterior, Bowen wandered to the warming room and entered through the south door. A meager fire burned in the corner of the room inside a primitive stone pit. He felt a wave of heat as he slipped past the flames and tiptoed out into the cloister or covered walkway.

Bowen shielded his eyes from the sun's rays with his paw and breathed in the aromas of the monks' hard work. The layout of the abbey's garden featured allotments for different purposes. A quarter of the green area flourished with lush vegetables and herbs like cabbage, leeks, celery, rosemary, and sage. The fragrance in the air smelled of onions and a hint of garlic. Bowen was hungry.

Another plot within the garden hosted a small water fountain shaped like a monk in prayer, its paws clutched close to his chest. The water trickled down into a small pond with simple drainage canals distributing runoff throughout the rest of the garden. A few footpaths of stone within the greenery offered the choir monks an area of reflection and a quiet place to search their souls.

Those smooth walking stones also led to the last quarter of the garden covered in rich flowers and aromatic blooms. The monks had carefully tended to these crops of roses, lilies, and violets, as evidenced by the cascades of blossoms on the shrubs. Each one brightly contrasted against the dark green leaves of the brushes. Overhead, tangly vines entwined themselves along a handmade trellis as the first signs of grapes emerged.

It was at this point that eight robed foxes rounded the corner on their way towards the nave to offer their afternoon prayers. Bowen followed quietly behind them. It wasn't that he was unwelcome in the abbey, or that he was forced to sneak about without being seen. Instead, he desired to see the monastic monks at work before requesting an audience with their abbot. It was his way... observation before action.

The monks marched into the narrow entryway, one by one, hands clasped in prayer. As they made their way towards the altar, Bowen slipped into a simple wooden chair positioned near the entryway. He could view the altar from where he sat, but stayed inconspicuous in case his presence caused a visible distraction.

He watched as the monastic monks lined up in front of the altar and kneeled in reverence. As they recited scripture, Bowen felt a peace and security for the first time in months. All the pretending and hiding....the exhaustion wore itself on his shoulders. He relaxed his posture and settled into the chair with a deep sigh.

But Bowen must have nodded off because the distant sound of bells startled him awake. He focused his eyes and noticed an empty room before him. *How long was I out?* Pulling his bag around his shoulder, Bowen stood up to investigate the bells he heard earlier. He stepped out into the cloister and passed the entrance to the library. But the tinkling sound caught his attention again. Over his shoulder, he noticed an older monk with a funny hat moving about in the library.

Bowen stepped inside and gently cleared his throat to get the monk's attention. The older monk turned around, surprised by the company. His robe was much more elaborate than the tired, brown color that the others wore. This monk had to be distinguished; his embellished hat or mitre was proof of that.

"Father?" Bowen asked.

"Yes, son," the other fox answered.

"Are you...?"

"I am the abbot here, my friend," he responded with a smile.

"Father Ennis??"

"I am," he paused and squinted his eyes a bit. "Do I know you?"

Bowen half chuckled. "Maybe. I used to come to services here as a boy...even sang in the choir." He stepped forward with his paw out, "I am Bowen Whitethorne. From the Redlan clan."

The abbot shook his paw and replied, "Ah, yes, of course. I remember your family. You still have relatives in the village?"

"Possibly," Bowen said stoically. "I haven't visited my birthplace in a very long time."

"Hmm," Father Ennis nodded. "What brings you here? Visiting?"

Bowen coughed a little, "No, uh, Father, I need to talk to you." He watched as two monks walked into the library and settled at the table to read. "Privately, please," he insisted.

The abbot and the fox moved out of the library and rounded the corner into the chapter house. The vibrant room hosted many wooden chairs, topped with red, tufted cushions that lined the walls. A small platform in the center of the room held a separate chair and small desk, for the director of notable meetings. Several gold framed pictures hung on the walls and a candle chandelier dangled from a wood beam exposed in the ceiling. And to the left, a medium-sized window let the daylight and fresh air in, so long as it wasn't raining.

The abbot sauntered into the room first and seated himself in a chair furthest from the door. Bowen followed closely behind. Once the fox felt safe to speak, he addressed the abbot in a low voice.

"Father, I need a safe place to store a few documents," Bowen said and patted his weathered bag.

"I see," Father Ennis responded. "What information do these documents contain?"

"I...I prefer not to answer. However," Bowen leaned closer to the abbot and whispered, "I am in a bit of trouble, and these papers hold truths that I am now aware of..." He looked to his right and then to his left, "...and responsible for."

"And these truths must now be safeguarded?" the abbot asked.

"Yes," Bowen responded.

"For how long?" the abbot asked.

"I don't know yet. But I am in need of a safe place to rest as well," Bowen looked into the abbot's eyes to determine his response. A weary, dirty fox shows up at this abbot's doorstep needing protection and a secure place to store evidentiary documents. *Would he house a potential threat to this community's peace?* Without a backup plan, this was Bowen's only chance to hide from those foxes trying to steal the documents he so vehemently held on to.

"You may stay with us," the abbot responded. "As for your papers, I will house them in the library with our other important documents."

Bowen sighed in relief, "thank you."

"On the condition that you tell me a bit more about your circumstances," Father Ennis instructed. He leaned back in his chair and explained, "It would be wise to prepare ourselves against outside interests."

Bowen's mind reeled. Flashes of the past few weeks flooded his brain. His eyes darted around the room and his heart pounded faster. Panic set in and the fox's breathing escalated. How much should he tell the abbot?

Father Ennis recognized the fox's panic and placed his paw on Bowen's shoulder to calm him. He said gently, "Why don't you start at the beginning?"

Bowen rubbed his face and whiskers with his paws. He felt the blood burning in his cheeks and slowly inhaled a deep breath. "Are you familiar with the rebellion within the Redlan Clan of foxes?"

"Yes, I heard that a council member overthrew Edwin's leadership. Such a shame; I supported Edwin's position of the clan," the abbot replied.

"Yes, well, I served Edwin as his accountant...and then as a negotiator. In the weeks leading up to the coup, Edwin asked me to survey land east of the river. A fairly mountainous area called, Swynton."

"I have heard of it. One of our lay monks arrived from Swynton only a year ago."

"Edwin claimed that he wanted to move our clan there, to a better environment with better resources and nicer neighbors," Bowen laughed a little. Speaking this out loud sounded silly, but Edwin wanted to get as far away from the black rats of Voldire as possible. He was tired of their raids. Though the rats didn't invade often, it was enough to strain the clan's treasury and render the economy almost useless. It was time to make a move. "Reginald, the former council member, hated this idea, claiming he had family in the area, and he didn't think it was right to take their territory from them. He compared the move to 'acting in accordance to a black rat'...all of this shouted in Edwin's face--in a council meeting!"

"Did you witness any of this yourself?" the abbot asked.

Bowen shifted his feet, "I was there, I saw Edwin's reaction. He was horrified!"

"What happened after that?"

"Well, within a few days, Reginald had garnered enough supporters to forcibly remove Edwin from leadership," Bowen replied.

Father Ennis sat in silence, consuming this information carefully.

"As you can imagine, all hell broke loose. Half the clan escaped to surrounding villages fearing repercussions from publicly supporting Edwin. Others remained to restructure the government and plan raids in accordance with Reginald's desires," Bowen said. He stopped for a moment before continuing, "The thing is, all this time, we knew Reginald pillaged occasionally from the area of Swynton, and he was chastised for it. He would be in trouble and restricted from performing certain duties...make amends and then return to the council. It was during one of those probation trials that I stumbled upon a notebook."

"A notebook?" asked Father Ennis intrigued.

"Yes, and as I read through it, the book revealed damning documents against Reginald himself. Information that doubted his identity. Documents outlining unknown trade agreements and family ties...or lack thereof. It's a mess, Father, and I just wasn't prepared for the truths I learned," Bowen's voice trailed off.

"I see," the abbot said.

"A few days ago, I found out that Reginald's guards searched my desk looking for the notebook in the drawer I hid it in. He then sent hunters out to find me. When I realized the severity of the situation, I ran," Bowen explained.

"And you came here," the abbot finished his thoughts.

"Yes. Now, I'm on the run; separated from my family, anxious, and holding onto critical documents that could render Reginald's power instantly useless. If his followers find out about his treachery, they'll hang him for sure!"

Father Ennis sighed with compassion. "You are in a very precarious situation, my friend." He stood up and stretched his back, "Come with me. You have refuge here."

Bowen stood up as well and rearranged his bag.

"Let's get those papers into the library so we can discuss further plans," the abbot suggested. "You look like you could use a good washing. I'll ask one of the monks to prepare fresh water for you as well as a clean robe and warm pottage."

Bowen chuckled half-heartedly and asked, "How about some ale too?"

CHAPTER 4

"I'm up here!" Beckett hollered from a high branch in an apple tree. Tegan shaded her eyes with her paw and watched the sandy-furred sombel scratch and claw his way down the tree trunk. Parts of bark and wisps of fur fluttered to the grass below as Beckett descended with a bag full of apples on his back. Once his paws landed on the ground, he turned around and smiled, "Apples anyone?"

Tegan and Kenna giggled. Beckett was a little taller than Tegan, even though they were the same age, relatively speaking. He wore a dark blue tunic along with a hat made of walnut shells. Beckett removed his helmet and showed it to the others, "Protects my head....in case an apple falls." He patted the scruff on top of his head for emphasis.

"Ohhhh," Tegan and Kenna replied simultaneously.

"Nice cloak you got there," Beckett stated as he looked Tegan up and down, admiring the new garment she sported.

"Thanks! I received it this morning," she said, then hesitated. "A thank you gift from the pixie clan." She glanced at Kenna and her face immediately darkened.

"Is anything wrong?" he asked noticing the change in his friends' demeanor.

"It's my father," Kenna jumped in. "We've received word."

As the little fox described what she knew about her father's disappearance to Beckett, a gust of warm, humid air blew by them and hovered over their heads. Rain was coming. Tegan searched the clouds for signs of a storm brewing. She nudged Kenna. "We need to get going if we're to make any progress before the rain gets here," she suggested.

"Well, I'm coming too!" Beckett said excitedly. "Let me drop these apples off at the house and I'll be right back." He paused and grabbed a few apples, turned them over in his paws, and stuffed them into Tegan's bag. "For later," he grinned.

As Kenna and Tegan waited for their friend to return, a small, dark cloud floated closer to the village. "It looks like the spring season is upon us," Kenna remarked.

The nation of Fellnore, in the spring, meant consistent, light showers instead of the winter's infrequent downpours. Though fruit grew year-round, villagers often enjoyed planting flowers and herbs during this time of the year. Handmade rain catchers lined the side of their well-kept bungalows, and small gardens popped up seemingly overnight. It was a time of renewal, a time for peace. However, Tegan felt deep down in her belly that something more was brewing, and not just this storm.

Once Beckett joined the group, they headed west--away from the rainy tempest. With their home village, Haven, behind them, the travelers walked down an old footpath through the beech trees and scrubby hedges. Willowy grass swayed as the moist air blew around them and the smell of earth lingered in their noses. Patches of sunlight splattered across the path, and the hikers enjoyed the warmth of the rays for as long as they could find it.

"Look over there!" Beckett exclaimed. The view suddenly opened substantially, leaving both the trees and shrubs behind them. "There's the lake!"

Indeed, the water of Lake Headley spread as far as the eye could see. Strong gusts of wind blew across the lake's surface and right through the travelers standing on the shore. As they padded along the bankside, their paws sank in the tiny rocks scattered along the water's edge.

"Should we cross it?" Kenna asked. She spotted a flat bottom boat tied precariously to a timber pier. The water slapped against the wood causing the boat to roll around violently in the water.

Beckett shook his head. "No, the water is too choppy," he replied. "We might overturn out there." He surveyed the area, looking for a break in the clouds. "The rain will be here soon though. Let's keep moving."

Little drops of water splashed against their cloaks. Tegan, Kenna, and Beckett trotted faster along the edge of the lake, following its shore for some time until they noticed another pier in the distance.

Then the sound of pitter pattering increased all around them. Cold rain pelted down on their ears and noses. Tegan pulled her hood over her head and wrapped her cloak tight around her, bracing against the wet weather. The travelers ran toward the distant pier, dashing down the bank in search of some kind of shelter.

It was Tegan who noticed another flat boat resting on the rocky beach. She motioned to the others and sprinted ahead. Once she reached the structure, the sombel grabbed the sides of the wooden boat and rocked it back and forth. She wasn't quite strong enough to force it one way or the other. Soaking wet, she heaved with all her might but slipped on the rocks and fell square on her bottom. By the time she stood back on her feet, Kenna and Beckett had caught up. The three of them rocked the boat again until it finally turned over to form a makeshift shelter. Kenna, Beckett, and Tegan scrambled underneath the small fishing boat to avoid the rain.

Under the shelter, Tegan gathered the bottom of her cloak and squeezed the water out with both paws. She huddled together with Kenna and Beckett, waiting in a wet heap for the storm to pass. Rain drops pounding noisily overhead made conversation difficult. So, Tegan sat with her thoughts, listening for any sign of the rain relenting.

It wasn't long before Beckett decided that he needed some air. He gently lifted the side of the boat to peek out. Light rain showered around them, but the travelers could now distinguish a few lights flickering in the distance.

"Is that what I think it is?" Tegan asked loudly. Her voice echoed around them once the rain drops, and noise, had tapered off.

Kenna stuck her paw out of the makeshift shelter to measure the rainfall. "It's only sprinkling," she said and shook the water from her paw. "Let's go find out where we are."

With a great shove, the travelers turned the boat back over and were free again to move. They scurried toward the distant lights, hoping it was their anticipated destination. While each step brought them closer, the travelers still felt trepidation in their hearts. Were they even headed in the right direction?

Then Beckett spied an old footpath marker. He approached the wooden sign and removed a bundle of leaves stuck to it by rain. Revealing they were only a short distance away from the village of Lansbury, Kenna sighed with relief. They were almost there.

The town of Lansbury was an established fishing destination. Located so close to the lake that it afforded the little community a bit of tourism as well as the opportunity for visitors to enjoy some anonymity. A few stores lined the main road: groceries, tackle and bait shop, two pubs, a post office, and a bakery. No doubt there were more businesses around the corner though; Tegan could see the thatched rooftops and smoke rising from their chimneys.

"Where should we look for Mr. Bridger?" Tegan asked Kenna. "Do you know where he works or which house he lives in?"

Kenna's whiskers twitched. "No, I don't," she replied.

"Wait, you don't have an address?" Beckett asked. "How are we supposed to—"

"Mommy! Look at those shiny swords!!" a young brown hare, or leveret, shouted. The little one with short ears tugged on her mother's apron and pointed. Apprehensive, mother hare pulled her baby close and whispered in her ear.

Beckett faced the leveret and showed off his sword. "It IS shiny!" He laughed and stepped closer. Kneeling to her level, he asked,

"Would you like to hold it?" The sombel held the end of the blade so the young hare could grasp the hilt. Her eyes widened with anticipation, and she gripped the sword with both paws.

"Weee!" she squealed and waved the weapon around her head. Both Beckett and the mother took a couple of steps back. "I am *fierce*!" she shouted and struck a mighty pose. Kenna and Tegan laughed at the precocious little hare. The leveret's white, frilly dress contrasted comically to the giant metal sword in her paws.

"Ginny! Give the sombel back his blade," the mother commanded and removed the sword from the leveret's little paws. She handed the weapon back to Beckett. "Thank you, sir, for your kindness."

Beckett smiled and nodded. "Say, do you know someone around here named Mr. Bridger? He's a friend of ours and we're in town for a visit. I'm told he lives in Lansbury."

The mother hare smoothed her light blue apron as she thought, "I don't know a Mr. Bridger. But the clerk in the post office might be able to help." She pointed to the store next door with a white awning out front.

"Ooh, can I get a lollipop, mommy? I want a red lollipop!!" Ginny begged.

"You had one yesterday, dear. Remember?" She looked at Beckett and explained, "I bought it when I mailed a package to her grandparents." The hare spoke gently to her daughter, "Besides, Daddy will bring you another one when he gets back from his business trip," she explained and smoothed the fuzzy hair on her baby's head. She looked at Kenna, Tegan, and Beckett, and chuckled, "Kids, right?" Mother hare held Ginny's paw and said to her, "Let's pick up our bread, dear, and head home." She waved goodbye to the travelers and opened the door to the bakery, disappearing inside.

Kenna shot ahead of Beckett and Tegan. The chiming of little bells hanging on the door tinkled as she stepped inside the post office. The room itself seemed just big enough to house a large hutch, which sat snugly against the back wall. Numerous cubbies (too many to count) spread across the entirety of the top half of the structure.

A short, prickly hedgehog stood on his tiptoes humming as he inserted mail into each of the cubby slots. With his tiny spectacles clinging to the end of his nose, the clerk studied each name on the envelope and then placed it confidently into the corresponding cubby.

In front of the hutch stood a table with a simple cash register, positioned conveniently for business. On both sides of the table sat wooden barrels containing hard candies and a few sweet breads. Small dishes holding bits of red licorice rested on top, providing a kaleidoscope of color.

Kenna waited at the register and rang the service bell. She heard the others enter the room but didn't look behind her. The hedgehog turned around and removed his glasses. "Can I help you?" he asked.

"I'm looking for Mr. Bridger. Do you know him?" the little fox asked.

"I can't say that I do," the clerk responded. "Has he lived here long?"

"About six months, I believe," Kenna said.

Tegan joined the fox at the counter. "We are just passing through town and wanted to say hello," she added.

"Well, there *have* been a few new residents over the past month or so. But I only get to know them when they request mail service," the clerk pointed to the hutch behind him.

"Looks like a full house," Tegan replied and nudged Kenna.

But Kenna did not respond. She was focused on something. Her eyes didn't move.

Under each mail slot was a printed name...or set of initials. Tegan followed Kenna's line of sight and narrowed down the targeted object to a few cubbies.

"Kenna, what is it?" Tegan asked her.

Kenna walked around to the side of the table to get a closer look at the name under one of the slots. But before she could reach inside the cubby, the hedgehog stopped her.

"Please stay behind the counter, ma'am," he insisted.

Tegan gave Beckett a familiar look as she and the fox backed away from the mail slots. Beckett knew this look. He understood what was needed in that moment. He then wandered over to the opposite side of the table and asked the clerk, "How much are these candies?" He pointed to the barrel closest to himself, knowing that he needed to provide a distraction of some kind.

"Those are 2p (pence)," the hedgehog replied.

Beckett nodded. He searched the barrels for lollipops but didn't see any. "Do you have a few red lollipops?" he asked.

As Beckett and the clerk chatted about the candy, Tegan asked Kenna, "What's going on?"

"It's him, up there!" Kenna said excitedly and pointed to a slot with the initials, W.B., listed below it. "Wadsworth Bridger!" There was no stopping the fox now.

The cubbyhole was high, out of reach. Tegan shot Beckett another look; this time, it was more intense.

"Uh, do you have anymore? Say in the back maybe?" Beckett requested. His eyes darted around searching for something, anything, to get the clerk's full attention.

The hedgehog studied Beckett, and then Kenna and Tegan. He sighed out loud and said, "Wait here." He stepped through a small door next to the hutch and into a modest storage room. Maybe he had extras in here somewhere.

Once the clerk shuffled out of sight, Tegan hoisted Kenna up on her shoulders. The little fox needed confirmation of the mail slot with "W.B." printed under it. She craved validation. Kenna shoved her paw inside the slot and grabbed what mail was in there. Pulling out an envelope, the fox rolled it up and stuffed the letter under her tunic.

The stubby hedgehog waddled out with a paw full of red lollipops. "Are these what you're looking for?" he asked.

Beckett was obviously pleased, "Yes! I'll take them all!" He scooped up the lollipops from the clerk and handed him a couple of coins in return.

"We best be on our way now," Tegan said as she and Kenna headed toward the door. "Thanks for your help, sir."

"You know," the clerk hesitated. "There is a particular area of town where newcomers tend to settle. It is in the eastern part of the village. You might want to check there for your friend," he suggested.

Tegan paused to process the clerk's counsel. "Good to know, thank you," Tegan replied over her shoulder. The travelers gathered outside on the sidewalk.

"Which way is east?" Kenna asked, looking for the sun.

"That way," Beckett pointed down the road ahead of them. He fumbled with the lollipops, selecting one in particular and inspecting it. "Go on without me; I'll catch up." He smiled, "I need to deliver this treat to a ferocious little hare in the bakery."

Chapter 5

Adler followed Reginald back to the longhouse where the councilmen waited for their leader. His paw clutched the crumbled paper he stuffed into his vest before leaving the pub. Tall and stocky, Adler stood out among the other foxes due to his muscular, sturdy stature. And because of these traits, Reginald demanded his employment as bodyguard; to which Adler accepted this 'privilege' under duress.

Once Reginald overthrew Edwin, the previous leader, the villagers either supported the new king's decisions, or left. But even the choice to leave was plagued with the possibility of capture...then definite enslavement. It all depended on Reginald's mood.

Adler remained in Reginald's service, not because he supported the new leader, but because he had a plan. A hope to bring back the fruitful economy and business integrity that Edwin worked years to establish in Chipping Farms. There was too much at stake to leave. And Adler's family had been an integral part of developing the infrastructure so that trade would not only be profitable for their clan, but safe as well.

Reginald stepped into the longhouse and seated himself at the head of the table, near the fire pit. He shuffled plates of food and cups of wine within his reach. Waving his paw as a sign for the bodyguards to leave, Adler closed the door and remained outside.

The fox king held closed council meetings in the longhouse to keep out nosy villagers and possible spies. Even the bodyguards were expected to step out and secure the doors. But Adler could hear faint conversation through the cracks in the wooden door. Surely Bin, the other guard, heard it too. As the wine flowed, Reginald enjoyed himself more and spoke louder and louder. Adler stood motionless, staring into the distance before him, but he concentrated on the conversations within. And this time, Reginald shouted out Bowen's name.

Then a crash and a great deal of commotion, growling and screaming council members. Adler burst through the door to check for danger and saw the table turned over on its side; Reginald standing on top of his chair. The other foxes cowered below as Reginald yelled at them in a drunken rage. He held a torch in his left paw and waved it around just to frighten them.

"You let him escape! All of you!" the fox king roared.

"Sir!" Adler called. "Hand the torch to me and come down."

Reginald looked horrified. "Are you telling ME what to do?"

"Sir, I only meant for you to come rest. You're not feeling well," Adler replied calmly and motioned with his paw.

The fox leader recoiled and held the torch tighter. Sensing imminent danger, Bin tiptoed around the leader and snatched the torch from behind, surprising him. Reginald stood in disbelief.

Helpless, he finally relented, allowing himself to be removed from the chair. Adler gently held his arm and escorted the leader out of the longhouse door.

"Sir, let's get you home," he said.

Reginald mumbled incoherently, but Adler didn't mind. If he could get Reginald home quickly, he'd have some free time to himself. Free time to look at that crumpled paper stashed in his vest.

At dawn, the sound of singing monks woke Bowen from a deep slumber. Apparently, he slept so soundly that he never once changed positions in the bed. Bowen quickly dressed and heard a jingling at his door. Alarmed, the fox picked up a large rock to arm himself and waited in the morning shadows.

Slowly, steadily, the wooden door opened, and soft feet padded into the room. Bowen smelled something wonderful...it was bread! The messenger laid a small tray on the dresser by the bed, and looked around, puzzled by the empty blanket.

"I'm over here," Bowen said and hid his paw with the rock behind his back.

"Your breakfast, sir," the monk replied. "Father Ennis asked me to deliver this to you. How did you sleep?"

"Very well, thank you," Bowen said. "Where is the abbot this morning?"

"He is in morning prayer," said the monk.

"Please tell him that I need to speak with him shortly," Bowen said. He lit a small lantern in the room to see the messenger. The monk stood wearing only a simple tunic and rope belt; his paws clasped together in humbleness. "What is your name?"

"My name is John Henry," the monk replied.

"Thank you for breakfast, John Henry," Bowen said.

The monk pulled the door closed on his way out, leaving the fox to enjoy his breakfast in solidarity. Bowen's mouth watered at the aroma of fresh baked bread, and he eagerly approached the tray of food. A chunk of brown bread, slices of cheese, and a cup of tea rounded out the menu. He scarfed it all down, gathered his belongings, and set out to find the abbot.

It didn't take long to locate him. In fact, Father Ennis rounded one side of the cloister just as Bowen stepped out of his room. The sun had yet to fully rise and the air felt cool and damp. But Bowen recognized the funny hat and waited for the abbot to join him. Once he caught up with the visitor, he greeted Bowen warmly and asked, "Is there something you'd like to speak with me about?"

"Yes, Father," Bowen said and pointed to the garden.

Long before he fell asleep the night before, Bowen wrestled with his thoughts. The conversation with Father Ennis in the library had triggered his anxiety. He recounted the details leading up to his escape. Why had he come across those notebooks? And why did he read through them?

"Stop beating yourself up," Bowen mumbled under his breath. Indeed, he realized he'd been a little nosy. But that makes a great businessman and negotiator, right? I mean, he needed to know everything that Reginald knew, if he was to successfully negotiate land contracts for the leader. There was absolutely no room for surprises.

But ironically, the notebook he found was full of them. If Bowen kept quiet, he could ride out the crazy plans Reginald concocted for expansion. And surely, another power-hungry soldier would eventually come along and knock the leader off his throne. Bowen could ultimately reunite all of his family in the same village and resume a somewhat normal life....reminiscent of the years during Edwin's reign.

But he couldn't ignore the nagging in his heart. The sadness that arose whenever he thought of those inhabitants of Swynton...the ones Reginald raided and stole from. The badgers, the hares, the hedgehogs...simple business creatures just working to take care of their wives and their little ones; their family. His heart ached when he thought of his own family, torn apart by the selfish actions of a lunatic. At least Edwin had some integrity.

Yes, Edwin. And these documents could restore his throne, but only if he successfully revealed the information at the right time, which meant a plan. In order to strategize, Bowen needed to confirm this information within the documents for himself.

In the middle of the garden, Bowen said, "Father, I need to visit Swynton for myself. Stay a few days and make inquiries. If I can confirm what is in that notebook, then there's a strong case for Edwin to reclaim the throne from Reginald."

"Not without a fight, I'm afraid," the abbot responded.

"That is true. However, I must do whatever I can to right the wrongs in my village. Our community suffers greatly under Reginald," Bowen replied. "And you know, it's only a matter of time before the entire nation of Fellnore feels his wrath."

The abbot searched Bowen's face and stared into his eyes. He saw pain, and he saw regret. But in the midst of this visitor's conversation, he also recognized redemption. Bowen needed to make amends and found a unique opportunity to do so.

"I see that this is important to you," the abbot replied. "But you must not go alone. I can send another monk to accompany you as well as a map."

"Thank you, Father, but that won't be necessary," Bowen said. "I just need directions."

"The path to Swynton is difficult to find. You should consider a companion; someone who already knows how to get there," Father Ennis advised.

A small group of monks walked by the garden on their way to the presbytery for morning prayer. Both the abbot and Bowen watched in silence as they shuffled down the sidewalk.

"John Henry," Father Ennis called out. "Come here."

One of the monks turned around and headed towards the garden.

"This is the lay monk I mentioned earlier. I believe you two have already met," the abbot said.

"Yes, this morning, Father," the monk replied.

"Really, sir, I just need directions—"

"John Henry, please describe to our visitor the way to Swynton," the abbot requested.

"Well, it's a day's hike to the base of the Arsa mountains. Look for a logging town and a small pond. Eventually, you'll see a white timber framed house. Nothing unusual, just an ordinary house. To the left of it runs a simple footpath into the woods and a passageway through the mountain. Swynton is on the other side," the monk described.

"So you see, Bowen, the directions are vague. John Henry grew up in Swynton, so he can help you navigate your way to the village," said the abbot. Then he told the monk, "Go gather a few supplies and meet us back here."

The monk looked curiously into Bowen's eyes. He nodded and trotted off as instructed. Bowen tried to hide his agitation. He didn't need a babysitter. And he was in a rush.

"Father, I'll be fine," Bowen said with false confidence and managed a smile.

"John Henry will be back soon. Just wait here until he returns," the abbot instructed.

The church bells suddenly rang. Father Ennis arranged his hat and patted down his robe, "That's my sign. I'm off to preach this morning's sermon." And with that, he strolled past Bowen and headed to the high altar.

Bowen realized his chance and darted out of the garden, across the cloister, and through an open archway to the outside of the monastery. He could get a head start before anyone noticed his absence.

But Father Ennis looked back over his shoulder at the same time John Henry showed up.

"He's already gone," the abbot told the monk. "Just wait a few minutes and follow closely behind him. Don't let him see you. We need to keep an eye on that fox."

The monk smiled in return.

Chapter 6

"426 Bean Street," Kenna read out loud.

Tegan shaded her eyes with her paw, surveying the land eastward. She pointed toward a clump of earthen houses and said, "That way. Let's go!"

Both Kenna and Tegan covered their heads with their cloak to stay as invisible as possible. The villagers walking along this road headed to the lake to fish. Foxes and hedgehogs held fishing poles, bait, tackle boxes, and nets while they chatted and laughed amongst themselves. Other villagers made their way into local stores like the food market and dress shops. Children zipped by on small bicycles and wagons. Even the pubs filled quickly with patrons ready for lunch. Down the road, construction continued slowly as the rain had now fully stopped. A few hedgehogs gathered near the base of a small bridge to repair what looked like a hole in the middle plank. Their tiny hammers whipped back and forth as the crew worked together to repair the structure.

Tegan and Kenna kept their eyes low. Then Tegan felt a paw on her shoulder; and she jumped.

It was Beckett. He finally caught up to the others.

"Hey! Where are we going?" he asked.

"The address is on Bean Street. Right over there," Tegan replied, pointing east.

The group turned off the main road on to Bean Street and continued hiking until they saw a cluster of small homes. For the most part, only the doors and a small window could be seen of each house. The roof and the sides were hidden by earthen walls and green mossy growth. The dwellings appeared to be hidden within the modest hills themselves.

A few wooden tables sat in front of the doors, accompanied by a chair or two. An apple, jam jar and bread slices, and empty cups had been left out since the breakfast meal. Above the door, each home displayed a series of numbers or the address...all of the doors but one.

Tegan stepped up to the window of this particularly anonymous house and peeked in. But she couldn't see anything as a hand towel covered the opening. Backing up, she turned to see Kenna knocking confidently on the door.

"Kenna, is this the right one?" Tegan asked in a whisper.

"Yes, 424 is over there and 428 is on the other side," Kenna replied. "This has to be the right one." She knocked again.

The door opened slightly.

"Is this 426 Bean Street?" Kenna asked the stranger behind the door.

To her surprise, the door slammed shut. A puff of air ruffled her fur and Kenna stepped back, shocked by the sudden action. She huffed and then knocked again, this time, harder and longer.

The door opened a second time, but only somewhat.

"Is this 426 Bean Street?" Kenna asked more determined than ever before. Then she added, "I'm not going away."

"Who's asking?" the voice demanded.

"Kenna. It's me, Kenna," she hesitated. "Bowen Whitethorne is my father."

The door squeaked open a bit more for the stranger to examine the fox.

"Bowen?" he asked and stepped closer to the opening.

Tegan noticed that this stranger was a badger; not a fox like she expected. His black and white fur lay slicked down on the top of his head. He wore glasses close to the end of his nose. And his deep blue vest and pants simply appeared wrinkled and creased. *Had he been sleeping in these clothes?*

"Mr. Bridger?" Kenna asked gingerly.

"Yes, I'm Mr. Bridger," his eyes darted from Tegan to Beckett and back to Kenna.

"Sir, these are my friends. I am looking for my father," Kenna explained.

The badger stuck his head out of the door, looked suspiciously around, and then hustled the travelers inside his home.

"Did anyone follow you here?" Mr. Bridger asked impatiently.

"No, we are alone," Kenna responded.

The badger's face relaxed. He leaned over the table and turned up the lantern light, allowing the visitors to see his small living area. A modest wooden table and a couple of chairs were the centerpiece of the room. Small shelves loaded with cups, plates, and bowls appeared messy and unorganized. To the right of the fireplace sat a sack of flour, a broom, and a kettle still steaming from the blaze.

The walls, covered with a form of clay, felt smooth to the touch. Except for a few pictures, there really wasn't much to see in the badger's home. Tegan wondered how long it had been since he moved in.

Mr. Bridger motioned for his guests to sit and checked the windows for any openings. He couldn't have anyone detecting his company.

Kenna waited for Mr. Bridger to sit down and then asked, "When was the last time you saw my father?"

Mr. Bridger scratched his head and replied, "It was a few weeks after Reginald took over. Your family moved out so quickly, which is understandable, considering your father's occupation. I said a few words to Bowen and wished him well. I haven't seen him since then. Has something happened?"

"Bowen has been reported missing," Tegan replied.

"Reginald had something to do with it, I know it!" Kenna stated boldly. "I need to find him. I need answers!"

"Missing, you say?" Mr. Bridger's eyes widened. He stood up and checked the window openings again. Paranoia set in.

"When did you leave Chipping Farms?" Tegan asked the badger.

"Well, it took some time for my family to leave. We waited a month or so to see how Reginald would manage affairs in the village. But we hated what we saw and left one morning at dawn. We didn't plan where to go and only stopped at Lansbury to rest and regroup," said Mr. Bridger. "And we never left."

"You said you hated what you saw," Beckett said. "What did Reginald do?"

"That fox is manipulative and conniving," observed Mr. Bridger. "Within the first few days, he formed a small party with the sole purpose of raiding a local town."

"How did he get other villagers to join him?" Kenna asked.

"Reginald pushed for 'volunteers,' but no one willingly came forward for the task. So, he waited until nightfall and sent soldiers to the remaining families in the village. His soldiers forced their way inside their homes and coerced the younger male foxes to join his raiding party."

"Sounds like we got out just in time then," Kenna remarked.

"Yes, you might have been subjected to one of many raiding parties under his command. Your father did what was best for you." Mr. Bridger reminisced as he watched Kenna's emotions bounce all over the place. She hadn't thought about the day she and her family escaped from Chipping Farms in a long time. She had hoped that moving back would be safe; the jobs (and the money) were there.

"Your family moved to Old Padley then?" The badger asked.

Kenna swallowed hard, "Yes, we stayed undercover there for a while. There's a community of foxes in that area that served under Edwin. Some are military leaders; others are business owners. We were just trying to survive."

"Is that where your parents are now?" he asked.

"No, we moved back to Chipping Farms recently because we needed jobs. It was simply worth the risk for the money just to get by," Kenna replied.

"Apparently, it wasn't," quipped Mr. Bridger. "If Bowen is truly missing, I guarantee you that Reginald had everything to do with it."

"Do you have any knowledge of where Bowen might be right now? Has he contacted you?" Tegan asked.

"I wish I could say that I know where he is; that he is in hiding and is safe. But I can't," the badger responded.

"Is there anything that might give us a clue as to where we can search for him?" Kenna pleaded.

"Look, Bowen and I had our disagreements, but we generally got along. I've been accused of many things during our time together. Unfortunately, most of the accusations are true. And I'm trying to rectify that. But the weeks after Reginald took over were pure chaos," Mr. Bridger said. "The only thing I remember is Bowen holding an old messenger bag packed with papers (documents I assumed) and eventually fleeing on foot. He took his time to gather what he needed before leaving. He was always thinking ahead. I imagine those papers were quite important."

"Some kind of security or insurance maybe," Tegan responded.

The badger sat motionless for a few moments, recalling the last time he saw his coworker. Frantically, Bowen had shuffled through notebooks and files while he watched in terror. The badger envied his courage....the steps Bowen took to secure his own importance.

The fox made sure he was more valuable alive than dead. And the truth in those documents he possessed proved that.

"Oh," Mr. Bridger exclaimed. "I've just remembered something. Does the word 'Firinn" mean anything to you?"

Tegan and Beckett glanced at Kenna. She stared at the ground moving her lips to words no one could hear.

"Kenna?" Beckett asked.

The little fox smiled. "I know the word from an old poem. Let's see":

> *"Out on the magnificent sea,*
> *A soldier gathered his courage to be*
> *Strong in the faith, mighty in firinn*
> *And sail back home with a victorious win."*

Kenna scratched her head, "Or something like that. We learned it in school." She waited for Mr. Bridger to answer.

"An old adage to the war in northwest Fellnore, across the shores of the mighty river," the badger mused.

"Is there something to that?" Beckett asked.

"To what?" Mr. Bridger quipped.

"Do you think it's a reference to where Kenna's father might be? Northwest Fellnore?" Tegan probed.

Before the badger could answer, Kenna jumped up, "Yes! It has to be!" She scrambled around the others and reached for the door.

The badger caught her paw before she opened it and said, "Kenna, if that is true, then you need to confirm with Edwin." Kenna stepped back with her mouth wide open, "THE Edwin?"

"Yeah, THE Edwin?" Beckett repeated.

Tegan covered her ears with her paws. She did NOT want to hear this. No way was she going back to Chipping Farms. Not unless....

"Edwin knows the most about the battle: the location, the dates, the strategy—"

"How is *that* going to help us?" Tegan asked indignantly.

"If the word Bowen repeated is indeed a clue to where he's hiding, then Edwin can send you in the right direction to find him. It's your best option," the badger replied.

Kenna nodded, "Right, are you coming with us?"

"Oh no," Mr. Bridger answered. "I couldn't possibly leave this village. You are on your own, but I do wish you good luck."

"Why won't you come?" Beckett asked.

"He's afraid," Tegan responded.

"Is that true, Mr. Bridger?" Kenna asked.

The badger sighed deeply, his head low, "Yes, the truth is that I am afraid."

"Afraid of what?" asked Beckett.

"Failure," the badger replied. "I let Bowen down once before. I can't do that again."

Chapter 7

Hours into the journey, Bowen finally gave himself permission to reflect. Was he doing the right thing? And if so, was it worth it?

His family had been torn apart by Reginald's insurgence. His wife confined to their house while their daughter sought odd jobs along the forest path between Chipping Farms and Old Padley. But the males fared far worse.... brothers and sons made to join the pillaging parties or march in a so called "exploration militia." Those that disapproved were promptly given heavy manual labor jobs like hauling stolen goods from wagons to storehouses. Bowen's uncles cleared land for a new two-story barn, and his own nephew required to serve as bodyguard for the outrageous leader. Every villager served Reginald's needs in one way or another.

Tired and sore, Bowen breathed heavy. Yes, he was doing the right thing. To bring Reginald to his knees and stop all of this chaos was well worth it. Bowen just had to keep going.

A small creek trickled over smooth rocks next to the footpath. Bowen squatted down and removed his bag from around his shoulder and neck with a grunt. Rubbing the side of his neck, he lowered his other paw into the cold water and splashed some on his face and chest. The cold liquid chilled his aching muscles. He sat near the creek for a while and watched the water swirl over and around the stones. His thoughts wandered to his daughter, Kenna. Had she received his letter? Would she understand the context and know to stay hidden?

Oh Kenna! Bowen rubbed his ears. Of all his kids, she was the youngest and most spirited. All his sons had served Edwin in some capacity.... soldier or scout. Even Declan surprised them by becoming the leader's full-time chef. He prepared meals for not only Edwin, but also for any of his visitors that stayed in the village. A highly trusted position indeed!

But Kenna, still very young, had just completed her formal education when Reginald overthrew Edwin. The chaos that ensued caused panic and turmoil within his family. Once they migrated to Old Padley, Kenna grew restless. She explored the forests despite her parents' warnings, spending days in the fields or in tall trees to survey her new territory. As weeks flew by and news of Chipping Farms seemed to settle, Bowen and his wife decided to make the journey back. They needed money, and those jobs remained in their old village. Their growing concern over Kenna's safety also spurred them to action. In fact, the desperation to reunite his family instigated Bowen to do something... anything to bring this madness to an end.

He remembered the documents stored safely at the abbey. Surely those papers would serve their purpose of revealing who Reginald really was to the clan. Then, and only then, would an uprising and prompt removal of Reginald be the justified means to end the misery his rule had inflicted.

Bowen secured the bag around his shoulder and neck. Rested and fully focused, he hiked along the footpath again. It wasn't long before the fox left behind a patch of vegetation and noticed several large wagons in the distance. Four large carts filled with a variety of lumber suggested that Bowen had reached the logging town. With no other creature in sight, he quickly moved closer. The smell of fresh beech filled his nose, making his eyes a bit watery. To his left, Bowen spotted a single empty wagon ready to haul a day's wage of lumber to town. Stumps and half trees surrounded him like a grassy, gaping forest.

And then he heard it. A high-pitched squeaking noise rolling his way. Like a caged animal with nowhere to hide, he panicked and jumped into the empty wagon before him. The fox listened as the screech drew closer and closer. The sound possessed him, and he popped his head up to see where the noise was coming from.

In front of him rolled an empty wooden wagon driven by a red squirrel. Propped up in the front, the squirrel wore a straw hat pulled down to shade his eyes. He barked at the miniature oxen pulling the wagon. Slow and sluggish, the creatures turned the cart and rolled up to the side of the wagon where Bowen sat cowering.

"You there!" the squirrel called out to Bowen.

The fox raised his head sheepishly and answered, "Yes?"

"What are you doing in there?"

"Sir, I apologize. I was unaware if you were friend or foe. I simply need a place to rest," Bowen explained.

The squirrel stood up and secured his wagon. He jumped off the cart, turned and studied Bowen. Chewing a blade of grass between his large front teeth, the squirrel grunted. "Well, I guess you're harmless enough. Still, no sudden movements!"

Bowen nodded energetically.

The red squirrel stretched his back and said, "If you follow the wagon path there through the forest, you'll reach the village. I'm sure there's a vacant room at the pub for one night's stay at least."

"Perfect!" the fox replied. "Food as well?"

"Yes, Fergie makes the best pottage ever," the squirrel smiled and removed the tethers from the animals so they could graze. Plucking a leaf stuck to his fluffy tail, he said, "If you hurry, you can get there before dark."

"Thank you, sir!" Bowen noticed the sun setting and quickly gathered his bag. "What is your name?" he asked.

"Gus," the squirrel replied and adjusted his hat.

Bowen nodded with appreciation and swiftly headed in the direction of the town. The path itself showed well-worn ruts dug deep into the packed dirt trail. No doubt these heavy-laden wagons caused the indentations over a long period of time. Whether locals hauled timber or sizeable rocks (removed for farmland) in those carts, Bowen appreciated the ease at which he could follow the trail in the failing sunlight.

Several mountains blocked the spill of daylight as the fox dipped in and out of the sun's last light. Instinctively looking over his shoulder, Bowen confirmed that he was alone....no one had followed him. Pleased that he managed to make good time, the fox smiled a little. And just ahead, as Gus suggested, he spotted a cluster of shops on the main road.

The narrow street straightened as small wooden store fronts lined the way. Bowen watched as several shops lit candles in their windows to signal business after dark. Up and down the street, foxes of all ages gathered the day's wares and headed home to prepare dinner for their families. But some of that foot traffic headed toward a particular establishment on the right: the Monk's Candle.

A wooden sign hanging outside the pub depicted a hooded monk holding a melted candle. Some of the paint was missing around the edges and a bit of the monk's hood had flaked off from years of weathering. Bowen peeked in the window just below it, curious and hungry. Groups of patrons shouted and laughed as they crowded near the bar to order drinks. Barmaids holding little wooden trays carried pints and small snacks to others sitting at tables near the window. He could almost taste the baked bread and butter the foxes consumed in front of him.

Dimly lit but full of life, the pub enticed Bowen to step inside. And the fox obeyed the calling, but with apprehension. He felt out of place and weary. Stacks of burning candles sat on every flat surface in the room, creating an almost ghost-like effect. He had never seen so many burning flames all at once and thought this quite odd.

In the corner of the pub, a trio of musicians set up chairs, ready to entertain for a good portion of the night. Bowen settled at a small table near them and ordered an ale and a bowl of whatever pottage was in the pot. He didn't care at this point. Fatigue had finally caught up with him and he was ready to call it a night.

The musicians played... a fiddler, a flute, and a bodhran drum. The melody, combined with patrons clapping, hummed through his head. Though the upbeat tempo delighted his senses, Bowen chose to meditate on his own thoughts instead.

He stared at the candles as he finished his meal. One last swig of ale and then he walked around a group of dancing couples towards the bar to inquire about a room.

"Pardon me," Bowen spoke to a small red fox standing behind the counter. "I'm looking for a room for the night. Do you have one available?"

The little fox brushed crumbs from her paws on her gray apron and replied, "Aye, let me check, sir." She turned to a small wooden box sitting on a shelf and opened it. Pulling out a large metal key, she playfully pointed it at Bowen and said, "You're in luck! Last room in the inn."

She smiled, pulling a thick book from somewhere beneath the small counter. Opening it before him, she instructed Bowen to fill out his name and address in the ledger. He thought for a moment and then carefully wrote "John Henry" on the line. He had to be cautious in case he was being followed.

"Here is your key, Mr. Henry," she said and pointed him in the direction of the room.

Bowen thanked her and then paused. An unusual candle stood on a simple brass pedestal behind the clerk. It caught his eye immediately. Not because of the candle itself, but that the flame burned an unusual deep shade of red. Intrigued, Bowen asked, "What is that?"

"It's the Monk's Candle," the clerk replied.

"As in the pub's name?" he responded.

"The very one."

"What makes it burn red?" Bowen asked.

"It's no ordinary candle. It is a relic; a symbol of trial and triumph," she stated. Seeing Bowen's confused expression, she moved closer and asked, "have you heard the story of our monk's candle?"

Bowen shook his head.

"Well," the fox slapped the countertop, "I'll tell you then. This candle shared a special role in the battle that took place over a hundred years ago. Do you know the legend of Petyr the Small?"

He shook his head again.

"Back when this village was just a dot on the map, a monk named Petyr lived and worked at a tiny church on the hill up there." The clerk motioned toward the window facing the east.

"This was during the time when the grey foxes raided villages, plundered goods, burned down structures, and killed any creature who got in their way. Word reached the monk that the foxes were only a day's march away. They were determined to bring destruction to this village and level every structure in their path.... including the church... on their way to the coast. Petyr was devastated.

However, one of the foxes in the raiding party had sought shelter with Petyr years before: an orphan who found both kindness and work from the monk. Recalling that compassion, that fox secretly advised Petyr to light a candle in his window. And as the raiding party marched through his village, the invaders would spare the little church and anyone hiding inside.

With this information, Petyr ran from house to house and gathered the villagers into his sanctuary. There they spent the night in darkness, except for a dim light emanating from this candle in the window. They huddled around it and prayed it stayed lit," the clerk said.

"I don't understand," Bowen replied. "What makes this candle so special?"

The clerk chuckled. "You see how there's hardly any wick left?" she asked.

Bowen looked closer. Indeed, most of the candle had melted over the stand in a cascade of wax, and the bit of wick left burned a very small red flame. "Yes, I see," he responded.

"The rampage was supposed to last one day; you know, march through, take what you want, start fires, and move on. But the raiders camped out in the village."

"What?!" Bowen was now entirely drawn into the story and the clerk knew it. She enjoyed retelling this tale for outsiders.

"They remained in the village for *eight* days!" she emphasized.

Bowen's mouth dropped open. "What happened to the candle?" He asked.

"The candle stayed lit for the duration of eight days. *That's* the miracle. It never wasted away or melted. The wick managed to burn without being used up. And as you can see," she pointed again to the relic on the wall, "it remains lit to this day."

Bowen stared at the candle and tried to imagine a scene of destruction. Raiders culling an entire village except for the little church. It was astonishing that the candle lasted as long as it did....and still does.

The clerk said, "If you need anything else, just ring me." And with that, she turned her attention to another customer requesting a drink.

Bowen played with the metal key in his paw and opened the wooden door just down the short hallway. Relieved to stay in a downstairs room, he quickly washed his face and paws in a bowl of water sitting on a table. As he wiped himself dry, he noticed a window just over the bed. A round glass pane stood slightly ajar. Chilly air wafted in from above. So Bowen stepped up on the bed and secured the window closed, pulling the curtains to block the light from a full moon outside.

As he tossed and turned in bed, Bowen tried his best to get comfortable. The blankets felt warm enough, but he was restless. Images of that candle floated around in his mind. And grey foxes overrunning villages with weapons and torches sent chills down his spine. He had to rest his mind in order to rest his body. So he counted slowly, but that didn't help. Squeezing the strap on his messenger bag, Bowen relaxed knowing that the bag was secured to his arm and not going anywhere without waking him up.

Besides, he thought, *I can escape through that window if necessary.* He closed his eyes tightly and hoped that he wouldn't need to escape. At least not tonight.

And then he fell asleep.

Chapter 8

A warm breeze blew across the moorlands, rippling through the purple heather that populated the landscape. As the thinly veiled moon peeked out from the behind the clouds, a shimmery glow settled on a stone path that snaked through the shrubbery. To the east, on top of the hill, a pack of gray wolves stood with their noses pointing upwards into the air. It smelled of rain...and something else. The animals circled each other and lifted their noses again. The lingering scent compelled them to search it out. So the wolves trotted down the hill and into the brush, determined to find the origin of the aroma.

But those predators weren't the only animals out there. Tegan, Beckett, and Kenna skirted the edges of the moors. Knowing they needed to cross quickly, the travelers held their lanterns close as they hiked along the pebbly foot path. Beckett's heavy steps on the gravel stones sounded like constant crunching noises. His lantern was running dangerously low on fuel. Nevertheless, they continued on foot resolute to make it to Chipping Farms before sunrise.

Tegan, in particular, dreaded going back into the town. Their first visit had resulted in a not-so-friendly introduction to the new leader there...plus a night in lockdown. And if they ran into Reginald again, would he remember them? No doubt their abrupt escape last time left a horrible taste in the fox leader's mouth. He would surely be more careful this time.

In the silence, a loud wailing, like a mournful call echoed from the hills. The travelers stopped and listened with attentive ears. Wide eyes scanned the landscape for any movement in the moonlight.

"What was *that*?!" Tegan whispered loud enough for the others to hear.

Beckett shook his head and motioned for quiet. He knew that sound and he knew it wasn't friendly. Readying his sword, he swung around and heard it again.

Ahhhwwwwwrrrooooooo!!!!

The howling sounded closer this time. Kenna shivered, "it's a wolf," she said flatly.

The other two stared at her processing what she just said. Tegan felt the blood drain from her head, making her dizzy and lightheaded. Fear gripped her in a way she hadn't felt since facing the rat king on her last quest. She drew her sword and planted it upright in the ground to steady herself.

"Let's keep going," Beckett suggested. "We can get to the river before they find us."

As the three quickened their pace, the sight of something else caught their attention. Ahead of them, near the forest line, a pair of glowing torches pierced the night sky. Tegan saw it and motioned to the others. She didn't know if the lights were friendly, but whoever or whatever behind those lights had to be safer than fighting off wolves.

The travelers ran toward the torches, their feet sensitive to the gravelly path. Loud crunching sounds from the small rocks and heavy hearts beating drowned out any other sounds of the night. As Kenna raced a few feet ahead, she abruptly stopped and fell over something in the dark, dropping her lantern. Breathing heavy, Beckett and Tegan raised their lights to see a pile of large lumber pieces on the road. Tegan reached over and helped Kenna stand up.

"Are you hurt?" Tegan asked her.

"No, I'm fine. Maybe bruised a little, but nothing is broken," Kenna said as she stood up.

Beckett and Tegan both exhaled in relief. As they stood there catching their breath, a rustling noise came from across the field. The travelers could barely hear it but knew what it was. The wolves were hunting them. And they were getting closer.

Panicked, Beckett and Tegan ran around the side of the lumber pile to join Kenna on the footpath. But something wasn't right. The earth under their feet gave way and the two tumbled backward into an earthen pit. Dirt and shrubbery fell on top of them as they shrieked and howled in fear.

What just happened? Tegan was in shock. She fell flat on her back, knocking the wind out of her lungs. Trying to speak, she managed a meager whisper, "Beckett, what happened?"

Beckett sat up and rubbed his head. "I don't know. Are you hurt?"

"I don't think so," she replied and sat up as well. Both of their lanterns were out so they couldn't distinguish their surroundings. The smell of damp earth lingered in their noses, and Tegan coughed and spit dirt out of her mouth.

"Tegan?! Beckett?!" Kenna squealed, "Are you there?" Kenna's head and small light from her lantern illuminated the two in the pit from above.

Beckett squinted in the dusty air. "We're good...just get us out of here!" He jumped up several times trying to escape from the hole. But the depth was just enough that they couldn't leap out.

"Climb on my back," Beckett instructed Tegan.

She stood up but immediately fell back down and cried out. "I can't, my ankle!"

Kenna reached down and felt around, "Reach up, Beckett!"

He raised his paw but couldn't quite reach her. "Kenna, find something, anything, to get us out."

She nodded and rushed to locate anything that could help the two out of the pit. She placed her lantern on a larger piece of lumber. Below it was a smaller piece....maybe this would work. Squatting behind the lumber, she placed her paws on the center of the wood and pushed as hard as she could. It moved slightly but not enough. She turned around and dug her feet into the ground, pushing with everything she had. The lumber dislodged and moved a bit closer to the pit. Kenna ran around and shouted down the hole, "Watch out! I'm shoving a piece of lumber toward you."

"We're ready, send it down!" Beckett replied. He looked at Tegan who held her leg and ankle in pain. "Don't worry, Tegan, we're getting out of here." She smiled weakly and nodded in agreement.

Kenna situated herself again on the backside of the piece of wood and shoved with her legs. The lumber teetered over the opening of the pit like a seesaw. She ran to the edge and pushed one last time. Sliding into the pit, the end of the wood piece landed slanted with a thud. The other end extended only a small bit out of the pit's opening. Kenna wiped the sweat from her brow and lifted her lantern to see down inside the hole.

"Come here," Beckett lifted Tegan up gently to stand on one leg. "Hold on to my shoulders and I'll get us out."

Tegan gingerly wrapped herself around her friend in a piggyback style while Beckett grabbed the wood with both paws. He shook the lumber a bit to measure its stability.

"Hurry!" Kenna whispered loudly into the pit. Looking over her shoulder, she saw movement in the bushes just across from her. "They're coming!" she shrieked.

With a burst of adrenaline, Beckett heaved himself up on the wood carrying Tegan on his back. Another step and then another, Beckett grunted under the weight while Tegan whimpered in pain. Near the top of the pit, Beckett steadied himself so Tegan could get off and out of the hole. Kenna grabbed her paw and pulled, yanking her friend off Beckett's back and onto the ground next to her.

In the hole, Beckett stepped up again on the lumber, but his foot slipped. He grabbed the wood with both arms trying to slow himself down. His tunic snagged on a small knob towards the middle of the wood, abruptly stopping him from falling any further. Beckett unhooked his garment from the knot and took a deep breath. Tired from exertion, he hoisted himself up one last time and managed to reach the opening of the pit. Kenna kneeled near him and tugged on Beckett's paw, pulling him out.

Kenna looked at Tegan and then Beckett, "We need to get out of here, the wolves are coming!" she squeaked.

Beckett nodded and lifted Tegan up, placing her arm around his shoulder. Kenna grabbed the other arm and did the same. They managed to carry their friend some distance down the path before noticing that the brush near them quivered with movement. Beckett and Kenna both turned and saw a snarling wolf behind them, head down, ready for attack. The two burst into a sprint, carrying their friend as best they could. The wolf and his pack bounded down the path toward them, quickly catching up with the travelers.

And just before the wolf leader attacked the wounded, a horrible shrieking noise bombarded their senses. A sound so terrifying that the travelers fell face first on the ground, covering their ears. The wolves stopped in their tracks and whimpered.

Two torches moved before them, almost as ethereal entities. As the fire got closer, Tegan could see a figure holding those torches, dressed in a colorful robe. The figure waved the fire at the wolves and shouted gibberish at them, causing the predators to step back.

Traces of smoke billowed in the air with a faint smell of sage, or perhaps rosemary. Tegan coughed again as the fragrance irritated her lungs and made her eyes water. She sat watching the scene unfold before her, like it was scripted. *Who is this creature?* she wondered.

The wolves stepped farther and farther back until the figure turned around and began walking towards the travelers. Beckett and Kenna scooped Tegan up again, ready to run. But the figure motioned to them and pointed to a stationary object parked on the side of the pathway. It was a caravan...an old tinker's wagon. With Tegan in pain and the wolves still out there wandering the moors, Beckett and Kenna decided the caravan was their best option for the night.

Kenna hopped up a primitive set of wooden stairs and tugged at the door handle. Wrapping her paw around the wrought iron handle, she pulled until the chunky wooden door swung free. In fact, the door itself was split into two parts, creating both an upper and bottom door. Kenna managed to open the bottom door and quickly crawled inside. She held her paws out while Beckett shoved Tegan's legs into the opening, cradling her head. Kenna pulled on Tegan's cloak as Beckett ducked in the wagon holding his friend's shoulders tightly. Laying the wounded sombel on a long bench filled with beige and blue pillows, Beckett wedged the door closed behind them. Finally, they felt safe.

Low light filled the small van as two lanterns, draped with thin scarves, sat on the table: their flames barely visible through the veil. Shadows danced on the walls as the flames flickered wildly. Across from the bench stood a black iron fireplace with a wooden cupboard built above the stove top. The skinny chimney disappeared into a hole in the roof of the caravan. A dark colored kettle and teacup rested on the stove, waiting for its owner to fetch a late-night snack. In the cupboard above, someone had curiously arranged sets of bowls, plates, and cups, securing them behind a glass door. No doubt those breakables were stored somewhere safe when the wagon began moving.

On either side of the iron stove was treasured storage space. To the left, a corner cabinet, and to the right, a wooden table. The table itself actually lifted to reveal a storage compartment beneath it. Most travelers stowed extra kitchen utensils, cooking pans, spices, and other ingredients there.

Towards the back of the wagon, against the window on the back wall, laid a hefty mattress decorated with plush, red blankets. Plump, purple and green pillows were heaped at the head of the bed, on the right side of the wall. The mattress, itself, rested on a stack of storage cabinets. Shiny iron handles adorned the furniture along with fancy scribblings and hand painted yellow flowers. The contents within these drawers most likely consisted of bedding, along with clothing and heavy garments, safeguarded for whoever lived in this caravan.

In addition to the back wall window, one other opening had been cut into the wagon. Much smaller than the bed window, the opening above the bench was decorated entirely of sheer yellow fabric and golden tassels; whereas the bed window had been layered with a thin, gauzy, white curtain with heavier, burnt orange fabric on top of it. Currently, the outer drapes were secured with a tassel, leaving only the sheer white drapes in view. Those layered, heavy drapes helped keep the cold out as well as the sunlight in the early mornings.

Then suddenly the door blew open with a *bang!* and the robed creature crawled inside with the torches. She snuffed out the flames, sending smoke swirling around her head. Tucking those torches under the iron stove, she closed the door and secured it tightly. Her visitors remained motionless, not knowing if the creature knew of their presence.

"Hello?" Beckett whispered.

The creature turned around and cinched her robe closer to her waist. "I see you found a place to hide," she replied in a crackling voice. An older raccoon with graying fur stood before them; her petite frame oddly disproportionate to the huge, roomy robe she wore.

Tegan's ears perked up and her whiskers twitched. She knew that laugh...but from where?

The raccoon sat next to Tegan on the bench. Beckett and Kenna hesitated, unsure of what to do or say. They were trespassers in a compromising situation, hoping for a little grace.

"Do...do you live here?" stuttered Tegan wincing in pain.

"Aye, child, I do," she replied. "This is home."

The raccoon motioned to Tegan so she could inspect her injury. Desperate for help, the sombel complied. Delicately feeling the bones around her ankle, the raccoon tilted her head and grunted to herself. Tegan was surprised at how gently the raccoon tended to her. She could barely feel the pressure from the raccoon's fingers.

"Have you done this before?" Tegan asked timidly.

"I have," the raccoon replied without looking at her patient. "I believe you have only sprained your ankle. I don't feel any broken bones." The raccoon leaned over and opened the table compartment, reaching in for a few fabric pieces. She ripped them lengthwise to form long strips. The visitors watched as the raccoon collected a bowl and fabric pouch from the cupboard. Then, she poured hot water into the bowl from the kettle and mixed in a spoonful of blue powder from the pouch. Placing the fabric strips into the mixture, the raccoon soaked the strips and then squeezed out the excess water. She then wrapped Tegan's ankle as tight as the sombel could bear.

"There, keep your ankle elevated tonight. You should have use of it by morning," the raccoon instructed.

Tegan felt a burning sensation in her foot. Panicking, she instinctively grabbed the bandage, pulling it away from her leg.

The raccoon seized her paws, "Don't remove it!" She placed Tegan's paws on her lap and said, "that burning sensation means the salve is working." She patted Tegan's shoulder softly to reassure her.

"May I ask your name, miss?" Beckett inquired. "We are grateful for your assistance."

The raccoon turned her attention to Beckett and Kenna, "I'm Sabreena," she replied. Observing Tegan in the dim lantern light,

Sabreena proposed, "You may stay the night and leave first thing in the morning."

"We appreciate your kindness; but we don't want to encroach on your hospitality," Tegan replied.

"Nonsense!" Kenna barked. "Remember the wolves we just escaped from? They're still out there salivating. Do you want to run into them again?"

Beckett shook his head emphatically, "Definitely not!" He turned to Sabreena with wide eyes and said, "We'll stay for the night."

"Good, then it's settled," the raccoon tinker responded and hummed a tune as she tended the stove. "I have soup in the oven, and it will be ready soon."

Tegan listened as Sabreena hummed the same tune over and over again. In a strange way, she felt like she'd heard the melody before. But where? The sombel closed her eyes and concentrated on the song. She pictured trees, then a forest, and then a ravine. "Oh!" she gasped and covered her mouth with a single paw. She pointed to the raccoon, "That's where I know you from.... the forest!"

"Aye, child, the forest," Sabreena smiled and tilted her head back to project a foreboding, guttural laugh.

Indeed, Tegan had met Sabreena months ago on her way to a wise man's cave. It happened during the prophecy of the blood moon. The tune the racoon sang gave it away. In that unexpected meeting, Sabreena confirmed the prophecy and gifted her green moonstones and athru berries—both deemed crucial for the quest. But how did she know that Tegan would need them?

And now? They'd crossed paths again... under coincidence. Or had they? Sabreena understood what Tegan required that day in the forest. Would she know what lay ahead of her now?

"How did you know I needed moonstones and athru berries that day?" Tegan asked the raccoon.

"The prophecy," Sabreena responded, stirring soup in a huge black pot.

"But I never saw you before that day," Tegan replied.

"Aye, but the prophecy knew," Sabreena turned away and hummed, a clear sign not to ask any more questions.

Tegan looked at Beckett and shrugged. Neither of them ever inquired about that day again.

CHAPTER 9

The wind picked up outside, howling through the trees and gusting against the walls of the little caravan. A few rain droplets echoed off the roof. Those inside the wagon knew a storm was coming. The visitors huddled around each other sharing a blanket in the low candlelight. With full stomachs and warm tea, Kenna, Beckett, and Tegan found comfort in each other's company amidst the noises they heard outside.

"That's some storm," Kenna said in a low voice.

Wind pushed against the caravan so that the loose items inside the tinker's shook a bit, jingling and jangling in the dark. The sound of rain pouring down reverberated in the wagon, causing those inside to keep watch instead of drifting off to sleep.

"Aye, but it will pass," replied Sabreena. Moving the curtains to one side, she peered out of the window. Sheets of rain shimmered against the moonlight and lightning flashed. The racoon quickly pulled the curtain closed and said, "Looks like we're in for a long night." She sighed and sat on a small chair just opposite of her visitors.

In the dim light, they studied each other. The old tinker pushed her little round glasses up on her nose. Brown tuffs of fur stuck out in between the folds of her cloak and her dark paws now lay folded in her lap. Gray whiskers lined her snout, but her large brown eyes revealed traces of kindness.

As Kenna and Beckett whispered to each other, Tegan opened her mouth to say something but then closed it. Should she mention Bowen? It seemed farfetched that a rambling tinker would know anything about Kenna's father.... or his situation. Or would she?

"Do you wish to ask me a question?" Sabreena offered.

The visitors looked at each other, but Tegan was the first to respond. "Have you heard anything about a missing fox...one that went into hiding, maybe?" She asked.

"He worked for Edwin of the Redlan Clan before Reginald took over," Kenna added.

Sabreena thought for a moment. "I don't know anything about a missing fox. What is his name?" she asked.

"Bowen Whitethorne," Kenna replied. "He's my father," she squeaked out.

Tegan rested her paw on Kenna's shoulder, comforting her. Kenna, though smaller than the other two, was feisty and bold. But it was in this moment that Tegan understood the little fox had a soft side too.

"I've heard that a Redlan fox escaped Chipping Farms with sensitive information. And Reginald is desperate to get those documents back," the tinker said. "Is this the same fox you mentioned?"

"Sounds like it," Beckett spoke up. "And if it is, do you know where he might have travelled?"

"The only clues we have are an old lullaby and the word 'firinn.' Apparently, my father kept mumbling that before he fled," Kenna said.

"Who told you this?" Sabreena asked.

"Mr. Bridger," Kenna responded. "Wadsworth Bridger. He worked with my father in Edwin's council."

"Ah, of course he did," the tinker replied.

Her tone caught Beckett's attention. "Do you know him?" he asked.

"Indeed, I do. Conniving little badger," she said under her breath.

"Pardon?" Beckett asked.

"Bridger is one of those creatures that plays both sides of the coin, if you know what I mean," Sabreena said. "For the most part, you can count on the badger to do what he says he'll do. BUT, if a situation suits his particular need, well, let's just say he only looks out for himself."

"I see," Kenna said softly.

"How do you know this?" Beckett asked.

"We go way back. I knew Bridger when he was still in school. Pretty decent individual back then. Once Edwin took him in and made him part of his council, I began seeing changes in him," Sabreena said.

"What kind of changes?" Tegan asked.

"He became more elusive and scheming," she replied. "Look, I'm an old raccoon. I've seen my share of war and conflict. But the matters Bridger fought over are far from done. Mark my words." Sabreena leaned back and closed her eyes. "I know the Branwell clan well. While they are related to the Redlan clan, the Branwells consider themselves separate from the Redlans and all their dealings. Not too long ago, I caught wind of a parcel of land that Edwin wanted to buy just north of the Arsa mountains. I believe he wanted to make it into an alternate trade route for those living by the sea. He was about to send Bowen to the coast to start negotiations with the natives; to make peace and work out an agreement for the land purchase. These negotiations were incredibly important! Not just for Chipping Farms, but for the county of Fellnore."

"What happened?" Tegan asked.

"Bridger heard about it and sabotaged the entire deal," Sabreena replied.

"What?! Why?" Beckett asked incredulously.

"Some believe Bridger wanted the land for himself. But I think there was another reason," Sabreena replied. "Jealousy." The raccoon sat up straight and continued, "See if the deal went through, your father's success would solidify his position as Edwin's number one employee, his right-hand fox. But if the deal fell flat, then Bridger might be able to step up and negotiate it for himself and be considered the hero."

"No doubt taking the top spot from my father," Kenna responded. "Oh, this is way more complicated than I thought!" She covered her eyes with her paws, cradling her head on her knees.

"So what finally happened?" Beckett asked.

"Nothing," she replied. "By the time Bridger stepped up to negotiate a deal, Reginald rallied his troops and overthrew Edwin. The village fell into total chaos."

Could the timing of the uprising be coincidence? Or was it planned?

Tegan swallowed hard. The more she thought about the events surrounding Reginald's rise to power, the more she smelled foul play.

Yes, Reginald turned greedy. Yes, he wanted power. But was it possible that Reginald AND Bridger concocted this plan together? A plan to cover a sneaky badger's tracks and hide the fact that he was in this all along? Afterall, Reginald would indeed inherit power and then Bridger could be the number one aid...once Bowen fled, of course. The truth, the 'firinn.'

Tegan scratched her head and rubbed her face with her paw.

"What was that?" Kenna asked.

Apparently, Tegan mumbled that last bit out loud. "Oh, I merely said the truth, firinn."

"Yes, firinn," Sabreena repeated.

"Remember the old poem about the soldier on the sea?" Kenna asked. Without waiting for an answer, she recited:

"Out on the magnificent sea,
A soldier gathered his courage to be
Strong in the faith, mighty in firinn
And sail back home with a victorious win."

Sabreena sat in silence. After a pause, she said simply, "There are many types of truth, you know. Firinn could be what your father is seeking. It could also symbolize truth in creature form."

"Like a living thing?" Kenna asked.

"Yes, or someone that represents the truth," the tinker replied.

"A religious leader, perhaps?" Tegan suggested.

Sabreena smiled and laughed her cackly laugh. "Indeed, an abbot or a monk."

A surge of rain pelted the wagon's roof making it hard to hear anything else. Sabreena waited for the rain to taper off and then suggested, "Or, it could refer to the Flag of Firinn."

"The flag of what?" Kenna asked.

"The Flag of Firinn," the tinker replied.

"The fairy flag?" Beckett asked.

"Yes, the same. It is said that the silk woven by the fairies into the flag was dyed with colors gathered from dawn and dusk," Sabreena responded. "The fairies also imbued a certain magical property into the fabric. Do you know what it was?"

The visitors sat fascinated, waiting for the tinker to answer her own question.

"A compass," Sabreena said.

"A compass?" Tegan asked. "How does it work?"

"The flag, when unfurled, reveals not only the location of the individuals you seek, but it can also be implemented as a moral compass—an exposer of truths," Sabreena explained and shook her head. "I've only seen this flag once in my life. It was truly magnificent."

"Where did you see it?" asked Kenna.

"Edwin's arsenal," Sabreen replied. "It had been secretly housed there and protected for over a hundred years."

Kenna looked at Tegan and Beckett, and then said, "That's what we need to ask him about."

"Yes," Beckett said. "We should be there by mid-day tomorrow."

"Oh, you plan to visit Edwin then?" Sabreena asked.

"That is our plan," Tegan said. "We should've been there tonight, but all of this happened instead." She grabbed her ankle, wincing.

"Well, he can answer all your questions about the flag, but you won't have the chance to see it for yourself," Sabreena offered.

"Why not?" asked Kenna.

"No one knows where it is. The flag was stolen a few months ago straight from the clan's arsenal," Sabrina said. "Edwin has been searching for it ever since."

"That might explain his need for purchasing land to the north," muttered Tegan.

"Indeed," Sabreena nodded to Tegan.

"Any idea of who might want to steal the flag?" Beckett asked.

"The only witness reported that they saw a monk holding an odd-looking candle looming around the arsenal walls the night before the robbery," the tinker said.

"And who wouldn't want a flag with those kinds of powers?" Tegan asked rhetorically.

"Exactly, it could be anyone," Beckett replied.

"Imagine if we could locate that flag," Kenna mused. "I could easily find my father and end this. I'm supposed to be participating in Edwin's return to leadership anyway."

"Aye, but the flag isn't the only way to pinpoint your father," Sabreena said. "And remember, the reason your father is missing is because he knows a secret. Those details must be revealed so the truth can prevail....no matter the outcome. And that is a treacherous spot to be in."

Kenna sighed a deep, deliberate sigh. She knew It. But if she could find her father, then the two could at least face the consequences together, as a family.

Adler fiddled with the lantern on his dinner table, making the flame burn a bit brighter. It had been a long day, but then, so was every day in the service of an eccentric ruler. Stacks of receipts lay in a pile near his light source. One by one, he meticulously recorded each in the ledger in front of him. Somehow, this fox had managed to be assigned part-time bookkeeper (in addition to bodyguard), recording purchases of staple foods for Reginald. But he didn't mind the task as he relished this time alone.

For most of his day, Adler listened to the leader drone on about his desire for more land. And the reason? As far as he knew, Reginald's plans to pillage and plunder far exceeded his want to govern this village wisely...something the fox originally promised. And that was the trigger that set Adler off. He knew Reginald would never honor his word. And now, Adler felt the burden... the need... the calling to do something about it. But what?

He laid the ink pen down and rubbed his eyes. Weeks ago, his Uncle Bowen had called him into the office. While they discussed a few business matters, Bowen seemed tense and on edge like he was being watched. His uncle told him in very few words that he had discovered sensitive information and might be in trouble for it. But before Adler learned the details, they were interrupted. Day later, Bowen disappeared.

Now Adler had to piece together what little information he had. He stood up and walked over to the window. With only the moonlight in the sky, the fox could see across the field and barely make out the palace that Reginald lived in. The other bodyguard, Bin, enjoyed every minute in that house, and stayed most nights in a room off to one corridor. But Adler preferred his little home in the woods.

The fox pulled the curtain closed and returned to the table. In a small vest pocket, Adler removed the piece of paper he'd been saving from the Boar's Nest. That crumpled paper might give him a clue about Bowen's disappearance. He opened it and furrowed his brow. It was completely empty, except for a small doodle in the bottom left corner... a flag.

Adler smoothed the paper flat with his paw. The paper, itself, appeared worn. But he also felt indentations on the surface, perhaps from a writing instrument used to compose a message on sheets of paper stacked on top of this one. The fox spun around. He reached for the small fireplace on the back wall. Picking up a small chunk of charcoal, Adler returned to the paper and began vigorously coloring over the indentations.

"There it is!" he exclaimed. "It's Bowen's handwriting for sure." The last message his uncle wrote from this stack of papers. As Adler read the words, he realized it was the last page of a letter. So he didn't know the context or to whom the message was written. But he gathered that Bowen had sent the message to someone recently.

The last few lines read: "I understand that I will only be staying for a week. Please gather as many citizens in Swynton as possible for interviews. I will be leaving soon but can't reveal the exact date as I'm being watched... even now. Yours, BW."

BW... Bowen Whitethorne. And then, further down the page, as if on another train of thought, Adler saw the address for Derwent Abbey.

"That's odd," he said out loud.

Adler folded the sheet of paper and placed it in between the pages of a book laying on the table. *Why would Bowen visit an abbey? And who were the villagers to be interviewed in Swynton?*

Adler yearned to pack his bag and run to this abbey tonight. Seeing Bowen would certainly answer a lot of his questions. But if he left now, his life and plans to reinstate Edwin would be over. Those bounty hunters would come after him in no time. And at least Reginald didn't suspect Adler of planning anything to relieve him of his leadership—just the way Reginald did to Edwin. So, in the meantime, Adler stayed and waited. He needed more information... and he needed sympathizers that would follow him into battle, if necessary.

Chapter 10

Bowen's eyes opened as he heard soft padded footsteps outside his door. Back and forth they walked, until a sudden stop at his room. He peered down at the small opening below his door but couldn't make out the feet. As the adrenaline awakened Bowen, he quietly stepped out of bed and into his shoes. No more sleeping; it was time to leave.

The door or the window? If he waited long enough, surely the feet would move on, allowing him an exit through the door. But what if they stayed? Or worse.... They burst through the only obstacle standing between them? Bowen shivered and pulled on the window curtain. Outside, the dark still hovered over the landscape, but a hint of sunrise could be detected in the air.

He grabbed the latch and shoved against the glass. The window creaked as if it had never been opened; a sound that eerily echoed in the early morning air. Securing his bag around his shoulders, Bowen squeezed through the tight frame and landed squarely on the ground. The grass, now damp with dew, felt cold under his feet. And as he breathed out, puffs of air visibly wafted around him, formed by the cool temperatures. He stepped out into the darkness, searching for the road he followed the day before. And there it was! Bowen skipped toward a mile post sign propped snuggly, and a little crooked, in the ground. An arrow pointed to his right; it said, "To the pass."

"The pass? That must be the mountain pass to get to Swynton," Bowen thought. Surely the white cottage John Henry mentioned must be ahead.

He hiked the trail for what seemed like an hour when he spied a small white house sitting at the end of an orchard. By now, the sun had peeked over the horizon, and Bowen could spot the cottage under a bramble of tree branches. As he neared the house, the fox could tell that the owners kept the little cottage in fine condition, the porch, free from leaves and dirt, and the windows, spotless and clean. Several apple trees framed the home, shading the porch with their brilliant green leaves. On one of the lower branches sat a small mouse on a makeshift rope swing. The boy, no older than a toddler, wore a short, green romper and giggled loudly as an older sibling pushed him up into the air. Bowen smiled.

Soon, three other children came out from behind the house and ran squealing onto the front porch. Each little girl, dressed in a pastel pink dress and matching bonnet, chased by another two boys holding tiny frogs in their paws. The screaming must've caught the mother's attention as she opened the front door and called out, "Stop being so loud! You'll wake the baby!" She looked around as if something seemed a bit off but then turned and closed the front door behind her.

As the kids resumed their games, Bowen's challenge was to find the mountain pass without being spotted. It was supposedly around here somewhere. And secrecy was imperative. He didn't want anyone to know where he was going, or where he had been.

The smell of sweet grass drew his attention to the side of the house nearest to him. He squatted and crawled from his hiding spot (behind a tree) to the large patch of tall grass directly behind the swing. Bees and other insects buzzed around him, but Bowen kept low. The fragrance from the fresh grass was intoxicating.

Around the base of the grass patch laid an opening to a footpath. The grass had grown so tall that the weight of the blades caused the leaves to lean over, covering the path like a grassy tunnel. Bowen waited until the little girl pushed her brother once again on the swing and then rushed through the grassy opening. Shady and cool, the fox hustled along the path, the soft padding under his feet. He could still make out the sounds of little ones playing only a short distance away from him. But right now, he thought only of Swynton.

An uphill climb left him a bit breathless. Ahead, he spotted what looked like a piece of timber laying across the path. It had fallen in such a way that half of the wood protruded through the grass towards the sky. Seeing an opportunity, Bowen scrambled up the branch to observe above the grass.

The view was amazing! Mountains girded him on both sides, formidable but stunning. Cool air tickled his ears, and the smell of rain seemed just a short breath away. It was here that Bowen decided to take a short break. He descended the makeshift wooden tower back into the grassy covering. Seeing a stone the size of a chair, he seated himself and opened his messenger bag. A bit of bread and cheese would make him feel like new. And so, he ate hastily, wiping the crumbs from his whiskers with an old handkerchief.

The wind had picked up, blowing the ends of the grass back and forth like a game of tug of war. Bowen gathered his things, ready to increase the pace. Instead, a line of ants emerged from the path before him, marching in his direction. Their spindly legs traversed the grass in a mesmerizing manner. The ant leader stopped as soon as he saw Bowen, and the other ants paused behind him.

"Good day, sir," the ant said to the fox.

"Good day to you as well," Bowen replied. "Say, do you know how far it is to the end of this trail?"

"Where are you headed?" the insect asked, scratching his head with one of his forelegs.

"I'm hoping to reach Swynton soon," the fox replied. "Am I on the right path?"

"I'd say you are." The ant looked back at the others and then added, "We've just come from Haddonfield only an hour ago. Keep following this path and you'll reach your destination."

One of the smaller ants squeaked something to the leader. He paused and walked a step closer to Bowen, "But be aware," the insect said in a low voice. "There are whispers of bounty hunters in the area." The ant stepped back and examined the fox. Bowen felt the blood drain from his face, his body paralyzed with fear. He tried to open his mouth and speak, but all he could do was grunt.

The ant leader continued, "I don't know why you're travelling the pass, but it doesn't look like you're on holiday. Be careful!" Then the ant summoned the others with a short whistle and left.

Bowen stood in the middle of the path, alone and dumbfounded. *Bounty hunters? Could they be looking for me? I must stay hidden for as long as possible.* He took a deep breath and ran.

"What's the plan?" Beckett asked Kenna. "We're not marching through town, right?" His voice seemed a bit shaky.

"No," Kenna replied. "It's best if we keep hidden. Besides, Edwin's under house arrest in the old rectory just outside of town, so we'll be out of sight." She motioned to her friends, "Follow me."

The group walked under the coverage of a hedgerow until it met with a simple creek, quietly flowing in a shallow ravine. Kenna followed the water upstream, deep in thought, while Tegan and Beckett trailed behind her. A sense of dread washed over Tegan as she neared a jagged boulder. They were close and she could sense it, a foreboding in the air.

Quietly, they trekked to the base of the massive boulder and stopped to catch their breath. The sun hovered overhead and the heat had reached its peak. Beckett and Kenna both leaned over the stream and splashed cool water on their head and necks. Removing a piece of cloth from her bag, Tegan dipped it into the creek and squeezed it out, applying the damp rag to her forehead, ears, and neck.

Beckett noticed Tegan's paws tremble, "Is the heat getting to you?"

"No," Tegan half laughed, "it's the destination." She untied the wrap around her injured ankle and stretched out her leg. All this walking was aggravating her injury, and she hoped they could rest as soon as they met with Edwin. Tegan quickly inspected her ankle and then wrapped it tight for the hike.

A series of small, square stepping stones lay gracefully on top of the stream. Kenna tentatively raised her foot and placed it on the first step, making sure it was sturdy. Turning around, Kenna waved to assure her friends. Tegan followed Kenna, then Beckett. They gingerly stepped on the little path of stones, one by one, making their way to the old rectory or priest's house. Around the other side of the massive boulder, the stones tapered off and then disappeared. The three travelers hopped onto the sandy shoreline and walked up a foot path, leading to a stone fence. Kenna found an opening in the fence and slipped through into the rectory grounds.

Following close behind, Tegan entered the same opening and walked out onto the grounds. She noticed the stone walls were still standing, but the roofs had collapsed long ago. Piles of stone lay on the ground in every corner, enduring years of harsh weather like wind and rainstorms. Only one area remained intact; a large room resembling a cottage stood on the far right of the grounds. It was the rectory, the official residence of the clergyman.

Several arched windows graced the side of the stone wall facing the courtyard. With fabric covering the openings, a soft glow penetrated from the windows. A bulky wooden door stood ajar while high musical notes emanated from within.

But as the group approached, they noticed two fox soldiers sitting outside the door playing with dice. The soldiers, Reginald's guards, monitored the front door...no doubt they were some of his best fighters. Keeping an eye on Reginald's rival would be the highest honor these soldiers could achieve. But still, was there a way to get inside without being seen?

Huddled together near a broken wall, the group stayed out of view. How could they get inside? And then Tegan saw something... a handle on what looked like an old door, hidden along the hedgerows on the opposite side of the rectory. She nudged Kenna and asked, "Does this old rectory have a cellar of some kind?"

"I'm sure it does. Maybe an old wine cellar from its heyday," Kenna replied.

"Look," Tegan pointed to the handle on the door, which was now shadowed by the leaves hanging over the structure. "That just might be our way in."

Excited, Kenna stood up, ready to run to the cellar door. But Beckett and Tegan both grabbed her arms and pulled her back.

"We can't be seen," Beckett whispered in her ear.

Kenna nodded, but her eyes were wild and fierce. Edwin was inside and she would meet with him no matter the cost. "I have to get inside!" She wiggled free of their grasp.

"Yes, but we need a distraction," Tegan responded. "Kenna," she tugged on the fox's tunic, but Kenna didn't respond.

"Kenna!" Tegan whispered harshly to get her attention, turning the fox around by her shoulders. Tegan looked into those wild fox eyes and spoke slowly, "We will get inside that building, but we must first have a plan. Got it?"

Kenna's gaze broke and her eyes softened. "Yes," she finally said. "Yes, a plan."

Chapter II

Bowen stood in the clearing taking in the view. After trudging through the tunneled pass, he finally made it to his destination. This is Swynton. And what a sight it was!

A small cottage rested under a grove of trees to his right. A wide front porch and open windows made this building inviting. But farther out, the grassy ground turned to rock, dropping deeply onto a shallow beach before touching the sea. Creatures of all kinds, in bright colored bathing suits, littered the shoreline as they played in the sand or swam in the salty water. The bathers bobbed up and down on the gentle waves as the surf carried them back and forth along the shore. Young hares and hedgehogs squealed as they splashed in the water, oblivious to anything else but their activities. A mother badger, wearing a straw hat, tossed a ball to her son, and several foxes built towering castles in the sand. Bowen felt a breeze blow past him. Its warmth and soothing salt aroma calmed him to an almost dreamlike state.

Out in the sea, just off the shore, stood a solitary rock structure. And in the center of that rock sat a simple stone building, two or three stories high. Bowen recognized it. He planned to meet his contacts there. The fox scanned the shore to locate a way across to the rock. A small canoe or boat perhaps? But there was nothing of the kind on the shoreline.

To his left, an old pier seemed to extend all the way to the rock. Curious, Bowen ducked out of the tunnel's protection and stood in the sunlight, ready to explore that option. With warm grass underneath his paws, the fox scampered toward the pier to get a better view. The wind howled around him as he ran.

And there it was. Bowen stood at the base of the pier and analyzed the structure for safe access. Could he get across without tumbling into the ocean? Quite a few planks were missing, however he reasoned there were plenty left to stabilize the structure. As he contemplated the risks, a family of mice exited the building and walked across the pier towards him. Two parents and three little ones, with the smallest riding on the father mouse's shoulders. The mother, dressed in a white sundress and matching hat, held a burlap shopping bag while the other two kids ran ahead of her.

"Come back here!" she called out, and the siblings begrudgingly returned to hold their mother's paws.

The family chatted with each other as they crossed the pier to the shoreline. Bowen stepped aside to let them pass and nodded his head to greet them. The father nodded back and the little one squealed with delight.

Assured of its accessibility, Bowen stepped onto the pier and carefully navigated the first few planks. Feeling the ocean air whip around his body, the fox paused to steady himself. He gazed into the horizon and marveled at the diamond-like sparkles manifesting on each wave in the surf. The sun overhead quickly warmed his brown fur, making it hot to the touch.

As he continued his journey, Bowen surmised that this pier had been transformed into a bridge many years ago. He could see the series of wide planks suddenly stop; and then dark, thin planks took over. The wide planks had to be the original structure as they were weathered from the sun and sea. But the thinner ones were definitely newer since they felt sturdier underfoot and didn't creak with each step! Plus, not one of these planks was missing. As the fox reached the end of the bridge, he jumped onto dry ground. Then, Bowen navigated a steep stairwell until he reached the door of the mysterious building.

Several open windows near the door enticed Bowen to peek inside. He poked his nose in one of them and saw walls of bookshelves holding piles and piles of antique manuscripts and books. Poor lighting made it hard to tell if there were any other items on display. But he could make out a few shadows walking around, indicating that customers were shopping inside.

Twisting the giant door handle, the fox pushed the wooden door open and stepped in. The smell of musty books hit his nose as his eyes struggled to adjust to the dim lighting. Cascades of bulky curtains rested on heaps of books near the window ledges, partially concealing the coveted sunlight pressing through the openings.

"Welcome in, sir," a gravelly voice said from behind a counter.

Bowen searched to find the voice. Stepping closer to the sound, he bumped into a tall, skinny bookcase stationed in front of him. A lopsided pile of books tumbled off the shelf and to the floor, pages flying wildly around him.

"I'll get that," the voice said again.

"I do apologize," the fox responded and kneeled to help the creature pick up the items on the wooden floor. "I guess my eyes still haven't adjusted from being outside."

"Yes, we like the shadows in here," he said.

The creature stood up, placing the books back onto the shelves. Now Bowen could see that the individual was an owl; a rounded feathered bird with curved tufts at each side of his head. The owl waddled back to the counter and the fox followed him.

"I have a reservation, sir," Bowen said.

The owl turned to peer at him over his gold rimmed glasses.

"I see," he responded. "Your name?"

"Bowen Whitethorne."

The owl struggled to open the registration book due to years of pages packed so densely into one resource. No doubt this book had witnessed world changing events over the decades! Even its brown cover with gold writing on the front caught Bowen's attention. Squinting, the fox struggled to read it without causing suspicion.

"The Milecastle Inn," he whispered.

"Yes," the owl paused to glance at the fox and then flipped to the most recent page in the reservations book. His long feathers brushed over the worn pages, smoothing the edges as he went. "This building is but an ancient gatehouse for the castle. What's left of the structure stands across the cove on that stretch of rock," he motioned over his shoulder. "Right, Mr. Whitethorne, you'll be in room number two; up the stairs and to your left."

The owl shuffled around and selected a key from the peg board hanging on the wall next to the register. Handing Bowen the key, he said, "Tea is at four o'clock on the back porch. Will you be joining us?"

"I don't know yet," the fox replied. "I have a business meeting this afternoon. Maybe if that wraps up in time..."

"Room service then?" the owl asked.

"That might be better, thanks," Bowen replied.

The fox wandered to the far window to get a closer look at the castle the owl just mentioned. A craggy black rock jutted out of the sea, topped with a thin layer of tall grass and patches of wildflowers. It always amazed Bowen that life managed to thrive on a cold slab of rock. Several stone buildings sat at the highest point of the stony island. From what he could see, only one of the structures appeared in ruins...a wall demolished with only gothic arches still standing upright. The others seemed fairly intact. In fact, as Bowen focused his eyes on the outcrop of buildings, it appeared the structures were still in use.

"A small university," the owl said over Bowen's shoulder.

The fox jumped. *How long had he been standing there?* Bowen's heart raced and he excused himself abruptly. Locating the staircase, he ascended the tight, narrow steps to the first floor. Unlocking the door labeled number two, Bowen rushed inside his room and slammed the door behind him, exhaling heavily.

Once Bowen caught his breath, he examined his tidy room. Sitting next to the wall was a small bed covered with a modest, brown blanket and two simple matching pillows. Next to that, a carafe of water and a cup rested on the bedside table. The fox laid his bag on the bed and carefully washed his face and paws in a ceramic bowl provided for him. The cool water felt delightful on his weary head. As he dried his face with a towel, he heard some commotion outside his window. Drawing the curtain back, the fox noticed several carnival rides just below him. Lines of young animals waited their turn while jumping and chattering excitedly. The squealing of pure joy coming from those kids made him smile.

It wasn't that long ago that his own kids had been young enough to enjoy the village fair. And let's face it, does anyone really outgrow them? Bowen chuckled. His boys always ran to the river front to race their boats along the shoreline. But his daughter? Well, Kenna loved the rope swings. And once she started, she would kick her legs out and lean back so the swing nearly touched the clouds! Or that's at least how Bowen remembered it. One time, Kenna swung so high, she flew off the swing at its peak and came crashing down on a roll of hay in the petting zoo. Fortunately for her, a farmer left it there that morning for his sheep. Good thing, too, as the fluffy hay pile broke her fall.

Witnessing her plummet like that terrified Bowen, but Kenna came up giggling and even asked to swing again. That day, the fox shook his head and told her, "You're supposed to stay on the swing, not jump off!" But he knew better; she would do it again.

And now, where was his daughter? *"Safe, with friends,"* he reassured himself. Even if it wasn't necessarily true, he had to convince himself that she was secure just to continue this mission.

A knock on the door interrupted his thoughts.

"Yes?" he asked.

"Sir, your tea," the voice replied.

Bowen made his way to the door and opened it for room service. Outside, the same creepy owl he spoke to before stood there with a tea tray in his wings. Stifling a cringe, the fox stepped back and indicated that the tray with tea and snacks be placed on the small table near the bed.

"Are you the bloke trying to sort out the raids?" the owl asked.

Bowen hesitated. *How did he know about this?* "I'm here on business," the fox stated matter-of-factly.

"I see," the owl responded and slowly poured tea into the two cups on the tray. "Milk? Sugar?"

"Sir, this isn't necessary," Bowen stammered, unable to piece together what was happening.

"Aren't you expecting someone?" the owl asked and turned to the fox.

"Yes, but—"

"Ulric the Learned?"

Bowen now had a pear-sized lump in his throat. *How does he know who I'm meeting? Have I been found out??*

The owl, recognizing fear in the fox's face, responded, "Relax, sir. I am Ulric and I am here to meet with you."

Chapter 12

Adler had been awake since dawn. Thinking about Bowen's trip to an abbey caused him to toss and turn in the wee hours of the morning. What could he possibly be searching for? Adler knew his uncle was in danger; but without any direct information, he didn't know how deadly the situation was...or how long he'd be gone. In the meantime, Reginald was like a rabid dog, snarling and snapping at everyone, including himself. Adler managed to dodge the bulk of his rage, but it was only a matter of time before Reginald's unbridled wrath engulfed the entire village.

And that's when Adler had an idea. If he couldn't follow Bowen to the abbey to get answers, the next best source of information was Edwin. But how could he justify a visit to Reginald's arch enemy while on duty? Adler stood at the doorway inside the palace waiting on Reginald to close this meeting. Usually, Adler paid close attention to the voices inside the closed-door meetings, but today, he was antsy and distracted. Until the discussion inside turned into a shouting match.

"That property is mine!" Reginald yelled. "I intend to build what I want on it!"

"You don't have the title to the land," retorted the other attendee. "And they won't sell it. The villagers refuse to tell me who actually owns the deed so I can negotiate with him."

Adler couldn't see inside, but knew both parties had to be standing on their feet and threatening each other.

"I've taken three other properties on that side of the sea, and I will own that one as well!" Reginald replied.

"Not if you keep this up," the other said. "The small villages along the coast rely on those areas for trade. Seizing the property will only incite war. And let's face it, you don't have enough military left to crush a resistance. Your ragtag team simply plunders resources wherever they can for your survival. You have yet to show them unity within your troops, only chaos."

The door opened and Bin, the other bodyguard, slipped out. Adler could see that the voice inside the meeting room was Reginald's newly appointed consultant, a hasty move since Bowen's disappearance.

"It's getting nasty in there," Bin whispered.

"I can tell," Adler replied. Reginald's new obsession focused on acquiring property to the north of Chipping Farms. According to the leader, it wasn't enough to plunder all the resources from those poor villagers, he wanted their land too.

"Bin, I need to do something. Can I trust you with a task?" Adler asked in a hushed voice.

"Sure, what do you need?" Bin replied, relieved to do something, anything, other than what he was doing now.

"I'm headed to the pub. When this meeting ends, bring Reginald there too," Adler said to his colleague and tiptoed down the hall.

The Boar's Nest pub was only a couple of blocks from the palace. And as he strolled down the cobbled stone road, Adler devised a plan to make Reginald think visiting Edwin would be the leader's bright idea. After all, Adler needed the Reginald's permission to leave the village without suspicion of his motives...or his loyalty.

Inside the Boar's Nest, customers talked amongst themselves at small tables while barmaids delivered plates of food and cups of fresh ale to those waiting for their orders. Adler zigzagged his way to the once hidden room behind the bar, the door now permanently opened since Bowen left. The fox rifled through several drawers of files in the cabinet near the bookshelf. *Nothing out of the ordinary*, he thought and sighed. Stacks of receipts lay on an aged wooden desk, as well as vellum, quills, a pot of ink, and a lamp. A pile of boxes near the fireplace overflowed in the small office. Adler smelled the fresh ash in the fireplace, felt a tickle in his nose, and sneezed.

"What are you doing here?" It was Reginald, and Bin stood right behind him.

Reginald strolled into the little office area staring warily at Adler, his chief bodyguard. Clenching his long blue robe in one paw, he swept his other paw over the bookshelves and played with the candles on the stand next to the fireplace. "Bin tells me you're up to something," Reginald stated coldly. "This had better be good."

"Sir, I've been searching for clues pertaining to the land acquisition… uh, the one you just met with the consultant about. Up north, right? So, what I'm about to ask…." Adler hesitated. "You know my loyalty to you is trustworthy."

Reginald whipped his head around and snapped, "Is it?"

Adler took a step back and feigned concern. "I have served you in every way you've asked, and never once questioned it," he said. "Why would you doubt my allegiance now?"

"I've watched you over the months in my service," Reginald squinted his eyes and raised a finger, "you are distracted."

This caught Adler off guard. He was unaware that his actions had been interpreted as divided faithfulness. It was true, though, he was torn inside. The only reason he served Reginald was because he had been forced to. It was either that or join the raiding parties to steal from other villages along the river. Adler couldn't make himself participate in that, so he agreed to be the leader's bodyguard. And this access to Reginald's inner dealings allowed him to see how truly evil the leader was. Reginald's thirst for power didn't stop at controlling Chipping Farms. That fox wanted dominance far beyond the nation of Fellnore. And he was well on his way to make it happen.

However, Adler's family and village was his priority. He respected Edwin when the ruler still governed the community. So in an effort to buy some time, Adler decided to play along with this charade, using any inside intel he attained to plan his own strategy for Edwin's return to the throne. And right now, he had to convince Reginald of his undivided loyalty.

Adler straightened his shoulders and looked directly into Reginald's eyes, "That distraction, sir, is my way of thinking things through. If I don't consider the outcomes, or question other creatures' motives, how do I know if the decision to blindly perform such assigned tasks will be successful?" He stopped to gauge Reginald's response. But the leader had nothing to say. Adler continued, "You must remember that you destroyed my family and my community, and then I was forced into this position. I would like nothing more than to return to the ways before you selfishly took over. But that time has gone and I have to accept it. I now understand that I must start a new chapter in life; a chapter that serves you. And if I can live in relative peace, then I am content. But I must figure out my place in life while I function as your protector. That is the only reason I am 'distracted'." Adler realized that some of what he said was actually true. He did want Edwin and his old life back. But if his plan to reinstate the old leader fell through, then he would indeed have to find contentment with this new chapter in life. Something he didn't want to think about, at least, not right now.

Adler glanced at Bin whose wide eyes suggested he was shocked at Adler's candid response. But Reginald smiled; a slow, wily grin that implied something sinister. Nodding slightly, Reginald leaned into Adler and asked, "Alright protector, what are we here for?"

"I've been thinking about your trouble with this new land acquisition," Adler said as he patted paperwork on the desk. "If the owners won't sell, why don't you send a few soldiers out there to shakedown the competition? You can save your military for ambush or raids, but these few soldiers can make it their priority to get that title."

"I don't need a title, I can just take it," Reginald replied.

"Sure, you could. But don't you want to rule with the deed in your paw? Don't you want your name on that land so that the inhabitants repeat it every time they refer to their home? Doesn't that sound...*royal*?" Adler laid it on thick.

For a few seconds, Reginald's eyes glowed and he ran his tongue along his lips. *Royal*. He craved that distinction as it would be the first in his line of ancestry.

"I must have it," Reginald responded.

"Then I will appoint a committee to seek the title to the land you desire," Adler replied.

"That is all well and good, but the consultant doesn't know who the owner is and the villagers won't talk," the leader said.

"Who else might know the ownership of the land?" Adler asked, leading the greedy ruler into his snare.

"Bowen knew, the dirty traitor!" Reginald fumed.

"Surely, someone else knows?" Adler shrugged and looked at Reginald. "A fox with a wealth of incredible connections throughout the nation of Fellnore?"

Reginald and Adler stared at each other for several minutes, although to Bin, it felt like an hour. Adler tapped his fingers along the books on the shelves as he waited.

Then Reginald professed, "What about Edwin?"

Adler pretended surprise, "Edwin?! That's a wonderful idea! He does have the network and the intel to know exactly who owns which pieces of land. Well done, sir!"

Reginald smiled smugly, proud of himself for suggesting such a splendid idea.

"Sir," Adler started, "allow me to remove any doubts of so-called 'distraction' and send me to Edwin to sort out this land ownership. I would be so humbled!" Adler bowed his head a bit and nearly gagged with this last line. But it was necessary to persuade Reginald of this decision.

"Fine," Reginald waved his paw around, "do it." He stiffened his posture and headed to the door. "Report your findings to me immediately."

And with that, Reginald swished out of the room in his royal robe and into the pub. Bin followed close behind him.

Adler relaxed his shoulders and felt the weight of his world melt away. He had no time to waste. Edwin was the only one with as much information as Bowen. And if he was going to plan an insurgence, Adler needed to know why his uncle ran for his life. *What information was in the records he took with him?* Adler swore everything his uncle did traced back to Reginald. It had to be about Reginald. But how?

Wadsworth Bridger sat huddled under a blanket in his chair by the fireplace. His eyes darted from left to right, to the window then the door, and back again. Shadows danced along the wall and flashed over to the straw covered floor. Clutching the blanket, the badger listened intently to the sound of birds chirping noisily outside.

Mr. Bridger's wife spent the morning at the farmer's market down by the lake and would be home soon. But in the meantime, the badger waited for his spouse to return, alone and jumpy. With thoughts running rampant in his head, a slight scraping noise outside caught his attention. He stood up hoping to hear it again. And there it was! Above the window he heard, scraaaaatch! Tiptoeing closer, Bridger peeked through the curtain but didn't see anything. His heart thumped wildly and his eyes immediately dilated. Bridger froze, still as a statue, for what seemed like forever.

As he slinked back to the fireplace, the badger heard the sound again. He whipped his head around. But this time, the scratching came from the door. *There's no way I'm opening that door! If I'm quiet, maybe it will go away*, he thought. He squeezed his eyes closed and tried to imagine himself at the beach...or a waterfall. Something, anything, to calm himself down.

A few minutes passed in silence. *Was I hearing things?* He shook his head a little, *I guess I'm a bit paranoid*. Then the door handle creaked and Bridger let out a high-pitched squeal.

"Are you alright, dear?" Mrs. Bridger asked as she opened the door.

The badger gasped. Behind his wife stood a figure wearing a cloak.

"What's wrong?" she asked. But Bridger couldn't speak, his vocal cords were paralyzed.

The figure glided in right behind Mrs. Bridger, startling her so much that she dropped her shopping bag full of vegetables. A bunch of carrots scattered over the straw while a large head of cabbage wobbled over the floor.

The cloaked figure closed in on the two badgers, grasping Bridger around the neck. Mrs. Bridger screamed, alarming a second figure sneaking in through the door. Jumping over the vegetables, the second figure landed in front of her, and blocked Mrs. Bridger from striking her husband's captor as she viciously tried to free him.

"Where is Bowen?" the first figure asked. His eyes pierced through the darkness of his cloak, glowing a burnt amber color. With his teeth bared, the creature pushed harder against Bridger's throat, making it impossible for him to speak.

The badger grunted, indicating he wanted to talk. Slowly easing his grip, the figure asked again, "Where is Bowen?"

"Who's asking?" Mrs. Bridger asked, fuming.

The two cloaked figures looked at each other with mouths open and snouts flared. The captor holding back the badger's wife remarked, "Are you serious?" He then turned to the other captor and asked, "Is she serious??"

"You barged into our home! What do you expect?" Bridger squawked at them.

The first figure growled at the badger, baring his teeth.

"Bowen isn't here," Bridger said and gulped.

"We can see that he isn't presently in your little house," the captor said and leaned in so close that the badger could smell death on his breath. "What I mean is, do you know where I can find him? Have you seen him?"

"No, he hasn't seen him. We don't know where he is, honestly, we don't!" Mrs. Bridger replied as she yanked her arms trying to free herself from the cloaked figure holding her back.

"She's right. We haven't heard from Bowen since we moved here, and that was months ago," the badger responded.

"Hmmm, I guess we're going to have to use this then," the first figure pulled out a shiny metal dagger and held it up to Bridger's face. "So, I ask you again, do you know where Bowen is?" The captor flicked the dagger and pushed the tip into the badger's neck, puncturing a small "warning" wound. A few drops of blood bubbled out and flowed down his chest.

"I don't know! I don't know!" Bridger shouted as his wife wailed hysterically.

"Oh wait, I know what will do the trick," the first captor said and pointed the knife at Mrs. Bridger. "What if we try this again, but with the blood of the missus?" Both captors laughed.

"No! No! No! No!" she screamed as the dagger touched her neck.

"One push of this blade and it's all over, Bridger," he pricked her skin and she cried out.

"STOP!! You can't do this to her! She doesn't know anything!" Bridger yelled.

"Aye, maybe that's true. But I think you know more than you're sharing," the figure said menacingly. Then he grabbed Mrs. Bridger's paw and remarked, "Or, we could start by eliminating one finger at a time until your husband speaks…" The captor laid the dagger on top of Mrs. Bridger's paw and she shrieked in terror.

"I'll tell you what you want!" Bridger shouted. "Just stop hurting her!!"

The captors relinquished his wife's paw and turned to listen to the badger.

"It's true, we haven't seen Bowen since we moved here. BUT…" Bridger looked at his wife and shook his head, "we had visitors though. They are looking for Bowen, too, and were here asking the same questions."

"Who were these visitors?" the second figure asked.

"Two of them were sombels. The other was a Redlan fox. Kenna was her name," the badger replied. "And she's Bowen's daughter."

The captors looked at each other and grinned. "Did they tell you where they were going?" one asked.

"To see Edwin," Bridger said.

The first captor whispered something to the second one, and both released their hostages with a shove. As the cloaked figures talked to each other, Bridger wrapped his arms around his wife and asked if she was injured. She simply shook her head.

And just as quickly as they had charged inside the house, the two captors fled: through the door and into the village to reclaim their obscurity. The Bridgers sat in shock for a few minutes without speaking.

"What just happened?" Mrs. Bridger asked.

"Reginald's bounty hunters, that's what," Bridger responded. He stood up and shuffled paper around on his little table. "I have to make this right."

"What are you going to do?" his wife asked.

"I need to send a message to Edwin," the badger replied as he searched for ink and a quill. "I have to warn his visitors that the bounty hunters are closing in."

CHAPTER 13

Bored, Tegan, Beckett, and Kenna sat hidden in the hedges just outside the ruins of the church rectory. As they waited for a distraction, Beckett rolled a blade of grass around in his digits while Tegan played with the petals on a pink flower. Kenna, on the other hand, kneeled with her ears perked upright, listening for any sound to give her a reason to run to that cellar door. Beckett pushed for more time so the late morning shadows could cover their movements, but Kenna couldn't hold out any longer. She stood up in full view of the cottage and sprinted to the cellar door just behind the building. Beckett and Tegan both gasped. *What is she doing?*

Kenna yanked violently on the handle of the door while the others watched in fear. Tegan looked back and forth from her friend to the guards several times, trying to decide when to join the fox. The metal handle squeaked and banged with each forceful tug, but Kenna didn't notice. She had tunnel vision, intensely focused to the point of tuning everything else out.

Then, the two guards stopped talking; each one lifting a finger to quiet the other. Tegan's heart raced and she looked to Beckett for ideas. But it was too late. Beckett jumped up and scurried over to help Kenna open the stubborn cellar door. With one giant heave, Beckett managed to wrench open the door just enough for Kenna to slip through. Sucking in his stomach, Beckett wiggled through the door as well. He stuck his paw out of the opening and motioned to Tegan with a wave.

Tegan bobbed her head up and down, unsure of what to do. Would the guards spot her? Could she make it to the door in time? "Ooooooh," the sombel squirmed and hesitated, releasing tension with frustrated sounds. She clenched her paws and squinted her eyes, "Oh, fine!" Up on her toes, she glanced once more at the guards. As they turned their ears towards the wall opposite of her, Tegan jumped out of the hedge and scurried across to the door. Just before she reached her friends, she heard a guard ask, "What was that?" She slid into the darkness behind the cellar door, and the others shut it tightly behind her.

Without light, the three friends fumbled in the cool blackness that was now their surroundings. Kenna held a match in her paw and struck it against the stone wall. A small flame lit the tiny entrance just enough for Beckett to find an old lantern.

"Bring it here," he said to Kenna. Once Beckett lit the lantern, Kenna shook out the match's flame and tossed it aside. They could now see wooden shelves situated around the room, some of which still held dusty bottles of wine.

"This is definitely a wine cellar," Tegan remarked.

Boxes littered the floor as well as a couple of large wooden barrels used for alcohol preservation. But those had been emptied a long time ago. The vaulted ceiling and thick stone walls caused sounds to echo in an erratic fashion. The trio padded over to a slim corridor on the opposite side of the room. Relics from another time lay abandoned on shelves carved into the stone. Before them, the door stood frozen in time. From top to bottom, ornate decorations had been carved into the wood, and bulky metal hinges held the door in place. Tegan reached for the lantern in Beckett's paw and held it up to a tiny opening to see what was on the other side of the door.

"Do you see anything?" Beckett whispered to his friend. He watched as the lantern's flame caused her pupils to dilate.

Tegan turned her head and whispered back, "It's too dark in there, I can't see a thing."

"Let me try!" Kenna busted through the two of them and stood on her tiptoes to catch a view of the inside room. "Edwin?" she called out through the opening. "Edwin, are you in there?"

Beckett shushed her, "Are you trying to get us caught?!"

Something inside moved near the door.

"We're so close! I know he's in there!" Kenna replied.

"Yes, but we can't let anyone know we are on the other side of this door," Beckett stated, he looked back through the opening and shrieked. Two eyes stared back at him through the blackness, a terrifying sight in the dark. A sound like chains jangled near the floor and a horrible squeaky noise notified the travelers that the door handle was engaged.

Before Tegan, Beckett, and Kenna could flee, the secret ancient door opened just wide enough for someone to squeeze through.

"Come in," whispered a voice from the other side.

Kenna ran in first, "Edwin? Edwin, is that you?" she asked repeatedly.

Tegan slid through the opening, pushing aside a large blanket that covered the entrance from the inside. *No wonder I couldn't see anything!* Beckett followed his friend and pulled the ancient door closed as best as he could and returned the blanket to its original hiding position.

Once inside the abandoned rectory turned holding cell, Tegan admitted to herself that the missus had definitely made the inside as comfortable as possible. Two rocking chairs positioned by the fireplace each held worn yellow blankets, while big soup pots sat near the flames. Fresh wildflowers decorated a table centered in the room, complete with simple white plates, teacups, and matching cloth napkins. Even the single window hosted a simple covering, offering the couple the only privacy they could get.

As Tegan walked closer to the fire, she noticed Kenna chatting with a graying fox wearing a brown tunic and round glasses. He moved slowly and seemed to know Kenna by name. They spoke briefly before Kenna introduced him to her friends.

"Tegan, Beckett, this is Edwin," she smiled as she stood beside him.

"Pleasure to meet you, sir," the two responded.

Edwin nodded and motioned with his arm for the travelers to sit at the table. As the three friends gathered to question the former king and prisoner, another figure moved from the fireplace to the table area. "My wife is serving tea," Edwin explained. "We don't have much here, but we are making the best of it." All three travelers offered their teacup to the older lady wearing a dark blue apron. She tipped the pot and poured tea for her visitors.

"Milk and sugar are on the table, dears," she said with a wink and returned to her rocking chair near the fireplace.

"We don't have much time, sir, but we have a few questions," Kenna said. "And your answers may help me find my father."

"Yes, I learned of his disappearance from your cousin, Adler. He visits me from time to time and gives updates on what's happening in the outside world," the older fox replied. "How can I help?"

"Do you know anything about the situation that caused Bowen to flee?" Tegan asked.

"I understand he found something he wasn't supposed to," Edwin replied.

"But that's the thing," Kenna said. "What did he find? What was so confidential that he had to run?"

"We know it implicates Reginald, but we're not sure how he's involved," Beckett replied. "There is a land dispute that we know of—"

"And a flag—" Kenna suggested.

Edwin held up his paw, "How did you find out about all of this?" the older fox asked.

"Bridger," the visitors stated at once.

"Yes, well," Edwin positioned both paws on the table and said, "let's start at the beginning."

"The land?" Beckett suggested.

"So, the land in question is a small area just north of us; a port on the shores near Swynton. Have you heard of it?" Edwin asked.

"In northwest Fellnore?" Kenna asked.

"Aye," continued Edwin, "Reginald's raids to the north started out in secret. My council warned me something was going on, but we didn't realize the depth of his pillaging until a few months ago. Seems he went from trespassing to full blown destruction." He scratched his chin and leaned into the others, "I planned to send Bowen to sort things out. He's such a natural when it comes to negotiations. I figured he'd have it under control, peacefully, and the villagers would see our enthusiastic support for their wellbeing. But Bridger stepped in before our plan could take effect and proceeded to incite chaos."

"What did he do?" Kenna asked.

"That badger told all the villagers that I intended to seize their land and mercilessly rule over them! Can you believe it?" Edwin asked sarcastically.

"So the villagers cancelled all plans to lease the land," Tegan said.

The older fox nodded and sighed, "It would've been a glorious partnership."

"What's so important about the land there?" Beckett asked.

"The area we looked at provides direct access across the sea to Oren Plum. Many travelers use it; we wanted to build near the port to better manage our trade business," Edwin explained.

Beckett's eyes communicated confusion.

"Meaning we build storehouses, bait shops, markets, and more to aid business transactions there," Edwin clarified. "The council even suggested a tavern with individual rooms to house individuals working long hours and seeking a place to rest."

"A legitimate business proposal then," Tegan mumbled. "No wonder Reginald freaked out when he heard about this plan."

"All his plans for looting and robbery in that part of the world would come to an abrupt end," Kenna finished Tegan's thoughts.

"That's when Reginald flipped and conned Bridger into doing his dirty work...sabotage the entire deal so he could continue seizing what's not his," Beckett stated glumly.

Edwin sat back, satisfied that his visitors understood the predicament. It felt so good to talk about it now, especially since he hadn't had many creatures to talk to since the mutiny.

Tegan's head raced with thoughts about the port near the sea. Bowen's disappearance was definitely tied to the deal, but how?

"Now the question is, do you know where Bowen is right now?" Tegan asked.

"Is my father safe? Has he contacted you?" Kenna asked.

"Your father is a smart fox," Edwin said gently. "I don't know where he is. But I'm certain he is working things out so he can come home safely and keep his family out of danger. That I am sure of!"

Frustrated, Kenna growled to herself and crossed her arms. "I guess we need that flag after all, since no one knows where my father is."

"Are you referring to the Flag of Firinn?" Edwin asked.

"Yes, we heard it can help locate someone," Beckett responded. "Kenna is determined to use it to find Bowen. However, we understand it was stolen from here not too long ago."

"The Flag of Firinn is a very special flag, you know. Fairies wove it together from silk and dyed it with colors from the dusk and dawn," Edwin recited. "It can help locate loved ones, sure, but it also serves as a protector and a moral compass. The flag is extremely valuable and will warn its owners of injustices." The room fell silent. The older fox looked each of his visitors in the eyes. "The night Reginald had me arrested and locked me in here, I heard it."

"You *heard* it?" Beckett asked slowly.

"A wailing sound echoed from the inside of the remaining wall, just over there," Edwin pointed towards the covered window. "It went on for about an hour before it stopped. I couldn't sleep that night, so I watched from that opening. Around one in the morning, a mysterious figure appeared near the south entrance of the wall. He wore a monk's robe, hood covering his head, and carried a short candle. I could see the tiny flame flickering in a strange reddish color. The figure pushed on several parts of the stone wall, like he was looking for a secret opening. But just as I laughed about that, the shadowy form suddenly disappeared through the wall! I couldn't believe it!" Edwin shook his head. "And I knew the flag was gone."

"Did anyone else see the figure?" Beckett asked.

"Yeah, how do you know the flag is *really* gone?" Kenna asked suspiciously.

"One of my trusted colleagues checked on the flag the next morning," Edwin winked at Kenna. "Your father confirmed its disappearance."

Kenna gasped. *My father knows about this flag? Why didn't he tell me?*

"And to answer your question, Beckett, yes, a few soldiers witnessed the figure along the wall. However, they were unable to find and arrest him once he disappeared through the structure," Edwin replied. "There was no trace that anyone had been there." He paused a few seconds to let the information sink in. "You will need to know where to locate the flag in order to help your father. Fortunately for you, I am one of the very few keepers of this secret. I can tell you who the flag belongs to and where to retrieve it," Edwin said. "What I'm about to tell you is completely confidential, do you understand?"

Tegan, Beckett, and Kenna nodded in unison.

"I'm revealing this because I trust that you will use the information for the good of our nation," Edwin eyed each one of his visitors. They nodded again.

"The Moin fairies are the ones entrusted with the flag's protection. We signed a legal contract with the leader, Cormac, to house the flag while our clan built defensive lookout towers around the village perimeters. It was simply insurance protection. But when Reginald took over...," Edwin sighed. "My theory is that the fairy clan sent their soldier, dressed as a monk, to collect the flag and protect it from malevolent use," Edwin explained.

"The flag can do that?" Beckett asked.

"It can," Edwin stated. "My worry was that it could be sold to the highest bidder in an attempt to control foreign nations."

"How do we find this flag?" Kenna asked. She imagined holding the magnificent Flag of Firinn and unfurling it as she marched toward her father's location.

"The fairy clan that protects it lives in Heathersage; on the eastern corner of Chipping Farms, about a day's walk from here," the older fox said. "You must cross back over the moors and search for a mushroom ring there."

"Sounds simple enough," Beckett stated.

"But beware--," Edwin started.

"Oh no..."

"The Cu Sith protects those fairies."

"A Cu what?" Beckett stammered.

"Cu Sith or fairy hound," Edwin explained.

"A fairy *what*??!" Tegan asked alarmed.

"A fairy hound," Edwin repeated. "It is the guardian of sacred fairy grounds. According to fae legend, the fairy hound is bound by fae law to act as the living protector of the flag. You'll have to get past the beast to talk to Cormac."

"Now how are we supposed to do that?!" Kenna wailed.

"My advice?" Edwin asked rhetorically. "Don't tell a lie."

Chapter 14

Ulric handed Bowen a cup of tea and sat at the small table.

"I...uh...I didn't expect you to be my first meeting," Bowen said as he pulled out another chair to sit opposite of the owl. Nervous, the fox stood up and covered the window with the curtains. It wasn't much privacy, but he couldn't take any chances. "Right," Bowen settled back into the chair and opened his tiny pad to take notes. "As I explained in my letter to you last week, I'm following up on a report of suspicious activity in this area that was reported to our council. I have a few open-ended questions related to the investigation that I need clarity on. I promise to keep your name confidential, so please speak freely. Are you willing to speak with me?"

Ulric swallowed his sip of tea, "Yes, I am."

Bowen smiled, feeling relaxed for the first time all day. "What can you tell me about this town? What are your concerns?"

The owl pushed his gold-rimmed glasses closer to his face and said, "There is an oppression here, but I am unable to pinpoint the source." He leaned forward and spoke in almost a whisper,

"Villagers have seen a troop of foxes marching across our land, pulling wagons that carry who-knows-what to the port."

"A troop? Like an army?" Bowen asked.

"Yes, except there were only about nine or ten of them."

"So a small unit carrying miscellaneous goods to a port for some kind of transport. But why and to where?" Bowen knew these raids were facilitated by Reginald, but the fox always brought the loot home to Chipping Farms. What he didn't keep for himself, he distributed amongst his supporters; payment for a job well done. But this sounded like something else.

"How often do you see these troops with wagons?" Bowen asked.

"At least once a week; they gather near the shore. Troops load the wagons onto foreign cargo ships that moor here and sail westward, possibly to Oren Plum," Ulric stated.

Bowen wrote as fast as he could. "So this foreboding feeling you have.... you mentioned 'oppression,' what makes you feel this way?"

It was Ulric's turn to stand up and pace the room. Peeking through the curtain covering the window, he asked, "Did you notice how many families were playing in the surf today? And all the young kids on the rides?"

Bowen nodded.

"Well, that's the first time in weeks that the villagers have ventured from their homes to play in the sun," Ulric said.

"Why is that?"

"Everyone feels it...something is about to happen, and folks are staying close to their home," the owl replied.

Bowen was confused. The only thing he could think of "happening" to this community was Reginald and his goons robbing and looting from these villagers. But hasn't this town already felt the sting of Reginald's criminals? Surely, Swynton was attacked before. Ulric just mentioned wagons of goods and foxes marching to the town's port. The reports Bowen received while still holding office flatly stated that Reginald was stealing from this town's inhabitants. And when you looked around the village, all you noticed were families of badgers, hares, hedgehogs, and a few birds...but no foxes. The general consensus was that Reginald was shaking down these civilians for valuables. But with this new information, could he be stealing from another clan or community instead?

"Ulric, has your town been the target of theft lately?" Bowen asked.

"Do you mean by a group of criminals? No," replied the owl, shaking his head. "We haven't experienced *that* kind of disturbance in years. And to be honest, I wouldn't be surprised if the bad feeling I have is actually warning me of some kind of trouble like that coming our way."

The fox sat motionless, stumped by the owl's information. If the reports were true, then Reginald had been raiding this village for months, yet this resident showed no knowledge of that. So, what was Reginald doing on these long journeys then? He informed Edwin he was scouting for real estate but returned with wagons of loot. Bowen didn't hear Reginald's explanation to his boss, but instead, witnessed the carts filled with furniture, housewares, expensive clothes, tools, and more.

"Were you involved in any of the negotiations regarding the Redlan's clan to lease property near the port??" Bowen asked.

"No, but you should consult Sybil Verdun about land management. She works directly with the owner and was intimately involved in that debacle," Ulric motioned with his wing.

"Mrs. Verdun is on my list to interview. I'm supposed to meet with her later this evening at the pub," Bowen said. "Anything in particular I should know about her?"

"Look for a fox. She'll be the only one in the room wearing a red hat," the owl said.

A thumping on the door startled Tegan and her friends. She could hear the guards talking with someone outside and easing the front door open. Panicked, Edwin motioned for his visitors to hide behind the blanket hanging against the back wall. Each one stood as still as possible so no one would suspect their presence there.

"Edwin? I apologize for visiting unannounced." It was Adler.

"Adler, my friend, come in!" Edwin said.

When Kenna heard her cousin's voice, she sprang out from behind the blanket, "Adler!" She called out and ran over to him.

The others shushed her as they stepped out from behind their hiding place. Kenna hugged her cousin tightly as it had been a long time since she'd seen him.

"Kenna, what are you doing here?" Adler couldn't believe his eyes.

"My friends and I are trying to find my father," Kenna replied. "We just had to speak with Edwin." She introduced Tegan and Beckett to Adler and continued to tell her cousin about the meetings they had participated in so far. She explained how Edwin described a flag that could locate a missing person like her father, and how they could find it in Heathersage. "We're leaving soon so we can get there before nightfall."

"Heathersage, huh?" Adler asked. "That's a journey over the moors." He glanced from Tegan to Beckett and then to Kenna. "Some harsh countryside out there. Are you sure you're up for it?"

"We have to," Tegan replied precariously. "We don't have time to wait for Bowen to just show up somewhere. Reginald is looking for him."

"That I *do* know," Adler agreed. "He sent bounty hunters to find Uncle Bowen and bring him back with the stolen information. But no one knows where he went, and I'm worried about him. I was hoping Edwin might have some answers."

"That's why we're here too," Kenna said and touched his arm. "Edwin's been gracious enough to explain the land contract that sent Reginald into a frenzy. My father must have information implicating Reginald or else he wouldn't be missing."

"The fact that Bowen disappeared without a trace is unsettling," Edwin admitted. "I told Kenna about the Flag of Firinn—"

"It will help us find father!" Kenna said excitedly.

Adler looked at Edwin and then Kenna, "A flag?"

"More like a magic flag," offered Beckett.

Edwin laughed a little, "Yes, well, that is true. However, they must retrieve it from the Moin fairies in Heathersage. And there is a problem...."

"What problem is that?" Adler asked, his head tilted to the side.

"A fairy hound protects the Moin village. They'll have to get past the creature to speak with the clan leader," Edwin said.

Adler wasn't expecting that bit of information. "There's no way I'm letting my little cousin take on a furry hound to get a flag!" He motioned indignantly with his paws.

Kenna giggled, "Fairy hound, Adler, not furry."

"Whatever!" he snapped.

Tegan listened as the two cousins discussed Kenna's safety. No one wanted to be in this particular situation, least of all, Tegan. She yearned to go back home, work on simple chores, drink tea, and talk about silly things like clothes and who's going to the midsummer festival ball. Instead, thoughts of snarling hounds and magical flags danced around in her head. Did she want to risk it all to find her friend's father? Not really. But it was the right thing to do. The inhabitants of Fellnore deserved deliverance from Reginald's continued attacks on their communities.

Tegan stood up and walked over to Adler. "We are caught up in a situation where the odds are not in our favor. It's indeed unfair," her poignant words calmed him. "However, Bowen's survival will determine the outcome of your village, your home. Those valuable documents he carries will somehow change the course of Reginald's dominance over your family. And while I wish there was an easy answer, it looks like we've been forced to accept this course of action." Tegan stepped closer to Kenna, "We must obtain this flag to locate Bowen for the good of Chipping Farms, as well as every resident in the nation of Fellnore." She laid her paws on Kenna's shoulders.

"Adler," Kenna softened, "haven't we spent many nights talking about the rebellion? What we would do to take back Chipping Farms from Reginald, if only we had the chance?"

"I remember those nights," he responded happily. "Your mother always cooked the most delicious dinner! And after we ate, we'd sit out on the front porch and watch the fireflies light up the night sky. We'd joke about your brothers playing ball in the dark—"

"—and your oldest sister getting stuck babysitting baby Cyr! Remember how he'd crawl away from her when she tried to feed him?" Kenna asked.

"Yeah, and spit up on her clean apron the minute he swallowed anything!" Adler laughed a little.

"We spent hours discussing how different our lives had become since playing in the forest as kids." Kenna paused to let the memories sink in. "Remember your mom's cider? We sipped fresh mugs of homemade cider on the porch. Then the rest of the family would eventually join us in the moonlight. All we had on that deck were our dreams to restore what we lost," Kenna said. "This is our chance."

"Restoration sounds like the perfect motive to get us to Heathersage," Tegan mused.

Adler smiled. "I wish I could be there to see the look on that hound's face when he catches a glimpse of you."

"So why don't you join us?" Beckett asked.

"I can't," Adler replied. "Reginald would question something if I left my post. For this proposal to succeed, he must suspect nothing!" The fox sighed deeply and wiped his paws over his face in uncertainty and frustration. "If we are to plan this restoration, then we need to find Bowen...and make sure he's safe."

"I think we can all agree on that," Tegan said.

Voices outside the window alarmed the visitors. The two guards argued with each other as they rapped on the door. "Who's in there? Open the door, Adler!"

"They must've heard us!" Kenna squeaked out.

"Go now!" Adler motioned with his paw. "I'll distract them long enough to give you a head start."

Edwin moved to the door, "It's only Adler and me discussing business in here."

"Nonsense! We hear others. Open up!" the guard demanded.

Kenna squeezed her cousin tightly and then joined the other two as they slipped through the hidden back door into the cellar. As soon as the blanket covered the opening again, Adler unlocked and opened the front door. Both guards poked their heads through and looked around for company. But no one else was there.

"Our discussion got a little out of hand. My apologies for that," Adler said calmly.

The guards were not convinced, and Adler had to think quickly. He lowered his voice so the two had to lean in to hear him, "Just between us...." He looked back at Edwin and then to the guards, "I think this isolation is affecting Edwin, you know, mentally. Do you understand what I'm saying?"

Both guards relaxed their stances a bit. "You mean...his sanity?" one guard asked.

"The poor old fox is hallucinating," Adler offered. "He's seeing things and hearing voices that I don't hear. Then he responds in bizarre ways each time he hears them calling out!" He shook his head in pretend sorrow. Adler didn't like this line of lies, but he needed to protect his cousin and her friends at all costs. Plus, who's to say that being isolated like Edwin was, for a long period of time, *wouldn't* cause one to lose their mind?

"I see," the other guard replied. "Is the wife struggling too?"

"Not yet," Adler said. "But give it time, she'll succumb to it as well." He honestly believed that given enough time, both Edwin and his wife would suffer some kind of mental breakdown. It was just a matter of how long.

As the guards grumbled to each other, a raven flew by and perched on a tree branch near the building, catching Adler's eye. It called out and flew closer, landing on a stone column that had once stood tall but was now mostly toppled ruins.

"Sirs," Adler said to get the guards attention. "Let me settle Edwin back into bed and then I'll leave."

"You have ten minutes," the first guard barked.

Adler nodded and closed the door. And just at the same time, the raven poked his beak through the side of the window's curtain and flew in through the opening, landing on the fireplace mantel. It tilted its head to the side and flapped its wings. Then Adler saw it.... the raven carried a message. He retrieved it from the bird's leg and handed it to Edwin. The older fox unrolled the tiny scroll of paper and read it to himself, his lips moving as he silently digested the information.

"Who's it from?" Edwin's wife asked from her chair.

Still looking down at the scroll, Edwin replied in disbelief, "It's from Bridger."

"What does it say, sir?" Adler asked, but Edwin handed him the paper so he could read it for himself.

"I can't believe Reginald's bounty hunters tracked down Bridger," Edwin said as he paced the floor.

Adler continued reading, "And they know about Kenna and her friends too." He slammed his fist down on the table and shoved the paper into his pocket. "So what's the plan now?" He asked, knowing full well that things were worse than he originally thought.

Edwin placed his paw on Adler's back and whispered in his ear, "Gather as many supporters as you can...and get ready."

Adler turned to face the fox. "Ready for what?" he asked in a low voice.

Edwin patted Adler's shoulder in consolation, "You'll know when the time comes. I believe in you."

Chapter 15

Bowen poked his head inside the Milecastle Inn pub and searched for a customer there donning a red hat. Beside the fireplace sat a brown petite fox; one paw holding a menu while the other steadied her glasses. Bowen watched as she adjusted her simple red hat down further over her forehead, covering her eyes just a bit. This had to be Sybil Verdun.

"Pardon me," Bowen said gently to keep from startling her, "Are you Ms. Verdun?"

"Yes," she removed her glasses and asked, "Mr. Whitethorne?"

Bowen nodded and asked to sit down. She motioned with her paw for her guest to join her and signaled to the barmaid for two orders of cream tea with scones.

"Thank you for meeting with me," Bowen stated. "It's a pleasure talking to you in person."

Sybil smiled briefly and asked, "What is it that you want to discuss?"

"I understand you work for the owner of the land that includes Swynton's sea port?" Bowen asked. He needed confirmation that he had the right contact.

Several months ago, Edwin assigned Bowen to contact the landowner of this seaport and arrange a tour of the property. Bowen prepared a letter of intent and included a suggested purchase order. And while the raven that carried the message confirmed its delivery, Bowen never heard back from the owner. He waited another week and then sent a follow up letter as a courtesy, but still no response. It was around that time that Reginald sauntered into Edwin's office showing off a new tunic, embroidered with green and gold. He bragged about receiving it after another successful "scouting trip" with his gang. "Just another perk of my job," Reginald claimed as he escorted a wagon of goods down the main road in town.

With all this commotion, Bowen assumed the messages he sent had been lost in the midst of Reginald's chaos. And in some ways, they had.

"I manage that property for the owner, yes," Sybil replied as the barmaid delivered their trays of tea and scones to the table.

"Tell me about the plan to purchase that area of land. Did you receive a letter of intent?" Bowen asked. "It also came with a contract," he added.

"A few months ago, I received your letter requesting a tour of the property near Swynton's port. You indicated interest in purchasing the land for Edwin—something Mr. Ollie, uh, the owner, was not agreeable to." Sybil sipped her tea and continued, "Instead, I sent a message back to you suggesting you prepare a leasing contract in the hopes that Mr. Ollie would agree to a short-term solution."

"I never received that letter," Bowen tilted his head, his mind swirling with thoughts.

"Well, someone did!" Sybil looked around the pub suspiciously. "The next thing I know is we are being inundated with Reginald and his thugs trying their best to 'persuade' us to change our minds."

"Bridger!" Bowen whispered to himself. Bridger must have been the one to intercept the message. *That traitor!* It made sense now. Once Bridger seized the letter, he went straight to Reginald with the bad news—the owner would not sell. Since Reginald wanted the land for himself, he immediately marched into Swynton with a few soldiers to shake down the landowner. Only Mr. Ollie didn't budge. Instead, the plan backfired and the owner canceled all negotiations allowing Redlan foxes access to the seaport, as well as the surrounding land.

Bowen reigned his thoughts back into the conversation at hand. "How did Reginald's crew use persuasion? Did they utilize force?"

"No, not yet at least. Reginald indicated that the raiding to the east of us would transition to our community if we didn't give in," Sybil replied defiantly. "Plus, he kept telling us that Edwin's true intentions were to conquer this village and rule over it."

Bowen laughed at the thought. Edwin's interests lay only in business, not conquest.

"I know," Sybil grinned. "It seems silly when you actually know Edwin. But a lot of villagers were afraid. That's another reason why Mr. Ollie canceled the negotiations. He wanted to meet with Edwin in person to discuss Reginald's behavior towards our community."

"But that never happened," Bowen stated.

"Exactly. I learned that Reginald convinced his soldiers THAT same night to relieve Edwin of his duties...and the throne," Sybil said. "And here we sit today, in fear and in chaos."

"I've heard that fox soldiers have been loading wagons of goods onto a foreign boat at the seaport," Bowen said. "Is that true?"

"I've only seen it once, but yes, it's true," Sybil said.

"Do you know how often the boat docks at the pier?" Bowen asked.

"It used to be once a week," she replied. "But from what I heard this morning, the visits are happening more frequently. I wouldn't be surprised if the boat sailed into the dock later tonight." She cleared her throat. "I know what you're thinking, but I'd watch out for those soldiers, whoever they are!" She stared a little at Bowen, but it was long enough to make him squirm.

"Only..." she started.

"Only what?" Bowen asked quickly.

"I've just realized something," Sybil stated and adjusted her hat again. "I noticed those soldiers at the dock wear blue badges." She looked around nervously and continued, "What color badge does your clan wear?"

"Red," he answered.

"Right, so the badges worn on the dock must be from the Branwell clan. They were the ones moving goods into the boat," Sybil sat back in her chair.

"How do you know that?" Bowen asked.

"Well, I'm a Branwell fox. I moved to Swynton as a kid, but I still have family in their community," Sybil said. "And I remember those blue badges."

"But why would Branwell foxes be loading wagons of stolen goods onto a ship?" Bowen asked out loud. He sat there puzzled. What does this other fox clan have to do with Reginald? Sure, the clans were distantly related, but the Branwell clan?? Could they have helped Reginald raid villages to the east?

Sybil wiped the crumbs from her mouth and glanced at her watch. "Oh dear, I need to go!" She stood up and pushed her chair under the table. "I'm so sorry Mr. Whitethorne, I have another meeting. Please send word if you have any further questions."

Sybil left before Bowen could say anything. But now, he was left alone with his thoughts. Two things bothered him the most: the possible involvement of the Branwell Clan and this mystery boat. Branwell foxes, though distantly related to the Redlan clan, were a very industrious group. They made money the old-fashioned way—they earned it. Mostly farmers, the foxes excelled in both growing and selling their crops. The clan kept to themselves, and Bowen had never had any issues with them. This report of Branwell foxes carrying stolen goods didn't sit well with him. It felt...off. And this foreign ship? Bowen scratched his head. The only way he figured he could get answers would be to scout out this boat and observe the situation for himself.

He left the table and headed back to his room. "I just need a few things," he said to himself as he filled a bag with items like a rope, compass, matches, knife, bandages, snacks, and a few coins. *I have to see this boat for myself.*

The two fox guards questioning Adler outside the rectory returned to their post. As they picked up their playing cards to pass the time, the first guard remarked, "Shame about Edwin. I mean, hallucinating?"

"I had an aunt that came down with that," the second one said. "Scared the village kids. Ended up in a hospital not too far from here." He placed a card on the makeshift table between them.

"Still, Edwin seemed in his right mind the last time I spoke with him," the first guard said and put one of his cards down.

"It comes and goes," the other replied.

"Something feels off though," the first one said. He put all his cards face down on the table and sat back.

The second guard looked at him intensely, "What? Do you want to search the area?" He chuckled. "You think there's a ghost or something?"

"Not a ghost. But we should check one more time in case Edwin actually had a visitor," the first guard replied.

"In that small room? Come on!" the other guard said. "We didn't see anyone other than Edwin, his wife, and Adler. Where would they even hide?" He scoffed as he placed a card on top of the others.

"Yeah, I don't know. It's just a feeling," the first guard added.

"Go search then, I'm staying here," the second guard replied and stretched out in the shade, placing a hat over his eyes to block the sunlight. "Let me know what you find," he laughed and then yawned.

The first guard growled at him and stood up. He needed to check the area in case Reginald asked him about the incident. Besides, this post was a straightforward job, and he didn't want to lose it based on Adler's version of the noises he heard.

Walking around the side of the building, the guard stepped over a few stones and wandered near the forest line. He sniffed the air and noticed a change in the scent. Kneeling, he ran his paw over the grass and searched for anything out of place. A dark color caught his eye across the field. The guard leaped over to the object and picked it up; a strip of wet, blue cloth had been left behind. *This is what I'm talking about!* He hissed through his teeth. Sniffing the cloth, he sensed the animal that had worn this bandage was not a fox, but possibly a sombel. He sniffed the cloth again. *Yes, a sombel!* But he hadn't seen any creatures since his last patrol. *Where did it come from?*

Racing back to his post, the first guard shoved the cloth in the second guard's face and shouted, "Do you see this?"

The other guard moved his hat to open one eye and take in the view. "What is that?" he asked and placed the hat back over this face.

"You idiot!" the first guard snatched the hat from the other guard's face. "Look closer!"

"It's a wet cloth, so what?" he answered.

"It's a bandage, I can smell the herbs," the first guard threw the hat back to the second one. "And it smells like a sombel."

The second guard sat up, "A sombel?"

"Yes, well, it's definitely NOT a fox," the first one replied.

"What does this mean then?" he stared at the cloth and then at the other fox.

"It means," the first guard sighed, "Edwin had a visitor."

The second one nodded, "And Adler knew about it."

"Right," the first guard spoke. "We need to report this to Reginald immediately or he'll have our heads!"

Chapter 16

Bowen stood on the beach surveying the sea. The sound of waves rolling and crashing on the nearby cliffs made him sleepy. As he searched for a boat on the horizon, the fox found a cozy stone arch to sit under and wait. He was low enough to the ground that the shadows of the setting sun covered him completely. The salt in the ocean air rested on Bowen's lips. He licked them with anticipation; hopeful that tonight would bring another sighting of the mysterious ship.

As he played in the sand, it wasn't long before Bowen heard voices reverberating over the noise of the ocean's waves--a low humming sound. Then he spotted a large wooden wagon, covered with a white tarp, and pushed by five or six fox soldiers. Bowen's heart pounded as he watched the wagon roll over the rocks toward the seaport. The two soldiers in the front helped steer the cargo onto the pier, while the other soldiers pushed the cart from behind, and cleared any debris that might entangle the wheels. One soldier shouted orders to another and pointed to the sea.

To get a closer look, Bowen crawled out of his shelter and scampered across the beach to the pier. Once he reached the dock, he saw it: a large wooden fishing vessel with a tall mast and its sails tied down. A collection of wagons and carts sat parked on the starboard side of the boat. They looked exactly like the wagon on the pier.

Bowen's whiskers twitched. It happened when he felt anxious. *What's in those carts?* His curiosity consumed him. *If I could just get a peek....* He tiptoed even closer. The soldiers at the end of the pier shouted at each other as they pushed the heavy wagon from behind; but it wouldn't budge. Something on the boat ramp kept the wheels from moving forward. The wagon rocked several times before finally tipping back, spilling cooking pots and drinking cups all over the pier. Bowen jumped up and ran down the pier to the wagon. As the soldiers struggled to push the cart back to its upright position, Bowen slipped in and helped reposition it.

"Get all the wares," the captain of the soldiers barked.

All the soldiers scrambled to pick up the pottery and pewter pieces and return them to the cart. Bowen retrieved several cups and handed them to a fox loading the wagon. Once the goods were accounted for, the captain draped the tarp back over the top and commanded the others to load the cart onto the boat. Bowen ducked down to blend in with the soldiers, and they shoved the wagon up the boat ramp and onto the boat's deck.

"Oi! You there!" the captain shouted at Bowen.

Bowen stood completely still.

"Who are you? Where did you come from?" The captain demanded.

"Sir, I, uh, was enjoying the beach and I saw your foxes struggling with that wagon...and, uh," Bowen struggled to answer. He swallowed hard, "I thought I could help."

"Hmmm, for that I am grateful," the captain replied and walked around Bowen, analyzing him from top to bottom. "You're a fox, I see. What clan?"

Bowen hesitated. *This was not going to end well*, he thought. "Redlan, sir," he half whispered.

"What clan?" the captain demanded.

"Redlan clan, sir," Bowen said a bit louder.

"The Redlan clan?!" the captain asked loudly. All the soldiers and boat workers stopped what they were doing and turned to look at Bowen instead.

"Y-yes," he replied.

"Where did you come from, Redlan fox?" the captain asked.

"Chipping Farms, sir," Bowen replied.

"Chipping Farms? The village where Reginald lives?" The captain's eyes widened with disbelief and the soldiers grumbled to each other.

"He's a traitor too!" One soldier shouted while the others cheered him on.

"Who me? No! You have the wrong idea!" Bowen panicked and sprinted toward the ramp to escape.

"Don't let him get away!" The captain commanded. Two blue-badged soldiers caught Bowen's arms and prevented him from leaving the boat. "Keep him confined until we've left the shore. I have more questions for him."

The soldiers nodded and shoved Bowen down the stairs and into a makeshift meeting room on the first floor. They managed to secure him to a chair with rope wrapped around his shoulders and bag, tying his paws and feet with the last of the cord.

"Captain's got questions for you," the first soldier laughed.

"Why? I haven't committed any crime!" Bowen said.

"Knowing Reginald is crime enough!" the second soldier joked.

Bowen felt the ship move and cursed himself for helping these soldiers out. Now he sat trapped on a boat, tied to a chair, going who knows where...and for how long?

"Sirs, I can assure you that I am no friend of Reginald!" Bowen exclaimed.

"How's that?" the first soldier asked.

"He overthrew our leader, my boss, and wrecked everything precious to me," Bowen choked a little on his words but kept talking. "I'm here because I've lost everything to that monster and I want to get my life back."

The two soldiers, silent, looked at the fox tied to the chair. After a pause, a voice echoed from behind Bowen, "That makes two of us."

It was the captain.

He untied Bowen's restraints and then sat across the table from him. "Tell me your name," the captain stated.

"Bowen Whitethorne."

"Bowen, you worked for Edwin, right?" He asked.

"Yes, for years I served as his council and accountant," Bowen replied.

"How were you affected by Reginald?"

"When Reginald took over the throne, I lost my job," Bowen explained. "My family and I had to escape and hide out in a village farther south. Eventually I moved back for work," Bowen said. "because I needed the money. But life was so much better when Edwin was in power."

"Edwin is a good leader," the captain agreed.

"Sir, if I may, what is happening on this boat?" Bowen asked timidly.

"The wagons, you mean?" the captain stood up and grabbed two teacups. "Tea?"

Bowen nodded.

As he poured the hot tea, the captain simply stated, "We're moving."

"We? We who?" Bowen asked.

"I have orders from our leader to relocate," he replied. "Our clan needs to start somewhere new, a place where we can thrive."

"But, why?"

The captain sat down and handed Bowen a cup of tea. "What do you know about this area of Fellnore?"

"Not as much as I should," Bowen said. "I know Reginald has a lot of interest in the seaport."

"Exactly. Is that why you're here?" the captain asked.

"Edwin asked me to investigate negotiations for land purchases here, but that never happened. Reginald—"

"Ah yes, the rebellion."

Bowen tapped his fingers on the table, considering how he would ask the next question. "Have you witnessed or experienced any...aggression from Reginald in this area?"

"And there you have it," the captain sipped his tea and set the cup down. "The constant raiding on our land is the reason we're leaving."

"Raiding?"

"Yes, we're an agricultural community," the captain said. "We cannot survive any longer with the threats of invasion."

Bowen's mind reeled. *What is he saying? How are they in danger?*

"You asked about aggression," the captain said. "Well, our community is fed up with Reginald and his goons coming after our crops, our homes, and everything we've worked so hard for. We have fought long enough," he shouted. Then lowering his voice, he explained, "We're simply tired."

"What are you saying?!!" Bowen cried out. "Reginald has been raiding *your* villages?!!"

The captain nodded. "We're shipping what's left of our belongings to a new community in Oren Plum. That's where we're headed now."

"But why would Reginald raid your villages?" Bowen asked incredulously. "I thought he had family in the Branwell clan. That's what he's always claimed. The fact that he's a Redlan fox with family ties to the Branwell clan is the *ONLY* reason he has followers now." It was true, Reginald bragged about his connections with both the Redlan and Branwell clans, but some of Edwin's council members had their doubts; one of them being Bowen.

Laughing, the captain cleared his throat, "Is that what he told you?"

"It's what his followers believe."

"Then why are you here? Do you believe Reginald?" the captain asked.

"I don't have to believe him. I'm here to uncover his real identity as well as his true intentions for power over this land," Bowen replied. "If I can prove what I think is true, Reginald will no longer be in charge. Edwin can resume leadership and I can get my family back."

"How do you plan to accomplish this?" the captain asked.

"Before I left Chipping Farms," Bowen said, "I stumbled upon some sensitive documents that point to Reginald's actual ancestry; documents that could terminate his reign based on the ancestral lineage. But I'm having trouble confirming it."

"Well, what do you know?" the captain asked casually.

"There's a missing piece, a link that I can't connect," Bowen scratched his head. "Do you know anything about Reginald's background or identity that could help me piece this all together?"

The captain grinned and said emphatically, "Well, he's not a fox."

Chapter 17

The moorlands, in the late afternoon, radiated under the lazy sun like no other landscape in Fellnore. Tegan, Beckett, and Kenna stood at the top of a paved stone footpath admiring the beautiful purple heather around them. Under the scruffy lavender brush, a couple of wheatear birds chatted with each other about the weather. Tegan couldn't help but eavesdrop as she soaked in the breathtaking landscape before her.

"I feel the rain coming, George," a little wheatear said to her husband.

"Yes, the breeze is westbound," George replied. "It will be here tonight, no doubt about it, Allie."

"We best get home and secure the chicks," Allie said. "Will you stop by your brother's nest and tell him I'll come in the morning for the wool?"

"Sure thing—"

Suddenly, a howl broke through the skies and lingered over the moors. The travelers, and the birds near them, froze in fear.

"What was *that*?" Tegan whispered to the others.

"Is it him? The hound??" Beckett asked terrified.

"That's a pack of wolves," Allie said to the group. "You should go." She waved her wings, signaling for the visitors to leave. "Sounds like they're just over the hill there."

"Do you know this land?" Kenna asked the bird.

"Yes, we live not far from here," George answered. He stretched and flapped his wings, preparing to take off.

"Oh, before you go...tell us, please, where is the village of Heathersage?" Tegan asked. "We are looking for Cormac, the leader of the Moin fairies."

Allie laughed. "You know there's a fairy hound prowling around out here, right?"

The three travelers nodded solemnly.

Sighing, Allie replied, "Walk this path and head north, over that hill. Look for the fairy ring near the creek. A villager will find you there." She tilted her head and spoke again, "You'll need to find thyme if you want to camouflage your scent." Flapping her wings, Allie jumped and flew off into the sky.

"We should've asked her more about the hound," Beckett lamented.

"Yes, but she did give us important advice," Kenna commented.

"Thyme," Tegan stated and looked around. "And there seems to be patches of it growing wild everywhere."

As the travelers climbed the path toward the top of the hill, they gathered as much of the herb as they could find. By the time they reached the summit, the group heard another howl. This time the vocalization sounded deep and mournful, more like a song than a warning.

"That's not the same howl we heard before," Tegan said as she gripped Beckett's arm tight.

"I know," he surveyed the land around them and pointed in the distance. "We need to make it to that mound over there before the hound finds us."

"Can we make it?" Kenna asked.

Beckett hesitated, "We have to."

The travelers rubbed the thyme all over their fur and stuffed the bundles into their bags and sacks. Searching for the best route down the steep hill, Tegan spotted a large slice of bark resting close to the rocky edge. She walked closer and observed it for sturdiness, turning it over and then back again. It was fairly thick and curled up on the sides, making for great protection against trees and scrubs.

"Beckett! Kenna!" she called her friends over to see what she had discovered. "What if we ride down the slope on this? We can get there faster."

Beckett analyzed the bark, rocking it back and forth. Kenna jumped up and down in the middle of it. "The only thing I can't make out is how to hold on," Tegan said.

"Kenna, do you still have rope in your bag?" Beckett asked. He was the best at figuring out a solution in a tight situation.

"Oh, I do," Kenna opened her bag and handed it to her friend.

Beckett stepped back and measured a length of rope to secure across the front of the bark. Envisioning something similar to a sled, he used his knife to cut the exact length of rope needed to stretch crosswise. He then proceeded to punch out a small hole on each side of the bark. Feeding one end of the rope through the hole, he knotted it securely on the outside. Then he poked the other rope end through the second hole across the bark and knotted it. Now his makeshift sled was coming together. Beckett stood up and pointed to his creation with a huge smile on his face. "Ladies first!" he stated proudly. "Are you ready to ride?"

Kenna and Tegan nodded emphatically. While this "sled" wasn't much of a comfort ride, it would get them to the bottom of the hill a lot faster than if they traversed it on foot. And Tegan was thankful since she was still a bit sore. She instinctively felt her ankle again and rubbed it. Then she rubbed it again. Patting around her foot, she noticed something was missing and examined it closely. The bandage was gone. She had lost it! But before she could say anything, Beckett directed Kenna to sit first up front, just behind the rope. Directing Tegan in position behind her, Beckett pushed the bark sled to a perch along the grassy edge.

"Hope this stays off the rocks," he grunted. And with that, Beckett shoved the bark sled over the edge and jumped on the back, squeezing in behind Tegan. The trio leaned forward as the sled bumped over the first few patches of grass and small rock. As it picked up speed, Tegan buried her head behind Kenna while Beckett shouted out directions like, "lean to the right!" All three riders leaned right to steer away from a jagged rock pile.

Bumping down the slope, Kenna suddenly stiffened her arms and squealed. Tegan jerked her head up and saw a huge boulder in their path. "Lean left! Lean left!" Beckett yelled. All three leaned to the left, but the sled didn't quite clear the rock. Instead, the back half of the sled hit the boulder, causing the bark sled to swing around backwards! Now Beckett was in the front, but his back faced the downhill path. Sliding at a frantic pace, Kenna held the rope as tight as she could while the others clung to her.

About halfway down the massive hill, Beckett directed the others to lean left again to try and reposition the sled. Tegan, Kenna, and Beckett all leaned sideways as Kenna tugged at the rope. The sled tilted and rocked side to side; the riders shrieking.

"Again!" Beckett shouted. As the three leaned all their weight to the left, the sled lost control and rolled over and over along a mossy area on the side of the hill. Beckett propelled out of the sled and continued rolling until he stopped near the foot of a young willow tree. As he sat upright and caught his breath, he watched the bark sled strike a huge boulder near the bottom of the hill. The sled and its two riders hurdled through the air, with both Kenna and Tegan screaming in terror. Rotating once, the sled landed squarely on the bank of a small creek winding through the moors tall grass.

Beckett gasped and took off running to the bottom of the hill and across the field to the sled. "Tegan!" he yelled out. "Kenna!" As he approached the sled, he rolled over the bark and stepped back. It was empty. Panicking, Beckett searched for his friends in the grass. He found Tegan's messenger bag, but no Tegan. He wrapped her bag around his shoulder and walked on.

"Beckett!" The voice came from the creek.

"Tegan?" Beckett called out. "Where are you?" He hurried in the direction of his friend.

"Over here, by the creek!" It was Tegan. She kneeled beside the bank with her paw outstretched to a very wet, Kenna. The fox sat waist deep in the cold water, her tunic floating in the gentle current and the fur sticking up on her head. She looked miserable, but otherwise in good health.

"Bad landing, eh?" Beckett asked and stretched to help Tegan pull Kenna out of the creek. He smiled at his friends, relieved everyone had survived that crazy ride.

"Yeah, and what happened to you?" Kenna asked in return.

"A willow tree stopped me," he replied laughing.

Tegan pulled grass pieces from his fur. "It sure did," she said.

Shivering, Kenna squeezed water from her tunic and asked, "What do we do now?"

A low, reverberating howl interrupted their reunion. It sounded close, a few kilometers away.

"I think we make use of the thyme," Tegan responded, pulling the herb from her bag. "Hurry, rub more of this all over your fur!" The three used their paws to scrub thyme fragrance all over their torso, arms, and head. They each took turns helping the other reach their back with the herb.

"Let's follow the creek and look for that fairy ring," Beckett said in a guarded tone.

"Maybe those fairies will have a warm fire and pottage too." Tegan said to Kenna. The little fox nodded and walked behind Beckett as they set out for the Moin fairy clan.

After a few minutes into the search, a wolf-like howl wailed across the sky and echoed throughout the moors.

"It's the hound!" Kenna shrieked. "I know it is!"

Tegan, Beckett, and Kenna ducked into a small stone grotto near the creek bank. Pulling moss and fern leaves down over the opening, Tegan stood motionless and watched for any movement outside their hiding spot. The sun barely illuminated the moorland as it slipped farther under the horizon. But Tegan and the others surveyed the creek and the terrain just beyond it from their shelter. As the breeze picked up, grass swayed back and forth, and the heather bounced in the wind. The clouds shifted around in the sky until finally, only the glow of the sun remained.

And in a moment of silence, Tegan saw it. A green blur that streaked across the landscape on the other side of the creek. All three travelers gasped in unison and held their breath. The creature backtracked as if it heard the sound emanating from the grotto. Walking steadily along the creek, a giant hound with dark green, shaggy fur paced back and forth. Its glowing eyes tore through the darkness and pierced into their soul.

It was the Cu Sith, or the fairy hound.

The creature's nose sniffed the ground as it wandered around, its large paws and sharp nails padding on the grass. Recognizing a scent, the hound raised its furry head and howled a long and disturbing cry, with breaths of air swirling against the sky. Beckett, Kenna, and Tegan clutched each other and shook in fear, wondering if the hound somehow sensed them nearby.

Then the hound turned its head, staring directly into their hiding spot, and growled. Tegan stood mesmerized by the creature's golden eyes. The longer she stared, the more she felt something. It was almost like she could read the hound's thoughts.

Jumping over the creek, the fairy hound approached the grotto, smelling the air around it. Inside, the friends squeezed together as tight as they could but were backed into a wall with no way of escape.

As the hound inched its way closer to the opening, Tegan stared directly into its glowing eyes again and mumbled.

"What?" Kenna asked in desperation. "What are you saying?"

"I know what it's thinking," Tegan replied. "We need a way out now!"

Beckett shook Tegan out of her trance. At the same time, a ball of fire swooped down and struck the lurking creature, knocking it over. It yelped and rolled away from the grotto entrance. Tegan's eyes darted around the landscape, trying to make out what just happened.

"Over there!" Beckett exclaimed.

To the left of the stone grotto stood a petite river otter with a torch. He motioned to the travelers, "Come here, follow me!"

Kenna darted out of the shelter while the hound was down and joined the otter, while Beckett and Tegan followed behind her. Staying close to the creek, the group hiked through the tall grass, briefly passing by the confused and injured hound.

Then the otter faced the beast, holding the torch in front of him. "Keep going," he instructed the others as they walked in a line behind him. As soon as the group passed by the hound safely, the otter resumed his role as the leader. "There," he pointed. A large, circular stone reflected the early moonlight, with a ring of mushrooms growing to the side of it.

"The fairy ring!" Tegan gushed.

The travelers ran to the inside of the fungi circle, waiting for the otter to join them. He sprinted over to the ring and jumped inside, shouting, "A síoga, cosain sinn!" (Fairies, protect us!)

Behind the mushroom circle, a tiny flicker emerged from a fallen tree laying cattywampus across the creek. That flicker glowed intensely as several more lights materialized from the log. "Here they come, stay put," the otter whispered.

A buzzing sound surrounded the travelers as they waited, huddled inside the circle. Three fairies, armed with bows and arrows, whizzed around their heads. One fairy, dressed in dark green breeches and a white tunic, flew to the otter and spoke with him. Tegan tried to eavesdrop on their conversation but couldn't make out any of the words. Within minutes, the otter said to the group, "They will shelter you for the night. Follow me."

With that, the fairies and the otter scrambled to the tree log and entered at the base. Beckett, Tegan, and Kenna stopped abruptly when they reached the tree roots, confused as to where the opening was. Kenna pushed and pulled on a curling root; and Tegan unsheathed her sword, swatting at the tangled mess of roots that hung down before her. *How did he get inside?* She wondered. But before she could hit another root, the otter poked his head out of an opening and said, "This way."

CHAPTER 18

"Sir!" a fox guard ran past Adler and into the dining room of the palace.

Reginald sat in a gilded chair at the end of the table, devouring his salted fish. His long blue robe tucked around chest and hips; he swirled the last of the ale in his cup. Adler could see he was deep in thought and chose to remain outside the room while the leader ruminated. But this guard interrupted Reginald's reflection with news of his own.

"Sir, a minute of your time?" the guard requested as he drew deep breaths.

Reginald wiped his mouth with a cloth napkin and asked with irritation, "What is it?"

Adler recognized the guard as one of the two foxes posted outside Edwin's holding area or rectory. *What news could he possibly have? Is he tattling on me?* Adler stepped forward to make the guard aware that he was in the room too. The guard did a double take but continued to speak with his leader.

"Sir, I found this at the end of my shift," the fox guard reported and opened his paw to reveal a tattered cloth bandage.

"And what does this mean to you?" Reginald rested his chin in the center of his paw.

"Well....well...it means Edwin had a visitor today," the guard stammered. He placed the bandage on the table in front of Reginald as evidence.

Adler stepped forward, "Reginald's rules say that no visitors are allowed to see Edwin."

"That is true," the leader responded, pointing to Adler in agreement.

"Wait! Adler was there today. He was a visitor!!" the guard squealed trying to make his case.

"Yes, I authorized that meeting," Reginald replied curtly. "By the way, Adler, did you see anyone else there?"

Adler thought for a moment about how he would answer that question. "Just the family, sir." Hopefully that was vague enough to answer Reginald's question satisfactorily. He didn't want to outright lie, but Kenna was technically his family; and the other two probably felt like family to his cousin. So, there he had it.

Reginald stared at Adler for a moment without speaking, causing beads of sweat to erupt on the bodyguard's forehead. "Fine," Reginald agreed and waved his paws around. Adler released a huge breath he had subconsciously been holding.

"But he was there!! He must've seen something!" the guard shrieked. "Or someone!!"

Reginald lifted his paw to shush the guard. "Adler had an official meeting with Edwin; he is not responsible for patrolling the area like you and your associate are."

The guard began to protest but Reginald held his paw up again to silence him. "Go back to your post now. I will examine this bandage before bedtime." He pushed his cup back on the table and said, "You are dismissed."

The fox guard cursed under his breath and left the room furious. Adler immediately stepped back into his position in the hall to avoid further questioning from Reginald. In fact, he wished he could be invisible right now. The less Reginald asked him, the better.

Tegan couldn't see anything at first, but she felt warm and safe, which was the most important thing right now. The smell of burning wood and leaves tickled her nose. As her eyes adjusted to the light, she noticed a considerable fire glowing in the center of the room with both male and female fairies huddled around it.

"Come here, Benji," one of the fairies motioned to the otter. "Warm your paws and I'll make you a drink."

"Cheers, Lyra," he replied.

Benji sat near the fire and signaled to Beckett, Tegan, and Kenna to join him. Several of the fairy archers knelt beside the otter and asked how he was doing and about his family.

"Aye, they're fine, my friend," Benji said. "Well, the little one was asleep until these three caused a commotion...woke the baby right up!"

Tegan and Kenna winced.

"Right, well, I could tell they were in trouble—" the otter pointed to the visitors.

"The hound?"

"He was right on their trail…" Benji stated.

Lyra appeared with mugs of ale for Benji and the visitors. Beckett swallowed the beverage in one large gulp, thankful for anything he could drink. "Thank you for your hospitality," he said wholeheartedly. The fairy smiled and poured another cup for him. Beckett continued, "I thought we were going to be hound snacks out there!" Beckett threw his head back and drank the ale; this time, he actually tasted it. "Mmmmm," he rubbed his stomach, fully contented.

Tegan smacked her lips. The ale tasted like heaven! "This ale is exquisite!" she remarked. "What's in it?"

"Honey and a dusting of cinnamon," Lyra replied and grinned, pleased that her new visitors enjoyed her craftsmanship.

Tegan turned to the otter and said, "Sir, on behalf of my friends and myself, thank you for helping us out there." Beckett and Kenna also echoed her sentiments in between sips of the honey-based ale.

"You're welcome," Benji replied and set his empty cup down. "But now, I have to return home and help my wife get the baby back to sleep." He stood up, stretched, and shook hands with the archers. Facing the guests, Benji stated, "This clan will take care of you until it's safe to venture out again." And with that, the otter set out in the dark.

"Will he be safe out there?" Beckett asked. "From the hound?"

One of the male archers replied, "He will swim home; the hound won't bother him."

Lyra put her serving tray down on the table and asked the visitors, "What are your names?"

"I'm Beckett and this is Kenna and Tegan," Beckett replied. "You are Lyra?"

She nodded. "And these are our archers on duty tonight: Ember, Lumi, and Quinn." Each of the fairies nodded to their guests. "We have a few clan members in the kitchen." Lyra called and two fairies poked their heads out of a back room. "Here is Aine and Iris." The two curtseyed in their long skirts and aprons and returned to the kitchen.

"Most of our clan is still asleep. But we take turns keeping watch at night." Aine carried in a basket of barley bread and handed it out to the visitors. Finally relaxed mentally and physically, hunger pangs struck with a vengeance. Each traveler gratefully gobbled down the bread and finished it off with the ale.

The archers whispered to each other as they waited for their guests to finish eating. Once their bellies were full, Lumi asked, "Why are you here, friend?"

"We're looking for Cormac, leader of the Moin clan. Do you know him?" Tegan asked.

"Yes," Lumi replied skeptically. "Who sent you?"

"Edwin of Chipping Farms," Tegan responded. "Have you heard of him?"

"No, but Cormac may be acquainted with him," Lumi replied. He studied the guests from head to toe, then whispered to another archer. "Quinn will request an audience with Cormac. You can ask him that question yourself." Quinn left to find his leader.

Within minutes, Quinn returned with another fairy that appeared older and more regal. The gold embroidery along the hem of his white tunic suggested leadership and royalty. With a crown of heather resting on his shaggy brown hair, Cormac greeted his guests with a firm handshake.

"I trust you were treated with the utmost in hospitality?" Cormac asked his guests.

"Yes, thank you," Beckett answered as Tegan and Kenna both nodded in agreement.

"Good. Then what can I do for you?" Cormac asked and sat alongside the visitors near the fire.

"We're searching for the Flag of Firinn," Tegan offered. "Edwin of Chipping Farms told us you have it under your protection."

Surprised at the request, Cormac tilted his head a little and asked, "Why do you want our flag?"

"I need to locate my father," Kenna busted out.

"Gone missing, has he?" Cormac asked.

"There's more to it than that, but yeah, he's disappeared—" Tegan replied.

"And we've been told that when the flag's unfurled, it can locate someone," Kenna finished.

"It's true, the flag can be utilized in that way. But why would I loan out this precious artifact to you lot?" Cormac asked with his eyes squinted.

"Sir, are you aware of the invasions happening in and around Swynton?" Tegan asked. "We have it on good authority that Reginald in Chipping Farms is behind those attacks—"

"Reginald?"

"He's been in charge of the Redlan Clan of foxes for months now," Tegan replied. "His guards overthrew Edwin's leadership. And since that coup, he's been brazenly attacking villages in this area for quite some time."

Beckett added, "And you know it's only a matter of time before his soldiers discover Heathersage and all its splendid bounty...rivers of freshwater fish, open moorlands brimming with bilberries, wild garlic, and mushrooms..."

Cormac drew a deep breath, "I suppose it will happen eventually. But what does the flag have to do with Reginald...or your father?"

"My father worked for Edwin long before Reginald took over," Kenna spoke clearly and slowly. "And he discovered something, I believe, that could render Reginald's power useless, even reinstating Edwin back to the throne. That is why he is missing." She pounded her fist on the table, rattling the empty cups.

"And that is why we need the flag," Beckett added. "To find Kenna's father before Reginald does. We need to know what we're up against before the attacks become so widespread that no village within Fellnore is safe."

"I see," Cormac replied and sat quietly processing the information. Motioning to Lyra, he requested another ale and asked Kenna, "What will you do when you find him? Your father?"

"Find a safe place for him," Kenna said softly.

Tegan quickly added, "Of course we want to find out what he knows and make sure he's out of harm's way. But the thing is…" she looked at Beckett and then Kenna, "we really don't know what we're going to do after that."

"The only way your father will remain unharmed is if he acts on the knowledge in his possession," Cormac offered. "Just knowing something dangerously valuable will not guarantee his safety. In fact, it's quite the opposite. Whatever it is that he holds close must be removed from under the bushel and placed on a stand, in the light, for all to see."

"I was afraid you might say that," Beckett mumbled.

"Then it's settled!" Kenna blurted out. "We'll do just that…find my father and release the information." She clasped her paws together in victory.

"Yeah, but to whom?" Tegan asked. "Who should we trust with these details?"

"It would be wise to seek council on who should receive the information," Cormac said. "If it's as sensitive as you believe, your lives will be in danger too."

The room fell silent. The thought hadn't crossed their minds. If they find out what Bowen knows, the travelers will be wanted as well. Anxiety gripped Tegan by the throat and she struggled to breathe. Maybe they should let someone else accept this job after all? She glanced at Beckett who was pulling a loose string on his tunic. Winking at her, he stood up and addressed Cormac. "Sir, we would like to see the Flag of Firinn now."

"It's not here," Cormac smiled a little. "It's at Derwent Abbey."

CHAPTER 19

"What do you mean Reginald is not a fox?!" Bowen squealed, his mind reeling from this revelation. "What is he then?"

"Reginald is a wolf."

"As in...a cousin to the fox?"

"As in...your typical shapeshifting wolf."

Bowen sat for a few minutes thinking about this. It would actually explain why he fit in so well with the Redlan Clan—he shapeshifted to a fox to look like everyone else. But if anyone found out that he was an imposter, this information would destroy him as the leader of a fox clan. "How do you know all of this?"

"My son witnessed it one night."

Bowen leaned in closer to hear the details.

"It was a couple of years ago," the captain shifted in his chair. "Reginald used to live around here, frequented the Crown Inn pub down by the water. One night, a group of trolls came through the village looking for their friend. They stopped in the pub and drank ale all night. In fact, they drank so much that they eventually turned rowdy—throwing chairs around, bullying customers, and fighting with each other, which was when Reginald intervened." The captain sipped his tea and set the cup down. "My boy, Gamel, saw Reginald shift from wolf to troll right there."

"To a troll?"

"Yeah," he laughed. "After witnessing all that fur shedding, Gamel was never quite the same!" The captain scrutinized his visitor for a reaction. All Bowen could muster was a wide-eyed stare and screwy mouth expression. He was horrified!

"So Reginald turns from wolf to troll...just like that?" Bowen asked.

"It only took a few minutes...enough time to open the pub door and step inside. Of course, by then, the trolls were wrestling and punching each other in a drunken stupor."

"So why did he shapeshift to a troll?" Bowen asked.

"It was well known at the time that these particular trolls guarded a secret stash of gold somewhere in the Arsa Mountains. There had been rumors of the treasure for decades. Creatures slipped away from home and work, just to search for it on their own. Sometimes, they didn't return home. But when they did, they had changed...become morose and despondent. And what do you think Reginald was after?" the captain asked.

"The gold."

The captain nodded. "We believe Reginald shapeshifted to drill those trolls in the pub about the location of that treasure. Unfortunately, my son got spooked and ran home to tell me what he'd seen. I don't know what happened after that," the captain said.

"So Gamel actually saw Reginald shift?"

"Yes, and I've heard of two others that can corroborate his story. Though both of them spend the majority of their time these days drinking in the pub."

Bowen now had a better understanding of Reginald, the current leader of the Redlan clan of foxes: a shapeshifting treasure seeker, which explained his desire for green moonstones not long ago. But a wolf? Would anyone believe him?

Bowen's stolen documents exposed Reginald's shady ancestry, his plans to seize control of several lands, and his financial exploitation within the clan, but nothing to confirm his shapeshifting identity. *How can I expose him for who he really is?* Bowen needed a plan.

"What are you thinking about, friend?" the captain asked.

"Strategy," Bowen replied. "See, I have information on Reginald's misuse of funds, his intent to seize and control lands, even a dodgy family lineage...." he paused to carefully craft his words. "But I need a way to reveal his true identity to those who serve him faithfully. A way to lift the veil of corruption and shove Reginald's fate back into the hands of those who ought to revolt once they witness the truths I expose." Bowen tapped his head with his paw. "But how??"

The captain lowered his head, "I see your predicament. However, I know someone who may be able to answer that question. There's a leader in Oren Plum that's known for her wisdom. We sail all night but will arrive in the morning. You can ask her for advice then," The captain stood up and smiled to his visitor, "Come on, let's eat and listen to music. We'll be there before you know it."

John Henry stood with his hood pulled tightly over his head, covering his face from view. Dusk casted shadows over the cobbled stoned streets and lanterns began flickering along the main thoroughfare. The monk kept his distance from anyone on the street, hiding instead in an alley near the pub, the Monk's Candle.

Instructed by the abbot to follow Bowen closely, John Henry kept his word. Sending messages back by raven, he informed his leader of Bowen's movements. The fox had checked in to the Monk's Candle for one night and left abruptly the next morning. The abbot, in return, sent a message back with new instructions.

As the moon peeked through the clouds, customers trickled out of the pub, stumbling and laughing as they made their way home. John Henry waited until a small group walked past him and then slipped in through the door. He quickly raced to the back room and down the cellar stairs, hiding in the dark, dank room behind two large barrels of aging ale. Squeezing as far back as he could against a cold stone wall, the monk sat completely still, waiting for the last of the employees to lock up and leave for the night.

The smell of stale hay and alcohol hung heavy in the air. John Henry shivered a bit and pulled his robe tight around him. The night air chilled him to the bone down in this room. Hearing the pitter patter of footsteps on the floor above him confirmed the last barmaid closed the till and would soon leave the tavern. He traced the grooves of the barrels in front of him with his fingernail, straining to see anything in the darkness without so much as a candle for light.

The sound of squeaking metal startled the monk. Someone twisted the cellar door handle and pushed it open. A figure holding a lantern stepped inside and cautiously walked down the stairs carrying a medium sized box. John Henry held his breath as his heart beat wildly, panicked that the figure would discover his hiding place. Looking left and then right, the figure shuffled further into the room and set the lantern on a small end table to free his hands. Stepping back, he leaned on one of the barrels that the monk was hiding behind and placed the box on a shelf above his head. The monk pushed his weight against the barrel to keep it from toppling over, while at the same time, praying the figure wouldn't see him.

Once the box rested safely on the shelf, the individual grunted with satisfaction. He retrieved the lantern and hobbled back to the stairs. As he made his way up, the stairs creaked under his weight. The figure closed the cellar door behind him and locked it with the same metal key as before. John Henry sighed and went limp; he wiped the sweat from his brow and scolded himself for not coming up with a better plan than this. *What kind of monk am I? Who does this but petty thieves and rogue robbers?*

The monk listened intently for noises or movements upstairs for at least half an hour. Once he felt safe enough to move again, John Henry gathered the bottom of his robe and stepped out from behind the barrels. A familiar scent floated around the room and tickled his nose. He raised his head and sniffed a few times. That's when he realized the box on the shelf contained tobacco leaves.

Climbing the stairs, John Henry produced a skeleton key from his pocket and unlocked the cellar door. Now in the back room, he tiptoed softly to the entrance of the bar. A gentle moonlight cascaded in through the windows, casting a magical glow on a few scarce spaces. He soon spied the counter and crept over to it. Curiously browsing through the guest book, the monk searched for Bowen's name. But the only recognizable moniker listed on those pages was his own, John Henry. *What?* And then he smirked. *Clever, old chap! Using my name instead of yours.* He chuckled.

Scanning the area behind the counter, John Henry locked eyes on the relic, the candle of Petyr the Small or the Monk's candle. *This* is what he came for.

The small wick burned red just like he remembered all those years ago. John Henry carefully plucked the wax relic from its stand and placed it into a small leather bag he carried. He took a deep breath and swore, "I'll only borrow it. I'll return it when our quest is over." He took out a scrap of paper and scribbled a message on it. Then he wrapped the bag around his shoulders and leaped out the front door. The note didn't say much, only that he required the relic for a great truth and it would be returned soon. It would have to do.

John Henry didn't waste any time. He headed south for the abbey.

Adler raced down the hall and out the south door into the courtyard; he needed fresh air to clear his mind. Now that the moon hung lazily in the sky, he could feel the chill in the air and tightened his tunic around himself. Walking down a stone staircase, he ambled along the well-kept gardens and strategically placed fountains adorned with chubby cherubs or detailed dragons and gnomes. The sound of water splashing in the fountain pools eased his chaotic thoughts.

Without wasting any time, Adler continued through the orange groves and overgrown hedgerows until he noticed campfires in the distance: the soldiers' encampment. There, soldiers lived and worked in the barracks, but afterhours were strictly for entertainment. As he approached the encampment, a small group of foxes gathered around the bonfire to play their instruments. One gracefully held a flute, while another played the bodhran in a rhythm so sweet that the others clapped in beat with the tune. A fiddler joined the two to make a trio, and then a soldier wearing a tattered vest jumped up with a mandolin. Cheerful melodies lightened the mood as the handful of onlookers broke out in song. Adler smiled; work hard, play hard.

Discreetly, Adler moved around as quietly as he could searching for a particular soldier; a soldier he had spent time with in school. This particular fox exemplified such athleticism that even Adler had been jealous. That was before Reginald's takeover, of course, when many villagers had hopes and dreams of making something of themselves other than a servant to the new radical leader. And Rolf was one of them.

And then he spotted Rolf near a handmade table holding a bowl and a spoon. The way he held the spoon between his two fingers reminded Adler of those memories in school where Rolf showed off his archery skills. Bent the bow and string like it was made of paper! And then there was the time Rolf played in a stoolball tournament. Adler had been his teammate and witnessed his friend's impeccable coordination. But the rebellion had severe consequences on Rolf's desire to pursue stoolball or archery professionally. Most days, the soldier powered through the day's requirements, but Adler saw defeat written on his face. And that's why he chose Rolf as his starting point; he knew he could ignite the fire within this soldier to push his plan to restore Edwin to the throne.

"Good evening, Rolf," Adler greeted him.

"Evening, sir," Rolf replied.

"Aye, just call me Adler. I'm off duty and we're just talking as friends now," Adler smiled at him.

Rolf chuckled and patted the seat next to him, "Join me."

Adler removed his belt with his sword attached and sat next to his friend. It was nice to have someone familiar to talk to. They reminisced a little about school, but then turned their attention to the hardship of life in the camp.

"Most nights, we sit out here and sing about the life we used to have," Rolf said and crossed his arms over his chest. "No one dreams anymore."

Adler hesitated, "Rolf, I have a mission for you but it's something that must stay between us."

Rolf turned to face Adler, unfolding his arms, "Aye, what is it?"

"I'm looking to recruit a group of soldiers with allegiance to Edwin. It's for a project I'm working on," Adler hesitated. That sounded odd when it came out of his mouth, but he chose to continue anyway. "Do you think you could round those individuals up for me? I'd like to speak with them as soon as possible."

Rolf leaned over and replied in a low voice, "I can say with certainty that the soldiers here would devote themselves to any plans of supporting Edwin.... And with passion!" He winked at Adler.

Adler searched the faces of the off-duty soldiers enjoying their evening with each other. But their distracted eyes revealed a gloomy contrast to their present unfortunate existence. It was true; these individuals wanted their old life back. But would they fight for it? Would they risk their lives for it? There was only one way to find out.

"Tomorrow morning, round up the soldiers before roll call and meet me here," Adler instructed. "I need to speak with them at first light."

Rolf nodded in agreement. "What's going on, Adler?" He asked tentatively.

"Something's brewing," he replied and patted his friend's shoulder. "I can feel it."

CHAPTER 20

Bowen lay tucked inside his hammock in a small but tidy room. He listened to the ship creak as it lumbered from side to side, riding the crests of the waves in the sea. Opening and closing doors on the floor above him kept him from falling asleep. But he didn't mind, he felt cozy for once and enjoyed the solitude and relaxation.

Occasionally, he heard the flapping of the main sail fighting against the west wind. Rain clouds had been spotted on the horizon and the captain predicted a quick, blustery storm. Suddenly, rain drops splattered on the deck, the floor just above Bowen's bed. To him, it sounded like gravel hitting the wooden boards above him. But the noise was strangely comforting. Bowen pulled his blanket over his shoulders and snuggled in. His bag packed with sensitive information tucked neatly into the bed with him so he could keep watch over it. Some of the blank pages he curiously filled with notes and illustrations from his journey.

It wasn't long before he fell asleep; and slept so deeply that he missed the breakfast bell. Bowen jumped out of bed, afraid he neglected something. Quickly dressing himself, the fox stepped outside his cabin to see soldiers lining up for the mess hall. Delicious smells of fresh coffee, roasted potatoes, and baked bread wafted through the hallway, making Bowen's stomach growl. Scooting through the line, he grabbed a chunk of bread and cup of coffee, determined to visit a second time if his morning schedule allowed it.

Bowen passed through the main corridor searching for the captain. Only a few soldiers dotted the hallway, while the rest had migrated to the top deck. One soldier stopped him near the staircase and asked, "Can I help you?"

"I'm looking for the captain," Bowen replied.

"He's not here. Early morning meeting with the locals," he pointed up and over his shoulder.

Bowen thanked him for the information and scurried up the stairs onto the deck of the boat. The salty air slapped him vigorously while the sun pierced through the clouds and onto the boat, highlighting the soldiers hauling wagons and crates off the vessel and onto the shore.

They had made it. Wherever this was.

With the boat docked, Bowen finally saw the land that the captain spoke about. The terrain beyond the shore hosted lush green fields and fruit trees as far as he could see. Rolling hills and stone clusters highlighted the horizon, with promises of waterfalls and secret gardens galore. It looked like paradise.

Spotting a soldier in between jobs, Bowen walked over to him. The soldier rested on a weather-beaten broom and fiddled with a button on his tunic. Bowen asked, "Where are we exactly?"

The soldier looked at him and smiled, "This, my friend, is our new home." He held out his arms as if hugging the air, "Oren Plum."

"It's beautiful, indeed," Bowen sighed and paused to take it all in. "Do you know where I can find your captain?" he asked, suddenly intrigued with this new land.

"Yes, there's a small village to the right of that plum grove," the soldier replied. "Captain is speaking with the leader there. He'll be at least another hour. But you can find him if you go now."

Bowen shook his paw and marched down the plank from the boat to the dock. Hopping on the sandy shore, he squished his toes in the wet sand, glad to be on solid ground again. The fox hiked along the shore until he discovered a foot path beside a hedgerow. Since it headed in the general direction the soldier mentioned, Bowen decided to take it. The path itself was only mildly worn, an indication of intermittent use. The long blades of grass and green leaves provided a welcomed shelter from the blazing sun. Bowen appreciated this shade since the temperature felt increasingly warmer the more he hiked the trail. He spotted a winding creek and turned to travel along it toward the village mentioned by the soldier.

On the hill, he spotted a water well, its misshapen roof sheltering the spring—the only source of water for nearby clans--for hundreds of years. A villager wearing a straw hat drew water from the well by pulling a rope attached to a bucket. As Bowen crept closer, he swore the creature resembled a frog; its long legs and webbed feet and hands gave it away. The creature sat the bucket full of water on the edge of the well. With a huge wooden ladle, the villager scooped the cool water from the bucket and drank it straight from the elongated utensil.

Bowen hung back on the path, near the hedgerow, to keep the frog creature from seeing him. He needed the element of surprise on his side. The frog's knobby knuckles wrapped around the rope as it guided the bucket down into the well again. After satisfying his thirst, the frog hopped off into the bushes. Bowen rushed to the very spot the frog had been sitting and surveyed the land around it. Curious about the abundance of fruit trees, the fox craved a taste of its bounty. He scanned the area searching for a tree with branches low enough for him to reach the fruit. Settling on one a few feet away, Bowen plucked a plum from the leafy branch and rubbed it on his tunic to clean it. The fruit smelled a bit like summer flowers and honey, and Bowen sunk his teeth into it. Slightly crunchy, he savored the honey-like flavor on his tongue, licking his lips as the juice dripped down his chin. *Delicious!* Bowen picked a few more plums and stored them in his bag for later.

Then he heard voices. A gathering of village leaders sat at a wooden table under a large plum tree. Bowen could see the ship's captain discussing something and pointing to a piece of paper. The frog on the other side of the table nodded in agreement with whatever the topic was. The fox couldn't make out the words, but figured the captain was negotiating an important issue like land rights or access to the well. Whatever it was, he believed the Branwell clan's decision to relocate here was the right one.

Twigs snapped and startled Bowen. Whipping his head around to search for the source of the noise, the fox saw a frog standing an arm's length away.

"What are you doing here?" the frog demanded. The intimidating creature held a spear in one of his webbed hands.

"I...I..." Bowen stammered.

"Who are you?" the frog insisted, now pointing the spear in the fox's face.

"Bowen Whitethorne. I'm...I'm...here with the captain of the ship there," his shaky paw pointed in the direction of the meeting.

"We'll see about that!" the frog jabbed the spear at Bowen's leg motioning him to walk.

Bowen clutched his bag with both paws and made his way to the meeting area, the frog hopping closely behind him.

As the fox came into view, the frog leader and the captain both stopped talking and faced Bowen.

"My apologies for the interruption, but I caught this fox in the woods spying on your meeting," the frog guard said.

"That is my guest," the captain said and looked at the leader. "He is simply a visitor on my boat."

"I needed to stretch my legs after sailing all night," Bowen offered. "I'm truly sorry for any misunderstanding." He bowed his head and stepped away from the table.

The frog leader stared at Bowen, her eyes squinted and a slight smile appeared on her wide face. She rubbed her chin with her webbed fingers and then pointed at Bowen, "I know you," she said.

"Pardon me?" that was the last thing Bowen thought she would say to him.

Behind the leader sat an elderly male frog with a cane and a tilted crown. He grumbled every now and then while an aid tended to him.

"Yes, I remember now. Father sent me to Fellnore on a business proposition," she said and turned to the frail frog behind her. "Remember father?" The old frog grunted and mumbled something under his breath. "Before I returned home, I stopped at this wonderful little watering hole to enjoy the last bit of sunshine and warmth this modest place had to offer. But two bounty hunters showed up and destroyed the peace by throwing rocks and threatening me. I panicked and swam away. Only I couldn't go anywhere because my leg became entangled in a water vine." Three other frogs in attendance gasped at the same time, including the aid. "It was frightening!"

The scene unfolded in Bowen's head. After everything he'd been through, somehow, he forgot about that frog. Now as he studied her closer, she certainly looked familiar.

The frog leader pointed at Bowen and announced, "This fox freed me from that vine so I could return home." The frogs cheered in support of their leader. A triumph!

All eyes focused on Bowen, making him feel uneasy. He lowered his head and shuffled his feet. "It was the right thing to do," he mumbled.

"Indeed!" the leader boasted. "And I am in your debt."

"I can't believe it," the captain said and shook his head baffled. "You already know the leader of this clan?"

"I guess I do," Bowen said. "It's Rana, isn't it?"

Rana laughed, "It is. Welcome to Oren Plum."

The cold morning air struck Adler in the chest as he stepped out of his home to meet with Rolf. Thirty minutes to roll call and he was already at the soldiers' barracks. Whistling to his friend, Adler waited just outside the door, rubbing his hands up and down his arms to get warm.

Rolf poked his head out of the barrack's door and smiled at Adler. Waving to his friend, Rolf said, "Come inside, we have a fire in here." Adler stepped in and joined him in the center of the room where the fire blazed in the simple fireplace. All around him, soldiers dressed and groomed themselves, took turns pouring coffee and reading the morning news. A somber atmosphere to start the day.

Rolf quieted the crew and introduced Adler to the soldiers. Adler didn't have much time, so he needed a quick and persuasive statement. "Gather close my friends," Adler moved quickly in the new morning light. "What I have to tell you must stay here, amongst ourselves." He looked around at the soldiers; their eyes fixed on him. "Do you remember a time when we didn't have to worry about finding food? We farmed it ourselves." The soldiers mumbled. "Or what trade our kids would pursue? We chose what our little ones studied and, later, what businesses they opened." Adler looked around the room, pointing to a particular soldier he recognized and asked, "Rabun, what does your son want to be when he grows up?"

Rabun shook his head and replied, "You know I owned the bakery on Lemon Street. My kid wants to be like his dad; bake the best bread you've ever eaten!" He stuck his chest out and pointed to his fellow soldiers who cheered their comrade on.

"But what happened in the wake of the revolution?" Adler asked cautiously.

"That monster seized my bakery and forced me to serve him here, in this God-forsaken capacity. Pillaging other villages for what we could very well make ourselves." He dropped his head.

"It's a crime," Adler finished.

"Aye, aye," the others agreed.

"And your boy, what's he studying to be now that Reginald is in control?"

"A soldier," Rabun said with disgust. "That's what Reginald calls it and that's what Reginald chose for him. But it's a disgrace! What soldier steals from innocent clans and calls it a victory? We have no complaint with our neighbors!" The soldiers booed and shook their fists.

"Indeed, a disgrace," Adler agreed as the soldiers mumbled. "And this same story applies to each and every one of you, doesn't it?" The small group of fighters agreed.

"What I am proposing is a small coalition supporting Edwin's return to leadership," Adler stated and the room fell silent. "I'm not requiring you to do anything...yet. I'm simply laying the idea at your feet and asking you to consider it."

Looking at each other's reactions, the soldiers squirmed as they whispered amongst themselves. Adler continued, "Rolf will be my point of contact. When I know more, I'll tell him and then he can inform you. I have to be extremely careful, you know."

"Sir?" a soldier raised his paw. Adler nodded. "What are we going to do? Are we fighting Reginald? Throwing him and his minions off the throne?" The soldiers cheered.

Adler held out both paws to quiet the group down. "To be honest, I don't know how we will dethrone Reginald. I don't know when Edwin will be reinstated. But I feel something is going to happen.... something is in the air."

Adler turned and spoke to Rolf, "We'll know when the time is right."

CHAPTER 21

Tegan strolled out into the morning sun, rested and ready to travel to Derwent Abbey. Holding a hand drawn map in her paw, she raised it close to her eyes to examine the landmarks indicated on the path. Just this morning, Cormac had graciously offered Tegan the drawing along with a loaf of bread and some cheese for the road. She respectfully accepted this kind gesture knowing the terrain would be unfamiliar to everyone in her group.

Of the three, Beckett seemed particularly perky this morning, which annoyed Kenna. The fox wanted nothing more than the ability to teleport to the abbey instead of walking a day's journey to their destination. She was over it already and showed it.

"Why are you so jolly?" the fox asked Beckett.

"It's a beautiful morning, what can I say?" Beckett spread out his arms and turned around a few times. Tegan giggled at his antics.

"Delightful," Kenna grumbled, "until that hound finds us."

"Nonsense! Cormac assured us the hound wouldn't be out in the morning," Beckett replied and flicked Kenna's ear with his finger. She swatted him back, smiling only slightly.

"I saw that!" Beckett pointed at the fox and then skipped closer to Tegan. Kenna just shook her head and laughed.

"What are we looking for?" Beckett asked his friend. Tegan handed him the map so he could have a look for himself.

"It's a pond in the middle of an apple orchard," Tegan pointed to the mark on the map in Beckett's paws. "A crab apple orchard, to be precise."

"Duly noted," Kenna quipped from behind.

"It looks like once we clear these moorlands, we'll see an orchard and a small village behind that," Beckett said and handed the map back to Tegan.

"Hopefully, a friendly village," Kenna mumbled. Tegan and Beckett looked over their shoulder at her and laughed.

"Oh, cheer up, Kenna!" Tegan replied. "Maybe they'll offer us some delicious apple pastries."

"Like apple scones!" Beckett offered and licked his lips.

The little fox smiled at the thought of apple scones. Just a bit of honey and good pot of tea--that was heaven right there!

The group hiked through the moorlands all morning, feeling the scrubby bushes and feathery soft heather as they passed by. Small groups of flat rocks dotted the pathway, almost like a stone trail had been arranged here by creatures years ago. The farther they walked, the higher the sun rose in the sky. By its position, Tegan figured it had to be noon by now.

In the distance, a crop of trees appeared; branches swaying in the soft breeze. Tegan studied the map again. "That looks like our orchard," she said. The faint aroma of crab apple swept over the terrain and greeted the travelers with a tender embrace.

The group scurried toward the grove, looking forward to a snack and a little rest in the shade. As they approached the trees, Kenna stopped abruptly and looked up. Branches stretched as far as she could see, teeming with small pink and reddish fruits. All three travelers ventured into the grove searching for a branch low enough to sample the apples that nature offered them so abundantly.

"Over here!" Kenna called to the others. She navigated around a tree trunk and hopped over a fallen branch. Waving to Tegan and Beckett, the fox jumped up to grab an apple from the lowest branch she could find. Kenna tossed an apple to each of her friends before picking one for herself. She rubbed it on her tunic and smelled the sweet fragrance.

"Not bad," Beckett said in between bites and chewing. "Tastes a bit sour, but I like it!"

Tegan nodded and motioned for Kenna to toss her another one. Kenna reached up for another apple and quickly shrieked, shaking her paw violently.

"What is it?" Tegan asked, struck with pure terror, her mouth full of apple pieces.

"Spider web!" Kenna replied. She waved her arms around wildly, desperate to free herself of the clingy substance.

"Ewww!" Beckett squinted his eyes and shook his head. Nasty, sticky spider webs were the worst, especially when you walked directly into them at night.

As if on cue, a sizable furry spider dropped from the branch still hanging by its web. Kenna yelped and hopped off the limb, landing in the sparse grass at the foot of the tree. She rolled over and sat up.

"Did you see that?" the fox asked the others. "It was huuuge!"

Tegan and Beckett stood stiff, nodding their heads in agreement. Two more gigantic spiders dropped from the tree, causing the travelers to panic and scramble toward the other side of the tree grove. Single file, they quickly maneuvered around tree trunks and over tree roots—Kenna first, then Beckett, and then Tegan.

The fox scrambled up a fallen tree log and hopped over the obstruction and out of sight. She cried out with a desperate wail, terrifying her friends. As Tegan and Beckett caught up, they saw Kenna completely encased in a silken cocoon. Her arms and legs wrapped tightly while only her head poked out at the top. The spider next to her worked feverishly to stabilize the fox in the web. There was nowhere to go, and Kenna couldn't escape her sticky prison.

"Hold on, we'll get you out!" Tegan shouted and unsheathed her sword.

Beckett also grabbed his sword and hacked at the slippery web ties holding his friend hostage. Vibrations from the chopping caused the spider to jerk its head around and scamper toward the interference. Clicking its fangs at Beckett, the insect jabbed him with its hairy leg. The sharp nail at the end of its leg slashed Beckett's arm; and he dropped his sword. Flinching, Beckett grasped the wound with his other paw while leaning over to gather his sword, desperately afraid of his vulnerability. Recognizing his helplessness, the spider seized the opportunity and launched itself on top of him.

Tegan screamed and hurled her sword at the spider, but the insect swiftly struck her back with its strong spindly legs. With fangs clicking and closing in on Beckett's head, Tegan swung again and sliced the spider's body; but the injury only made the insect angry.

Swinging around on its back legs, the spider now faced Tegan in a standoff. She positioned herself steady on both feet and held her sword upright, ready to defend herself. Taking a few steps back, Tegan tripped on Beckett's fallen sword and tumbled to the ground, knocking the breath out of her. As she struggled for air, an enormous shadow blocked her view. She couldn't see Beckett.

The spider crawled over her and pinned her to the ground. Without enough space between the spider and herself, Tegan couldn't hold her sword to fight. She whimpered helplessly. How could she protect herself if she couldn't hold her sword right?

As the spider's head lowered to look deep into Tegan's eyes, its fangs clicked. A foul, deathly smell emanating from the insect's mouth caused her to gag. She could feel the pressure of its legs pushing down on her and the hairs brushing against her face. Desperate for relief, Tegan turned her head to the side to avoid the razor-sharp protrusions brimming with venom. Her breathing turned shallow and quick.

Time slowed to an irritating pace, and she could barely see Kenna now. The fox screamed and fought frantically to free herself from the cocoon. Tegan closed her eyes, wondering what to do, how to escape her fate. Would she end up wrapped in a sticky cocoon too? Would they all become spider food? She squeezed a few warm tears from her eyes and gasped. Something heavy bounced on her chest.

Tegan frantically opened her eyes. A large, bulbous spider head rolled from her chest to the ground beside her while she lay trapped under a disgusting spider carcass. She whipped her head around and saw Beckett holding his sword, splattered with spider guts, and breathing heavily. Dropping his weapon, Beckett rushed to his friend and pulled her out from underneath the spider's remains. Tegan gratefully hugged her friend and then retrieved her sword.

"Kenna!" she squawked, her voice suddenly muffled by emotion.

The fox remained tightly wrapped in the web cocoon, her eyes wide with panic. Tegan and Beckett hacked at the web in vain. Their swords sliced through the silky strands only to witness the regeneration of the web. Frustrated, Tegan climbed up to Kenna's head and shoved her sword down in between the fox's body and the top of the cocoon. Using her sword as a wedge, Tegan pulled against the web as hard as she could, growling with emotion. The gemstone in her sword started to glow a deep green color.

"Hurry! I see more!!" Kenna yelped.

Beckett turned around to witness at least ten more spiders crawling their way. "Keep going, Tegan!" He climbed up the web on the other side of Kenna and frantically hacked at the strands holding the cocoon.

Determined, Tegan growled even louder, her paws sweaty with each yank. Without warning, the gemstone flashed a blinding green light that launched both Tegan and Beckett into the air. They landed hard on the ground, moaning as they each sat up. But it worked. The cocoon webbing broke in half and Kenna slipped out, hitting the grass under the damaged web. Beckett scooped her up and helped her steady herself on both feet.

"Let's get out of here now!" Beckett shouted.

Both Kenna and Tegan regained their composure and followed Beckett's lead. Hopping over tree roots and around tree trunks, the group scurried through the orchard toward the light at the edge of the grove. Tegan briefly checked over her shoulder, to see where the other spiders had gone. Only a few still trailed them, but she knew the others were close by.

And she was correct. The branches over the travelers swarmed with spiders. The insects dropped one by one from the limbs to chase after the group. Tegan squealed, "Watch out! Overhead!" Beckett and Kenna noted the spiders above them and kept running.

One of the grounded spiders swiped at Kenna's legs and tripped her. She fell flat on her chest and groaned in pain. The spider rapidly approached the fox. But Tegan jumped on its back, lifted her sword, and stabbed the insect with fury—straight through the head.

"Nice!" Beckett remarked as he helped Kenna up.

"I hate spiders," Tegan replied.

"Me too," Kenna said weakly.

"Come on, we're almost there," Beckett said to the others.

With the sunlight in view, the travelers sprinted until they reached the edge of the grove. Scurrying out of the trees, they were immediately met with a view of a small country village.

"There it is," Beckett stated solemnly.

"We made it," Kenna replied. Standing with an odd look on her face, the fox wavered and then collapsed.

"Kenna!" Tegan knelt down and shook her friend's shoulders. "Wake up! Kenna!!" Raising her eyelids and checking her pulse, Tegan frantically tried to rouse her friend.

The fox's body lay limp and unresponsive near the grove. Afraid the spiders would find them again, Beckett picked up Kenna gently and said, "Let's take her to the village."

The two ran frantically toward the town. Surely someone could help Kenna there.

CHAPTER 22

Bowen sat on the wooden dock swishing his bare feet in the sea water. Enjoying the warm breeze, he watched as dozens of fox soldiers loaded empty wagons and carts back onto the ship. The contents of those wagons now stored somewhere in the new village--the one the Branwell clan and its captain recently established. Only a few residents had officially moved into the new village though, mostly farmers and a few guards to watch over the construction of housing. Bowen had so many questions as he impatiently waited for the captain to return to the boat.

A group of fox soldiers marched toward the dock. Bowen moved closer to another soldier that appeared to be on break to make room for the unit.

"How's it looking out there?" Bowen asked the off-duty soldier.

The soldier lifted his hat that conveniently covered his sleepy eyes and replied, "Aye, it's getting there. This is our sixth haul in the last month."

"Six?!" Bowen had to ask again.

The soldier just nodded and slipped his hat back over his eyes. Fortunately, a handful of soldiers accompanying the captain stopped at the bottom of the dock. While the captain appeared to sign papers, Bowen rushed to meet him.

"Sir!" Bowen addressed the captain. "Sir! A few questions?"

"Yes, of course," the captain handed his papers to the assistant and motioned for Bowen to join him on the shore. "Let's walk," he suggested.

As the two headed down the shoreline, Bowen asked, "How many more trips do you have to make before everything is transported here?" The captain looked at him with a sideways glance. Bowen reworded his question, "Maybe I should ask when will you be officially safe from Reginald's raids?"

"Soon," he responded. "We're planting, we're building, we're rezoning for water...the list goes on. Most of the clan will arrive and move in by the end of the week," he scratched his head and continued. "We can still transport what's left behind, but at least we'll be safe here."

Bowen spotted a shady place and motioned for the two to sit down. For a few moments, the two watched the ocean's surf push and pull along the beach in silence: the ebb and flow hypnotic. Pulling out one of the plums from his bag, Bowen sank his teeth into the juicy orange fruit and smacked his lips. "These have to be the most delicious fruit I've ever tasted!" he said.

The captain smiled, "You know, the first time I ate one of those plums, I had the idea to relocate our clan here."

"Really?" Bowen was amused.

"I went directly to our clan leader and proposed the idea," the captain stated matter-of-factly.

"What did he say?" Bowen asked.

"Well, it took at least a week to meet with all the councilmen, but ultimately, they all agreed that relocation was our best option."

"Why was that?" Bowen asked again.

"No one wanted war," the captain stared out into the sea.

"I see. And all that came from eating this plum?" Bowen chuckled.

"Strange, isn't it?" the captain agreed. "But there is some truth to it. Rana's clan is the protector of the spring water as well as the plum trees. She's the one who told me that eating the orange plum gives you wisdom."

"Is it magic?" Bowen asked.

"Magic, science, folklore...whatever you want to call it. But the fact is the plums hold wisdom in the fibers of their fruit," the captain pointed to Bowen. "Eat one when you need to make a major decision."

Bowen let that settle into his soul. There were plenty of opportunities for heavy decision-making once he returned to Fellnore. "I better take a few of these back with me then."

"Smart fox!" the captain cheered. "I'll have one of my soldiers bring you a few plums for your voyage back across the sea."

"Speaking of which, when is the boat leaving?" Bowen asked.

"Sundown."

Bowen hesitated; he had another question. And one not so vital. "By the way, do you have a name? Or should I keep calling you captain?"

The captain smiled. "It's Oliver. But everyone calls me Captain O."

Beckett cradled the limp fox in his arms as Tegan banged on the first village door she could find. After a few brutal knocks, the door flew open and a hare stood there surprised at what he saw.

"Can I help you?" he asked.

"Our friend is hurt," Tegan explained. "Is there someone here who can help us?"

The hare studied both Tegan and Beckett to determine if they truly required his help. "Did you travel through the apple grove?" he asked suspiciously.

"Yes, we did."

He sighed noticeably. "That might explain this," the hare replied. "Bring her in and lay her on the blankets there by the fire." He opened the door wider for Tegan and Beckett to come inside. Beckett placed Kenna on top of the blankets and stepped back while the hare and Tegan examined her.

"Tell me what happened," the hare said.

"We were walking through the apple orchard when a spider chased us. It wrapped Kenna up in a cocoon and came after the two of us," Beckett explained.

"After we freed Kenna, we all ran out of the trees. She just collapsed as we cleared the orchard," Tegan explained.

The hare kneeled beside the fox and inspected her fur. Lifting her eye lids, checking her pulse, and feeling her heart, the hare grunted, deep in thought. "I'm not a doctor," he said to Beckett and Tegan, "but I have seen this before. Look." He showed them two puncture wounds on Kenna's left shoulder.

"Spider bite?" Beckett asked.

"I'm afraid so," the hare replied. "The mere fact that you made it through the orchard with only a bite is a miracle! The Marfach spiders are nasty creatures. We've been fighting them a long time."

"Will she recover from the bite?" Tegan asked.

"I'll ask the apothecary. She'll know what medicine will help your friend," the hare said. "In the meantime, I'll boil some water and you can clean the wound with this cloth." The hare handed a soft cloth to Tegan. Dashing around the corner, he brought in a kettle and filled it with water, placing it on the fire next to them. "Make yourself comfortable and I'll be back soon."

"Sir, may I accompany you to the apothecary?" Beckett asked and shuffled his feet. "It will give me something to do."

The hare hesitated but then agreed. "Let's go."

The two scurried out of the door and down the road. Foot traffic was heavy, hares driving carts and hares carrying boxes occupied the middle of the main road. The two zigzagged in and out of the crowds until they stood in front of an unassuming structure: a tall, thin building with exposed wooden cross beams and a small open window. The hare pushed the heavy wooden door open and a little hanging bell rang, notifying the owner that she had customers.

Beckett stood a bit behind the hare taking in the floor to ceiling shelves of potions, spices, and herbs. A modest-sized hare stood behind the counter wearing a dull yellow dress and round glasses. She cackled and coughed before she could speak to the hare in front of her, "Lester, it's been a while now, hasn't it?" the older hare screeched between her laughs.

"Yes, well, I have a situation that I need your help with," he replied awkwardly.

"Who's your friend?" she asked peeking behind Lester.

"I'm Beckett," he said and stepped forward.

"This is Rosamund," Lester offered and motioned to the old hare.

"Now that we have the introductions out of the way, what can I help you with?" asked Rosamund in a serious tone.

"Beckett knocked on my door earlier carrying a friend bitten by one of the Marfach spiders in the grove," Lester explained. "She's out cold and I need something to help her recover."

Rosamund shifted her focus to Beckett, "Is this true?"

"Yes, he speaks the truth. We desperately need your help," Beckett pleaded.

"Very well then, let's see what I have," she turned to her shelves and climbed a short ladder to reach a few particular jars. Mumbling to herself, the two waited and watched as she walked from shelf to shelf to find exactly what she needed. Balancing several jars in her arms, Beckett ran over to help the old hare carry her herbs without dropping them.

Rosamund pushed her glasses higher on her nose as she added some dried herbs to her mortar. A bit of mint, a clove of garlic; she ground up the ingredients with the pestle and pure muscle. Grinding until the result was a coarse textured pile of granules, Rosamund put the finished product into a cloth stringed bag and handed it to Lester. "For tea," she said.

"Is this everything I need for the wound?" Lester asked.

"Oh!" Rosamund started and put her finger to her mouth. "One more thing." She looked under the counter and pulled out a big jar, placing it on top of the table. Grunting and straining until she popped the stubborn top off, Rosamund reached in and picked two pieces of black and blue smelly substances and wrapped them in wax paper.

"What is that?!" Beckett asked, his nose outright offended by the smell.

"This here is just a bit of moldy bread, dear," she handed it to Lester as well. "Apply the bread to the wound after you've prepared the tea."

"How long before it starts working?" Beckett asked.

"Should only take a few hours," Rosamund replied. "But I'd let the patient sleep as long as possible."

"Thank you for your help," Beckett replied and dropped a few coins on the counter for the apothecary.

"I hope your friend feels better," Rosamund said. "To be honest, I'm actually surprised you survived those spiders at all."

Beckett nodded and the two left the shop. On the road back to Lester's house, Beckett commented, "That's the second time someone said they were surprised we survived those spiders."

"Yes, it is unusual."

"Then how do you harvest the apples in the trees?" Beckett asked.

"That's something we outsource," Lester replied. "We don't venture into the woods anymore."

"I can see why," Beckett mumbled to himself.

Tegan met the two at the door and hurried them inside.

"How is she?" Beckett asked as he sat beside the patient.

"She's hot...a fever, I'm sure," Tegan answered. "She's restless too."

Kenna tossed and turned on the makeshift bed, fighting the fever inside. Wiping the fox's face with a cool, wet cloth, Tegan comforted her by humming gently near her ear.

Lester picked up the kettle to feel if the water was still warm. Pouring the contents of the bag into a little cheesecloth, he inserted that into a cup and filled it with warm water. As the tea steeped, he watched as Tegan and Beckett fussed over their friend; Tegan wiping the little fox's brow and Beckett holding his friend's paw.

"Here's the tea," Lester handed Tegan the cup of medicinal liquid.

She held Kenna's head in her lap and angled the cup so the fox could take small sips. Slowly, Kenna managed to drink some of the tea, but she continued to turn her head back and forth, restlessly.

Tegan looked at Beckett with helpless eyes. "What do we do now?" she whispered to him.

"All we can do is wait," he replied.

"I agree," Lester offered. "Just give the tea some time and let her sleep. She's battling that fever, so let her body do what it needs to."

Tegan nodded naively; trusting...hoping that all Kenna needed was some time to fight. She fluffed a few pillows beside the fox and curled up. If there was nothing she could do, then she might as well rest. Beckett also sat beside her, as if on watch.

Lester handed Beckett the wax paper with the moldy bread inside. Holding his breath, Beckett took the bread out and placed it on Kenna's spider bite. The little fox shivered and turned over to face the fireplace. Then Beckett wet a small part of Kenna's tunic and laid it over the wound, holding the moldy bread in place as she slept. The sight of his friend in such a fragile state really shook him, but he couldn't show it. He watched and waited.

Over time, Tegan must have fallen asleep because she suddenly woke up to Kenna mumbling in her sleep. Alarmed, she sat up and poked Beckett, who had also succumbed to the warm fireplace and cozy blankets.

"She's saying something!" Tegan said.

Kenna lay on her back, eyes closed, but her mouth slightly moved. "What's that?" Beckett asked the fox. He looked at Tegan, "I don't understand what she's saying."

Tegan put her paw on Kenna's arm, "We're here with you. What are you trying to tell us?"

Kenna twitched in response. Then her eyes fluttered and she looked around the room. She was finally awake! Tegan felt the fox's forehead, "No fever," she said and smiled. Kenna blinked a few times. She recognized her two friends but felt uneasy in her new surroundings.

"Where...where am I?" Kenna managed to squeak out.

"We're in a safe home," Tegan answered and patted her paw.

"Yes, you've been out a few hours, my friend," Lester stated. "Glad to see you're awake."

Kenna held her head as she sat up. "My shoulder is sore," she stated.

"Yeah, because a spider bit you!" Beckett half laughed. "We fixed you up with some medicine though."

"You were talking in your sleep, Kenna. What were you trying to say?" Tegan asked her.

"Me? Talking?" Kenna's eyes were wide as she studied Tegan. "I don't know."

"Did you dream anything maybe?" she asked again.

"I...I...remember seeing an army of foxes....and," Kenna closed her eyes to concentrate.

"And?" Beckett asked.

"And a flag. I remember the soldiers holding a blueish flag with a cross on it," Kenna said and looked up at Tegan and Beckett. "What do you think that means?"

The two friends shrugged.

Listening to Kenna's conversation about her dream, Lester walked over with a weathered book in his paws. He opened it to a page in the middle and showed it to the fox, "Did the flag look like this one?" he asked her.

Kenna took the book and lifted it close, "Yes!" she said with awe. "Yes, this is the flag!"

Tegan and Beckett turned the book around to see for themselves.

"The Flag of Firinn," Beckett read.

"Yes, the Flag of Firinn," Lester repeated.

CHAPTER 23

Bowen sat on the bed inside his little cabin rifling through some papers from his messenger bag. The voyage back to Fellnore would take all night and he was not particularly sleepy. Busying himself with note taking, he secured a blank page to draw sketches of what he'd witnessed during the day: the water well, Rana, plum trees, and the boat.

With all the interviews and notes taken throughout his journey, Bowen wondered how he could ensure his own safety and still reveal what he knew about Reginald. The end goal, of course, was to restore power to Edwin. But in the meantime, he not only carried important information that could ruin Reginald's reputation, but the documents he stored back at the abbey were testimony to the leader's true intentions. And if those were revealed, the village would collapse in chaos. Bowen walked a fine line that was now starting to unravel.

How would he unseat Reginald without threatening his own family? Was there a way to unveil Reginald's identity without a fight? Could he somehow leave a trail of breadcrumbs for someone else to identify, and thereby secure his family's safety? All these thoughts swirled around in Bowen's head. "*I need proper advice,*" he thought. The only advocate he trusted right now was the abbot, Father Ennis. So he resigned himself to seek wise counsel and hike back to the abbey as soon as they landed in Fellnore.

Satisfied with his sketches, Bowen leaned back to admire them. He laughed as he was definitely *not* an artist, but drawing basic lines helped him remember the details of his journey.

Bang!

Bowen jumped at the loud noise and his drawings scattered to the floor. The sound came from just outside his door.

Bang, bang, bang!!

He slid off the bed and cautiously opened his cabin door. To his surprise, no one stood there. However, a brown basket loaded with orange plums laid at the foot of the entrance. He had forgotten about the captain's promise to deliver the fruit before docking in the morning. Delighted, Bowen picked up the basket and carried it inside his room, quickly shutting the door behind him. He gathered all his sketches off the floor and stacked them in a pile on his blanket. Selecting one of the plums, he hopped on the bed and sank his teeth into the fruit. *Now is a good time to get wisdom. Let's see how these plums work!*

As he savored the fruit, Bowen sifted through his interview notes again, organizing them for the trip ahead. And then something caught his eye, something he didn't notice before. It was a separate sheet of paper obviously borrowed from Derwent Abbey. On the bottom left corner, Bowen recognized a blueish-colored flag. *Is this....?* He turned the paper so he could read the fine print. "The Flag of Firinn," the fox read out loud.

Bowen laid the paper down and leaned back against the headboard. Could it be that the wisdom within the plum fruit directed his attention to the flag? He remembered Edwin talking about this before he was dethroned. The fox even remembered the legend of the flag from school. But was it true? Could the flag actually reveal someone's identity? Could it unmask the shapeshifting veil that Reginald so comfortably wore? And could it be implemented in such a way that no harm comes to his family? Or his village? *That would be a miracle!*

Bowen packed away his papers into his messenger bag. He had a plan. And that plan started with speaking to the abbot and learning the truth about this Flag of Firinn.

Adler still had one more meeting before he returned to his little room near the palace. The fact that Rolf chased him down to schedule the meeting made him nervous. And confiding in this friend weighed heavily on Adler, instead of lifting his burden of secrecy.

Councilmen from several villages gathered in the meeting room at Reginald's palace. Servants zoomed in and out of side doors with bowls of fresh fruit and bread while participants debated the details of additional land development. He poured water from a pitcher near him and drank it feverishly.

Adler stood close by to keep a watch on his boss. As he observed the attendants going through the motions, all Adler could think about was that meeting with Rolf. Would the soldiers side with him? Or would they turn on him instead, and report this treason to Reginald? The thought of what would happen to him if he was caught paralyzed him. The blood drained from his face, leaving him feeling light-headed. He struggled to focus and rubbed his sweaty paws together over and over again. Adler even second-guessed drinking all that water.

As soon as Reginald readied himself to close the meeting, Adler signaled to Bin to take over for him. At this point, he really felt sick and wouldn't have to lie about that if questioned. He slipped out the side door and through the noisy kitchen. Bursts of fragrances like garlic and turnips battled for his attention. But the onion smell almost took him out. Adler burst through the exit and into the evening air holding his breath. Leaning over with both paws on his knees, he felt nauseous and refused to move for a few minutes. Slowly, he regained his composure and decided to walk home before meeting with Rolf. Warm tea and a bit of ginger would help his condition for sure.

The fox took slow, steady steps to his home, avoiding any sudden movements that might exacerbate this nausea. "Almost there, almost there," he kept mumbling to himself. Finally, with his home in sight, he rounded the corner and noticed that the door sat ajar. *Did I close it this morning?* he pondered. Pushing the door cautiously open, Adler wondering if someone had entered his place while he was at work. Then a figure darted by the door and crashed into the table, knocking it over with a loud smash!

"Hey!" Adler shouted and pushed the door open wide. "Come back here!!"

The figure stumbled over spilled items on the floor and dashed for the window. Diving through the small opening, the intruder escaped from the home and into the night air. Adler chased the shadow through the window and landed on his right arm on the grass outside. He continued running until he found himself down in the palace courtyard. But the stranger had disappeared into the darkness and Adler was in no mood to continue pursuing him. Instead, he hurried back to his home to check for anything missing.

Once inside, Adler secured the door with a lock and shoved a heavy chair behind it, for added security. He also closed the window and secured it with a latch, hammering it into place. Finally able to relax, Adler inspected the damage and his belongings. The overturned table lay on its side on the floor with the candle, plate, cup, and various books splattered around it. Resetting the table, Adler replaced all the items to their original location. He then put the kettle on for tea and collected a stack of papers that had fallen in the chaos.

Everything seemed to be in order. The shelves and cabinets were left undisturbed, and the bed had only been used as leverage to jump out of the window. Adler checked his food stash and counted three bins full of the fruits and vegetables he ordered only yesterday. His clothing lay intact as well as his bedside trinkets and glasses.

Why was the stranger here? What was he looking for?

While he waited for the kettle to warm on the fire, Adler casually sifted through the papers he collected from the floor: receipts, work orders, a map. *Hold on! Something's missing...where's the letter?* Adler rifled frantically through the papers again. He scurried along the floorboards searching for Bridger's letter that the raven carried to Edwin's place. He remembered putting it in his pocket and then laying it on the table when he returned home. *It has to be here somewhere! If Reginald reads it, this mission is totally compromised!* He lifted the blankets and inspected under the bed. Nothing.

Adler slammed his fist on the floorboard and yelped in pain. *Why did I leave it here? Now Reginald will find out; I'm finished!* He held his stomach and groaned; something clearly wasn't right. Crawling back to bed, Adler laid with his chin to his knees on top of the blankets. This sickness had to pass before he could do anything. But what would he do? More pain, more groans, Adler turned over and glanced out of the window. *What is happening to me?!*

"You've been poisoned."

"What?" Adler looked around for the muffled voice he just heard and asked again, "What did you say?"

"You've been in and out of consciousness for the last hour," Rolf called out. The soldier stood at the window shouting at Adler and knocking on the glass to get his attention. "Let us in!" he finally demanded.

Adler blinked several times and reached over to pull the latch on the window. Once it unlocked, Rolf and three others came in carefully to check on the fox.

"What are you doing here?" Adler asked.

"You didn't show up for the meeting, so we came to look for you," Rolf answered.

The fox nodded and said, "There was an intruder in my house earlier."

"Did you get a close look?" Rolf asked.

"No, just a dark figure in the night," Adler responded.

"Did he take anything?"

Adler rubbed his face with his paws and moaned. *Of course he did!* But he couldn't tell Rolf that...at least not yet. "He managed to take a document; something I didn't want Reginald to see."

Feeling some relief from the pain, Adler stood up and poured a cup of tea, adding ginger to it for his ailment. "You think this is poisoning?"

"You have the classic symptoms: stomach pain, nausea, so yes," said Rolf. "Also looks like someone doesn't like you."

"Or doesn't trust you," another soldier commented.

"Do you think Reginald suspects anything?" Adler asked

"I doubt it. We would be the first to know." Rolf poured some water from the pitcher into a cup and drank it. "Which is why we need to talk. There's a rumor circulating in the camp that we'll be marching soon. Have you heard anything about that?"

"No, I haven't," Adler said and furrowed his brow.

"End of the week and my soldiers don't want to go," said Rolf. "They're ready to back you."

"Well, that's good news," Adler smiled a little.

"It is. But we need to move soon or they'll get antsy and make mistakes.... say the wrong thing, look too long at the wrong soldier, start fights, you know what I mean?" asked Rolf.

"Yes, I do," sighed Adler. "Let me work out this stolen document situation and I'll send word to you soon."

"And the poisoner?" suggested Rolf.

"I have a feeling that the intruder and the poisoner are working for the same individual."

CHAPTER 24

The figure stood near Reginald's bedroom addressing Bin, the bodyguard on duty. "A message for the leader," he said in a gravelly voice.

"I'll take that," Bin said as he reached for the carefully folded note.

The figure jerked his paw away and spat, "I am to deliver this information in person."

Eyeing the stranger up and down, Bin cautiously turned and opened the bedroom door slightly to see if the leader was awake. Considering the sun was still making its way over the horizon, he wasn't sure if Reginald was even up yet.

"Sir?" he whispered loudly. "Sir, are you awake?"

Deep within the room, Reginald responded, "I am."

Bin could hear some rustling of blankets and footsteps on the wooden floor. "Sir, are you expecting a visitor by chance?"

"Yes, send him in," Reginald stated.

The bodyguard opened the door wider and stepped aside, allowing the stranger to enter the bedroom. As he stood there watching Reginald greet the figure, the leader glanced over at Bin and instructed him to wait outside.

What seemed like an hour turned out to be only minutes. Suddenly, the bedroom door opened, and the stranger rushed out with the hood of his tunic covering his head. Before Bin could grasp the situation, the figure disappeared down the palace hall.

"Come in," Reginald commanded.

Bin followed his instruction and warily stepped into the room. Taking a position near the fireplace, Bin stood with his arms crossed while Reginald preferred to sit on a chair near his bed. The leader picked up an unfolded note and asked his bodyguard, "Have you heard anything about Bowen's whereabouts?"

Staring at Reginald with blank eyes, Bin replied, "No sir, I haven't heard from the scouts." He had no idea where this conversation was going.

"Well, I have proof that Bowen's daughter is close to finding him. She's been to Bridger's house and even visited Edwin recently," he shook the paper at Bin. "And if she's talked with Edwin, then we have another problem."

"Sir?"

"Confidential, of course," Reginald replied with a grin and laid the note down. Bodyguards were not to be trusted with such sensitive information. He knew Bin was clueless to the situation but babbled on anyway. "Let's just say, I think I know what Bowen is searching for and we need to stop him before he finds it."

Bin just nodded. What else could he say? He had no idea of what Reginald was talking about but went along with it anyway. "The note? It tells you that?" the bodyguard asked.

"Yes, if you read between the lines, that is," Reginald answered. "By the way," the leader straightened his tunic and repositioned himself in his chair. "Guess who had this letter in their possession?"

"The stranger that was just here," Bin stated the obvious.

"Well, yeah, but he found it in someone's home," Reginald loved drawing conversations out. It was a special talent of his.

"Whose home was it?" Bin asked.

"Adler's."

"What?!" Bin shouted with disbelief.

Reginald laughed boisterously, his head thrown back, mouth open to show all his teeth. The sight actually frightened Bin as he'd never seen his leader like this before.

"Yes! So, here's what we're going to do," Reginald rubbed his paws together and planned his strategy out loud, sinking deep into his own solitary world. "I'll select a unit of soldiers to march toward the only place Bowen will be headed now and destroy the object of his desire before he can find it and use it against me." The leader stared into the flames in the fireplace as if hypnotized by the movement. He stayed there, oblivious to everything around him.

"Sir? Are you feeling alright?" Bin couldn't think of what else to say in response to his leader's ramblings.

Reginald blinked a few times, forgetting he had company. "What? Oh, yes," he stood up. "Come with me."

Following orders, Bin marched behind his leader. He listened carefully as Reginald continued talking to himself. "The unit must leave this morning. No time to lose. Get that flag and…" he trailed off mid-sentence.

Bin tried piecing together Reginald's cryptic clues in his head to make sense of the situation. What just happened? Those closest to the leader knew he wasn't completely sane because something was always…off…about him. No one had pinpointed it yet, but they all felt it. And what was this about Adler holding information that made Reginald go nuts? Was Adler in on it?

The two marched methodically toward the soldiers' barracks. Squinting in the morning sun, Bin trotted to keep up with the leader and his determination to deploy the military on some "get there first" expedition. Whatever this was, it was urgent.

As soon as Reginald arrived at the building, soldiers gathered outside stood at attention. They rarely received an official visit from their leader and wondered why Reginald showed up in person.

"Where's your captain, soldier?" Reginald barked at the closest fox he saw.

"Inside, sir," the soldier replied and pointed to the door.

"Well, go get him!"

The soldier ran inside the barracks and, within minutes, returned with Rolf, the captain of the unit. Standing at attention, Rolf waited for instruction, his heart beating wildly.

"I want you to gather a small unit of soldiers to escort me north. And make preparations in case of combat," Reginald demanded.

"Sir?" Rolf stood dumbfounded, hundreds of thoughts running around in his head.

"Go now!" Reginald shouted. As he yelled out orders for artillery, food, and other necessities, the leader calmly turned to Bin and said, "Get Adler. He's coming with us."

"Us?" Bin asked.

"Yes, both of you will do your jobs, standing guard next to me," the leader replied. "Or you won't live to march home."

"Of course, sir," Bin answered. "May I tell him where we're heading?"

Reginald chuckled, "Just tell him we have business at Derwent Abbey."

Tegan, Beckett, and Kenna thanked Lester for his gracious hospitality as they ventured out of his cottage first thing in the morning. If they hadn't knocked on his door a day ago, who knows where'd they be right now...or in what state? Kenna seemed to be herself though, which was a huge relief for the others. A bit weak, but she ate her breakfast of oatcakes like she hadn't seen food in days.

"Which way are we going?" Tegan asked.

Beckett showed her the map. "Looks like the abbey is just before this mountain. Only problem is..."

"What?" Tegan and Kenna asked at the same time.

"We have to pass through a forest area," he replied.

"As in tall trees, unknown inhabitants...?" Tegan asked. She wasn't sure she could face another day like the one she experienced yesterday. And she was absolutely positive Kenna wouldn't step foot anywhere near a place that could house--

"Spiders?!" Kenna shivered. "No way I'm walking any farther."

"Well, there is another path around the forest, but it will take longer on foot. Maybe a few hours more," Beckett said.

"I'll take it, so long as I don't see another patch of trees for a while," Kenna grumbled.

Beckett looked at Tegan and said, "In that case, we need to take the southwest footpath to Wheatsheaf Meadows."

"Isn't that where—?"

"Shhh, we'll tell her when we get there," Beckett whispered.

"What was that?" Kenna asked from behind.

"A silly myth...a war with spiders fought many years ago," Beckett waved his paw. "No need to think about it now; it's been ages."

"Are you serious?!" she asked.

Beckett's paw rested on Kenna's shoulder, "What we need to focus on right now is that flag. Does anyone know how to use it? That is, if we actually find it."

"Of course, we'll find it!" Kenna shouted. "We have to," she mumbled under her breath.

"I just don't see how a flag is going to help us get rid of Reginald," Tegan commented. "I mean, how does revealing his identity benefit us?"

"Agreed," Beckett said. "Isn't he just a narcissistic fox?"

Tegan laughed at the simple description. "Yes, yes he is," she replied.

"What you left out is that this special flag can also help me find my father...like a tracker to reveal his location," Kenna added. "And I'm going to find him, one way or another."

They came to a fork in the road and proceeded to hike south, around the forest before them. What kept them moving forward was the fact that the abbey was within reach. They just needed to find Wheatsheaf Meadows before dusk.

CHAPTER 25

As the boat docked back in Swynton, Bowen hoisted his bag around his shoulder and neck and stepped firmly onto the ground. A quick visit to the Milecastle Inn so he could check for messages would be his only stop this morning. As the fox stepped through the door, he met Ulric in the lobby.

"Good morning, sir," the owl greeted him. "How was your trip?"

"Informative," he replied and sighed.

Ulric chuckled; his wing covered his belly that shook up and down when he laughed. "I guess so! Are you heading out?"

"Yes," Bowen responded. "Did I get any messages while I was gone?"

"No, not a one," the owl flipped through a few papers on the registration counter. "Oh, but I did get an inquiry about you. Someone sent a raven asking if you were currently staying at the Inn."

"What did you reply?" Bowen quipped.

"I haven't responded yet. I only received the message this morning," Ulric answered.

Bowen let out a heavy sigh. "Good."

"What would you like for me to say?" Ulric asked.

"Don't respond, just ignore it," Bowen barked. He hesitated, realizing his abrupt tone and said, "My apologies. I've got more than I can handle right now. I just don't need a nosy stalker too."

Another customer at the Inn descended the stairs and presented his key to Ulric for check out. The owl turned his attention to the present customer, a hedgehog, while Bowen finished preparing his bag for the journey.

"Heading out, sir?" Ulric asked.

"Yes, I have a keel boat to catch," said the hedgehog.

Bowen's ears perked up. He hadn't been on a keel boat in years.

"Where are you headed, sir?" the fox asked.

"I'm taking the noon transport down the Tana River," said the hedgehog. "It takes you around the mountain pass, which is faster than walking, depending on your destination."

Could this water transport get him to the abbey faster? The sooner he spoke to the abbot about the Flag of Firinn, the better. Bowen decided it was worth a try.

Once the hedgehog left, Bowen asked Ulric for directions to the transport station and walked out onto the street. Following the foot traffic, he made it to the fish market situated alongside a creek trickling with fresh water. As he waded across the icy water, Bowen turned and hiked along the creek until it led him all the way to the keel boat station.

Standing at the dock, he admired the passenger boat in front of him. The slender, wooden vessel carried a crew of foxes on both sides of the boat, holding oars and poles, ready to paddle into the main current of the river. The skipper hollered out in a high-pitched voice for all passengers to board the vessel. Several hedgehogs, a hare, and a few foxes waddled over a plank to join the crew of this keel boat. As he stepped into the wooden vessel, Bowen noticed the bow narrowed into a sharp point in the front leaving the middle of the boat wide enough to carry everything from a few bundles of hay to piles of coal. Seats were scattered along the sides of the vessel and consisted of simple wooden benches. After paying his boat fee, Bowen secured his belongings under the seat closest to the bow and settled in for the journey.

A cool breeze wafted over the boat as the crew pushed the structure away from the riverbank. The air smelled completely different than his recent ocean voyage. Instead of salty humidity, he inhaled a combination of wet dirt, grass, and the subtle aroma of fish.

The structure floated along the mostly calm water, ducking in and out of the warm sunshine. Insects dotted the shadowed banks as tiny bubbles erupted nearby. Sleepily, Bowen drank in the singing birds and hypnotic water as it lapped against the boat. He didn't know how far this vessel would take him, but it was much better than walking. And he needed time to think.

If the Flag of Firinn was more than a fairy tale...more than fiction, how could he use it to free himself and his family of this monstrous debacle he found himself in? If it indeed revealed true identities, how could he use the flag to disclose to the village...the nation...that Reginald was not who he claimed to be? He was no fox...only a shapeshifting wolf. How could he prove that Reginald planned to buy up and eliminate the communities along the seaport? The truth sounded preposterous! But it needed exposure.

The keel boat slowed as the crew gently guided it into a shady area covered with low lying branches. This was the boat's first stop down the river. A fox tied the vessel to the rudimentary dock and pushed out the plank for disembarking. The hedgehogs and one fox stood up, gathered their bags, and ambled off the boat, balancing themselves on slightly choppy waters. A few customers on the riverbank waited their turn to properly board the vessel. One, in particular, wore a long brown robe with a hood covering the entirety of his face. The figure kept his head low so no one could recognize him, which intrigued Bowen.

As the skipper secured the keel boat for travel again, Bowen suddenly felt nervous. The fur on the back of his neck stood up and that funny butterfly feeling hit him in the pit of his stomach.

"Sir?" Bowen called out to the skipper. "Sir?! How far does this vessel take passengers?" He needed to know how far he had to go feeling this anxious. Could he make it to the furthest destination? Whipping his head around, the fox noticed that the hooded stranger chose a seat only a few feet away from him. Bowen subconsciously squeezed his messenger bag tightly to his chest.

"Our final stop is Camden. Then we turn around and head back," a crew member replied near him.

"How many stops until Camden then?" Bowen asked timidly.

"Three more," the crew member said and began whistling under his breath.

Bowen didn't know if he could wait that long to get off the boat. He might have to walk the rest of the way to the abbey after all. Observing the hooded figure again, Bowen caught sight of something odd. The figure wedged himself on the edge of his bench, hunched over with his arms wrapped and folded in his lap. It appeared as if he was protecting something under his robe.

The fox's adrenaline spiked, *what was he hiding under there?* Bowen nonchalantly glanced at the robe again, but the stranger caught him in the act and turned sideways to avoid the attention. It was at that moment that Bowen swore he noticed a dim glow under the figure's robe...a light so faint that he convinced himself he only imagined it. But in his heart, Bowen knew the truth. The stranger had smuggled something of importance onto the keel boat, and he would escape the first chance he got.

Wheatsheaf Meadows was a typical farming village built on the agricultural importance of wheat, hence its name. Why was wheat so fundamental for survival in everyday life? Well, every villager ate bread made from harvesting this precious staple. Additionally, malted wheat became ale, which the community drank liberally with their meals. Wheat could also be used as thatch for their homes and fodder for their livestock. Over the years, Wheatsheaf Meadows successfully carved its own niche within the Fellnore area by providing staples needed by neighboring clans to thrive.

Derwent Abbey also relied on this village for necessary provisions.

"This is it," Beckett said. "The last stop before we get to the abbey." He lifted his nose and sniffed. "And I smell food!"

"Of course you do," Tegan laughed.

The main road before them hosted a multitude of market stalls with little tables and chairs underneath, complete with white fabric coverings to shield them from the sun. Villagers busied themselves as they loaded items onto their tables like baked goods, clothing, hats, herbs, tea, and more to sell at the night fair. There were also woodworkers in the corner and a tailor at the other end to hem and repair clothing.

Beckett spotted a stall offering pottage and baked bread. He hurried over and placed his order for a bowl of stew and a chunk of barley bread. The others joined him with their orders on a small picnic table near the candle making shop. As they enjoyed the warm soup, sopping it up with their bread, the group felt a sense of joy for the first time in days. Nothing like a full stomach to soften the throbbing pain of sore feet and muscles.

And this village felt festive! Little lanterns hung from shop windows and garlands of ivy cascaded in and around the storefronts. Happy chattering from residents as they walked up and down Main Street echoed in their ears. As the friends sat content, a badger ambled up to the group and handed yellow primrose flowers to both Tegan and Kenna.

"For your journey," the badger suggested. "For protection."

Tegan and Kenna thanked him but were confused. How did he know they were travelers?

The badger recognized their confusion and said, "I can tell you're visiting because we don't see many sombels here these days." He smiled. "We celebrate the markets with these primrose flowers. Legend says that the fairies originally gave them to villagers to protect them from evil spirits."

That made sense. Tegan chuckled and thanked the badger again. As he nodded and waddled away, another badger strolled by with a baby in a pram.

"Ma'am?" Tegan called out. The badger turned to see who called out to her. "Is there an event happening here?" The sombel motioned with her paws to point out the stalls.

The badger pushed her pram closer to the group seated at the picnic table. "Yes, tonight we're hosting the first night fair of the season," she said. "Our town celebrates the harvest season with night markets for two weeks. But you're lucky, the first one is always the most fun. You should stick around and see it."

Crying spilled out of the pram as the little one demanded attention from her mother. "Oh goodness," the mother badger leaned over and lifted out her baby cub, swaddled in a soft cream-colored blanket. With her lacy bonnet a bit askew, the little badger wriggled around until her mother found the milk she kept in a basket underneath the pram and offered it to her. She gladly gulped the milk down while the visitors watched with goofy smiles spreading across their faces.

"She's such a gorgeous cub," Kenna said. "What's her name?"

"Thank you, dear. Her name is Gertrude, but we call her little Gertie," the mother replied and cooed over her baby.

Tegan rested and mused in the moment, watching Gertie in all her innocence. *That cub knows nothing about the world,* she thought. *She is trusting and naive. It's only a matter of time before the impact of Reginald's terrible reign sorely affects her world...which is why he needs to be stopped. The next generation will have no future if Reginald continues his fiery rampages.* Tegan blinked away tears and cleared her throat, "For all the Gerties in Fellnore," she mumbled.

"Are you feeling well?" Beckett asked her.

"Oh, it's nothing," Tegan quickly wiped the tears with the back of her paw. "I'm just emotional."

Beckett patted her on the back. The realization of how the future might turn out if Reginald continued to raid and seize land caused her throat to constrict. She stood up quickly and paced around, trying to get the air flow back into her lungs. Her full-on panic attack set in and she couldn't turn it off. *What if they couldn't find the flag? If they were unsuccessful in locating Bowen, who held the information to dethrone Reginald, then how would they ever secure Bowen's safety, and subsequently, get rid of Reginald?* Her head spun like crazy and she unwillingly sat down on the grass beside the picnic table.

"Do you need to lay down?" Kenna asked hovering over her friend like a worried mother.

"I'm fine, just give me a few minutes," Tegan replied and smiled half-heartedly. She needed time to calm her racing heartbeat.

"Are you staying in Wheatsheaf?" the mother badger asked as she cuddled her cub.

"We are passing through actually," Beckett responded. "Headed to an abbey."

Rocking her cub gently, the mother nodded and said, "If you're walking to Derwent Abbey, I hear there are soldiers in the woods nearby."

Tegan's ears perked up, "What did you say?"

"Soldiers, my dear," the mother said and placed her now sleepy baby back in the pram. "My husband was summoned to that area yesterday as a lookout for his captain." Tucking the blanket around her baby, she pulled the top over the drowsy cub, shielding her from the sun. "And everyone knows a lookout means hostiles in the woods."

Kenna looked wide-eyed at Tegan, and she looked wide-eyed at Beckett, who was also staring at the mother badger in disbelief.

"Take care of yourselves," the badger said as she pushed her pram back onto the main road. "Pleasure meeting you."

The travelers mumbled amongst themselves something that resembled "pleasure meeting you too." What did they just hear? Soldiers in the woods? Now what?

With the air unimaginably tense, Tegan blurted out, "Ale anyone? I think I need a drink."

Chapter 26

"Leadon!" the deck hand called out.

This was Bowen's chance to flee. He jumped up and hurried to the unloading ramp. Unsure of where Leadon was, Bowen felt the need to put a considerable amount of distance between himself and the figure with the glowing belly. Maybe he could busy himself for a short time in the village until he could figure out how to get to the abbey?

The fox found a footpath and hustled into the brush, quickly glancing over his right shoulder. Although no one was there, Bowen still felt like he was being watched. He clutched his bag tight around his shoulder and hopped over a branch that had recently fallen across the path. Down and around he traveled looking for the town in question.

As he neared the next bend in the path, Bowen overheard voices. It was subtle at first, but they grew louder the farther he tiptoed forward. The voices were not military with commands barked at soldiers. No, these voices sounded gruff and rowdy. Bowen squatted under a tree branch to get a look at what he heard. Two scruffy-looking foxes sat in a clearing drinking what appeared to be ale. And they must've been sitting out there awhile as both seemed mildly intoxicated. With their swords resting against the nearest tree, the foxes called out, baiting each other, in slightly slurred voices. As they approached one another, the first fox pounced on the other and they proceeded to roll around on the grass slinging uncoordinated punches at each other. One punch missed but the other made contact, knocking a fox backwards.

The fox wearing a black tunic stood up and stumbled forward a bit, his stance swaying as he struggled to keep his balance. He motioned for the other fox (wearing red) to come towards him, his paws up in a fighting position. Seeing this, the red tunic fox growled and lowered his head, ready to use it as a battering ram into the chest of his companion. He pushed with one foot on the ground to get a running start. But just before contact, black tunic fox's eyes rolled back and he swayed to one side. And then he passed out. Falling backwards onto the ground, he laid there silently with his belly facing the sky. And since there was nothing to hinder the red tunic fox barreling his body forward, he tripped over his unconscious opponent and faceplanted into the ground. He did not get up.

Bowen winced on impact. He couldn't decide if he was amused or afraid of what he just witnessed. What were these two doing out here anyway? Who were they? Already ruling out military, the only thing Bowen could think of was...bounty hunters.

And then he remembered the ant's warning along the mountain pass. Bounty hunters in the area. He had forgotten about that. Now that he was travelling on foot, he had to make sure he remained unseen; and that meant staying off these bounty hunters' scent. For the time being, Bowen could take advantage of this situation and get down the road undetected. But once those two foxes sobered up, well, he refused to think about that.

Bowen crept around the base of the birch tree but felt oddly insecure. The fur on his neck stiffened and he felt prickly all over. Surveying the land around him for movement, Bowen finally stepped back onto the footpath, ready to continue his journey. But he sensed something was still off. He gingerly walked along the edges of the path in case he needed to seek immediate shelter. Someone or something was following him.

Thunder barreled across the sky and the sound startled Bowen. He instinctively raised his eyes to see where the storm was coming from. Black clouds hovered over the hills to the north of him. Mid-afternoon showers were common this time of the year. Only lasting a few minutes, storm clouds usually dropped buckets of rain quickly but heavily, soaking you to the bone unless you could find shelter immediately. Bowen panicked, searching for a place to wait the storm out.

As he trotted down the path, he noticed an abandoned barn to his left. Places like this always reminded him of his childhood. Spending his first few years on a farm with his family, Bowen thought of his father's little vegetable garden and livestock pen. He had eaten more cabbage than he ever wanted to because that's what grew well there. And that's what his father sold at the farmer's markets in the village. He ate meals consisting of cabbage and beans, cabbage and potatoes, cabbage and leeks...the list went on.

Now when he smelled cabbage, he only thought of his father. And his heart sank. It had been too long since his father had passed, and he avoided anything with cabbage in it since, because it triggered the memories.

Bowen jumped over the tall grass and a fallen tree, leaping over stones until he reached the front door. Most of the barn's structure remained intact; although the door itself had loosened from its hinges and was propped along the inside wall. The dirt floor revealed paw prints in the center of the room and empty crates were stacked along the corners. It seemed this structure had been a storage place for the neighbors over the years as broken wagon wheels, empty chairs, and firewood collected dust under its rafters.

Rain splattered against the patchy thatched roof as Bowen huddled in the corner where the walls and roof remained the most intact. He could smell the sweet scent of hay and the faint aroma of rotting wood, both familiar scents to this former farmer's son. Stretching out his legs, Bowen leaned back and closed his eyes to rest for a moment. A quick nap would do him some good.

And then the heavy rain poured outside along with a rumble of thunder. Water trickled through the openings in the roof on the other side of the barn; but thankfully, Bowen remained dry. He changed positions, curling up and tucking his tail around his neck and nose.

The fox must've slept for a while because he woke up once the storm had passed and the rain ceased to fall. Wiping his eyes, he slowly sat up. Streaks of sunlight squeezed through the door as well as the openings in the roof. It was the last few rays of sun in the day, but at least it was finally dry enough to hike.

Bowen straightened his tunic and bag, brushing any dirt off his clothes and paws. As he stood up, he sensed instant terror. A hooded figure sat beside him, a dim light glowing from underneath his robe. The figure stood up and took a step closer to the fox.

Bowen froze. He opened his mouth to speak but only a pitiful shriek came out.

The figure held up his paw and spoke, "Wait, I will not harm you."

Adler still wasn't feeling a hundred percent. His head throbbed and his stomach ached, but at least the nausea was gone. Whatever he was poisoned with had been flushed out of his system by now. But this sudden call to march wasn't helping him build his immune system at all. And no one had a clue as to why they were heading to an abbey. On top of that, Bin looked at him suspiciously, like he had something to do with this impromptu campaign.

Bin and Adler marched slightly behind Reginald; a handful of soldiers leading the unit ahead. The rest of the soldiers marched behind Reginald to protect the ruler cushioned in the middle. And Rolf, captain of this team, led the entire unit by himself. Adler could see the top of his head and the tip of his drawn sword from where he marched.

Heavy clouds made the air humid and difficult to breathe in. Traveling in this kind of weather always made him feel more spent than on a cool, crisp day. And since this campaign had been so spontaneous, Adler felt completely unprepared and ill-equipped to march. Instead, he focused his thoughts on some kind of strategy. What would he do once they arrived at the abbey? How could he use this opportunity to his advantage?

Shouting commands to the soldiers, Rolf dropped back from the front line and picked up the pace next to Reginald. Speaking to his leader as they walked, Adler couldn't hear what he was saying, but Reginald appeared pleased and nodded emphatically. Then the captain stepped back and marched in line with Adler. Once a little distance came between Reginald and himself, he said, "How are you feeling? Are you up for this?"

Adler nodded, "I'm as good as I'll get."

Bin looked over.

Rolf leaned in, "I gathered as many supporters as I could find for this unit. Reginald, of course, appointed some of his own." He looked around and then whispered, "I've got your back." The captain patted Adler on the shoulder and then dropped back a few steps to shout orders to the soldiers in the rear.

Feeling a bit more confident, Adler turned to Bin and said, "I know you think I have something to do with this."

Bin narrowed his eyes.

"And I do," he replied. Adler marched closer to Bin and lowered his voice, "But I am simply an ordinary fox caught between forced loyalty to a lunatic..." Adler nodded to Reginald and continued, "...and duty."

"Duty meaning rebellion?" Bin asked sarcastically.

"Duty meaning justice," Adler responded.

Bin studied Adler's face. He was serious...and he was right. While he might not understand exactly what virtues Adler sought, one thing was for certain, he was also growing tired of Reginald's antics as well as his blatant paranoia.

Adler and Bin continued marching in silence. When they arrived at a fairly flat grassy area, the soldiers chose different spots to sit and rest. Reginald made sure he stayed with Rolf, but the rest of the soldiers sat together in groups of five or six. Taking a brief respite to eat what they packed in their bags and drink a little ale, the soldiers welcomed conversation with each other as they struggled to comprehend the meaning of this campaign. In reality, the only instructions given to the unit were to gather a few provisions, fetch their weapons, and march to the abbey. Reginald purposely kept the commands simple and avoided clarifying the purpose of the mission.

Why did Reginald need soldiers to accompany him to an abbey? A house of God?

As the unit resumed marching, Adler turned his attention to the soldiers behind him. A long wooden wagon lumbered over the rocky soil, pulled by two muscular fox soldiers. They held thick leather straps across their shoulders as they leaned forward to guide the cart over the knobby path. The soldiers heaved and the wooden wheels bounced on and over stones in the well-traveled road.

Reginald's special instructions to Rolf (as to the wagon's contents) were orders that Adler had been purposely excluded from. Whatever was in the wagon was secured with a tarp and ropes to cover the mysterious contents.

Adler caught Bin's eye, "Do you know what's in that wagon?" he whispered loud enough for Bin to hear him.

"I've heard it's a lot of lumber and some axes," Bin replied without looking at him.

"Great, more work for us," he sighed. But what would the soldiers need lumber and axes for? Were they building something?

Bin saw the confusion in Adler's eyes. He actually felt a little sorry for him and softened.

"Look, I may have heard something about a char cloth when I was collecting the axes this morning," Bin said. He still didn't make eye contact.

"Char cloth? As in..." Adler flashed an alarming look at his coworker.

"Yes, a fire."

"But.... but what do we need a fire for?" Adler asked. "I mean, we'll need campfires once we find a suitable camping site but—"

"No—not for campfires, not for cooking," Bin shook his head.

"What do you mean?"

"Rolf showed us the char cloth and kindling this morning. I think Reginald wants a massive bonfire," Bin responded. He opened his arms and stretched them out, showing his estimate of the cloth's size. "He means business."

Adler's thoughts went wild. Why did Reginald want to build a monstrous fire? Was it to signal another clan? Or would the fire actually destroy something? And if so, what could they possibly burn that would require a char cloth of that size?!

CHAPTER 27

"Who...who are you?!" Bowen held his bag so tightly against his chest that his fingers went numb.

"Relax, my friend," the figure raised his paws, grasped his large hood, and lowered it to his shoulders. The face under all that fabric looked so familiar.

"John Henry?" Bowen asked in disbelief.

"It is," the fox grinned.

"Were you following me?"

"Yes, I've been watching you since Swynton," he replied.

"But...but WHY?"

"Father Ennis wanted to keep an eye on you," John Henry said. "The path you decided to travel was not an easy one. He was only looking out for you."

Bowen narrowed his eyes. "But why the extra attention? I mean, what does he care if I complete my mission...or not?"

The monk nodded and glanced around the area. "Look," he said, "we're both heading to the same place, with the same goal in mind. Walk with me and I'll answer any questions you may have."

The two hustled back to the main path, eager to make it to the abbey before nightfall. Bowen wondered why the abbot would invest so much time and resources into making sure he was safe if it wasn't for a mutual interest—like getting rid of Reginald.

"You mentioned the same goal," Bowen began. "Tell me what goal you have in mind."

John Henry released a deep sigh, "I knew you would ask me that." He leaned in as he walked and said in a low voice, "I'm only authorized to tell you that Father Ennis has interest in merely supporting those individuals that cast doubt on Reginald's power and rightful ownership of the throne." He cleared his throat and then spoke in a confident voice, "And he believes you are one such individual."

"Ha!" Bowen guffawed out loud. "I don't know what I am anymore. I used to be an accountant and a councilman to Edwin; but now I feel more like a crusader." He patted his bag.

Silence fell between the two travelers; not because they ran out of things to say but because both needed time to think. Running into John Henry on the road to the abbey seemed more of a nuisance than an advantage.... unless the monk knew something he didn't.

The long, even trail eventually led them to a cozy but lively village. Evening crowds rushed here and there while wonderful smells of roasted meats and smoked fish floated in the air.

"Let's get something to eat," the monk suggested.

Pointing to the closest pub, the Sword and Stone, the travelers quickly ducked inside and found a table near the fireplace. Sitting on uneven wooden benches, Bowen and John Henry stared across a thick wooden table at each other. While the pub smelled like sour ale and dried fish, Bowen didn't care... he was hungry.

"Two of the specials please," the fox ordered food at the bar, handing the barmaid a few coins to cover their dinner. As he sat back down at his table, the barmaid walked over and placed two ales between the visitors.

Once the two were alone again with their drinks, Bowen spoke first, "So, tell me about yourself, John Henry. Where are you from?"

The monk sipped his ale and wiped his mouth on his long, brown sleeve. "I'm originally from a little community outside of Swynton, called Carraig Bay."

"Near the water, huh?"

"Yes, practically on top of it."

Bowen savored the ale in his cup before asking another question. And just in time, dinner arrived: a plate of salted fish and a bowl of vegetable pottage. Bowen could smell the leeks and turnips as the steam wafted over his bowl, totally making his mouth water.

"How did you end up at Derwent Abbey?" Bowen slurped his soup from a wooden spoon and smacked his lips.

"You mean, why did I choose to be a monk?" he raised his eyebrow.

"Yeah, that too."

"I actually didn't have a choice," John Henry leaned closer to Bowen and said, "I got into some trouble, so my father thought the church would be a better career choice."

Bowen stared at him, wondering if this monk was telling him the truth or not. John Henry, reading his thoughts, placed his spoon on the table and leaned back in his chair. "Look, it's not something I'm proud of. I rebelled, followed the wrong friends, and ended up getting caught...mostly stealing. My father gave me an ultimatum: straighten up in the church or spend time at a work camp on the other side of Fellnore."

"Let me guess," Bowen pointed his finger, "you chose the church."

"I did. This was years ago, mind you, and I chose monastic life. My father knew the abbot at Derwent Abbey and called in a favor." He scratched his head and began eating again.

"Is that why Father Ennis sent you to follow me? Your colorful back story?" Bowen asked.

"I imagine so."

"Are you ever tempted to revisit the old you? The life you used to have?" Bowen felt the ale kicking in.

"Not really," the monk drank his ale. "I would be lying if I said I've never been tempted though. But I've turned my life around. And I do use my 'extra' skills to 'assist' the church at times," John Henry said matter-of-factly.

Bowen laughed wildly, clearly relaxed by the ale. The monk, caught off guard, began chuckling as well. Soon, the two sat across from each other laughing over a silly implication until their faces turned red and they couldn't breathe.

As John Henry leaned over to catch his breath, an object the size of a cabbage rolled out from underneath his robe and hit the floor with a *thunk*! Light spewed out from the item and caught Bowen's eye. It was the same object he noticed on the boat…the glow that illuminated from under the monk's robe.

"What is that?!" Bowen quickly asked.

The monk scooped up the item and tucked it under the folds of his robe.

"It's a candle," he replied curtly.

"Why does it glow like that?"

"It's a special candle…. I need it to find something," John Henry said.

The ale continued working its magic on the fox. Relaxed and warm, Bowen's words slurred a little as he slowly asked, "What, sir, could you possibly be searching for that would require the use of a magic candle?"

John Henry gave him an unusual look. "Have you heard of the Flag of Firinn?"

"The flag of Fi--of course I have!"

The monk shushed the fox in order to talk to him in confidence. Glancing around the pub to make sure no one could hear him, John Henry said, "I've been tasked to bring this candle back to the abbey. I need it to locate the Flag of Firinn."

"You lost a flag in your church?" Bowen asked with a deadpan expression.

John Henry dropped his head in exasperation and took a deep breath. "It's not that simple," he said. Was Bowen even able to comprehend what he was explaining to him right now? "Edwin protected the flag for many years, but around the time Reginald seized power, it mysteriously went missing."

"I remember that," Bowen replied. "I was the one who confirmed it was stolen. How did you find out?"

"We heard about it from the fairies of the Moin clan. Cormac, their leader, told us their hound sensed a shift in power and in truth when Edwin was ousted as ruler. The flag called out to the beast when the injustice happened. We believe the fairy hound fetched the flag from the arsenal in Chipping Farms before Reginald could find it."

"Wait, wait, wait," Bowen held up his paw. "A hound?"

"The Cu Sith. The fairy hound is the living protector of the flag. It prowls the moorlands bound by law to the fairies." The monk used his digits to imitate walking and then paused to see if Bowen was absorbing any of this information. "Anyway, Cormac informed us that the hound stashed the flag somewhere in the monastery."

"So now the hound decides where the flag lives?"

"Uh, sort of," John Henry didn't know how much of this information was getting through to Bowen. He patted his stomach, "This candle is said to have the power to find items of truth. I'm on my way to the abbey now to assist Father Ennis in discovering where the flag is hidden."

"So, the flag's magical properties are real," Bowen mumbled.

"They are," John Henry replied.

Bowen felt the fog lift in his mind and could now formulate his thoughts. "Remind me again, what's so special about this flag that I keep hearing its name mentioned?"

"The Flag of Firinn reveals truth, which is why I believe Father Ennis wants this flag so dearly," the monk said. "It acts as a moral compass as well, giving wisdom to those who need to make high stakes decisions."

"What are you going to do with the flag once you locate it?"

"That, my friend, is something I don't know yet," the monk said. "Father Ennis told me he would fill me in once I returned."

"And you believe him?"

"I do."

Bowen finished his meal deep in thought. Could this flag be the key to reveal Reginald's true identity? If he could get his paws on it and somehow unleash its power, then everyone would finally see Reginald in his true form...a shapeshifting wolf pretending to be a fox. Then, and only then, would his village believe what he said to be true and confirm the legitimacy of the documents he held on to so tight. Reginald, in fact, *could* be defeated.

The Flag of Firinn now called his name.

"Stay low," Beckett directed the others in a hushed voice.

Tegan and Kenna caught up to Beckett who was squatting under a bush near the tree line.

"What do you see?" Tegan asked him.

"Over there," Beckett pointed across the field.

"The abbey!" Kenna squealed.

"Shhhh!!!" Beckett and Tegan shushed their friend at the same time.

Kenna was bursting at the seams. The abbey was in view, and that could only mean the flag—the relic that could locate her father—was in reach too. Tegan spotted her friend's tense muscles and frantic pacing, aware that she must calm Kenna's nerves before the fox sprinted across the field, in the open, and disclosed their position.

"Kenna, look at me," Tegan gently held the fox's shoulders so she could focus. "We're almost there, but we need to be careful. You see that open land?" Kenna's eyes darted to the side, then she nodded slowly. "If we run across it now, we will be exposed. And who knows what's out there waiting for us. We can't make that mistake. Not when we're so close."

Just then, Kenna whipped her head around, her ears flexing back and forth. "Do you hear that?" she asked.

Beckett and Tegan stood motionless, listening for something, anything, in the air. Then they heard what sounded like voices coming from across the hedgerow. Diving under the closest bush, the three travelers huddled together in silence. Tegan gripped her sword handle with a sweaty paw, not sure if she should unsheathe it or not.

A small unit of fox soldiers marched along the foot path where the friends sat in hiding. Several rows of three soldiers wide hiked past the travelers, their feet kicking up dirt and small stones. As they passed, Tegan bent over to get a look at the individuals. Who were they? Where were they going?

Tegan recognized the fox wearing a blue tunic. It was Reginald.

She pointed out the leader to Beckett, "Reginald," she mouthed to Beckett.

A paw gripped her wrist so tight that Tegan felt her digits go numb. It was Kenna. She sat wide eyed and stiff, unable to move. "Adler," she stated in a low but controlled voice.

Marching a half-step behind the ruler, Adler kept his head down low. And as they made their way along the path, Kenna studied Adler's face. He was miserable, she could tell.

A massive wooden wagon rolled along the path, signifying the last of the unit. Its thick wheels and mysterious contents seemed out of place within this group. What was Reginald hauling in there?

As if on cue, Beckett pointed to the wagon rolling past him and said, "Whatever's in there is bad news for us."

Tegan nodded. "Looks like they're heading to the abbey too."

CHAPTER 28

As the sun held on to its last light, Bowen and John Henry made their way to the abbey in the dusk's shadows. Bowen surveyed the landscape around him and spotted the army just over the horizon.

"Get the lantern ready," John Henry said.

The fox leaned over and lit the candle with a bit of flint. The dull glow only offered a little light along the path, but it was enough for now. "Won't they see us coming?" Bowen asked.

"This road hosts travelers from all over the county," the monk replied. "We'll be safe for a while."

Their footsteps crunched over gravel and small stones laid on a mostly dusty path. But when the seasonal rains hit, those stones kept feet mostly dry from the muddy mess underneath.

Bowen fumbled with a chunk of cheese he had stashed in his bag, tossing it awkwardly into his mouth. Creamy and strong, the tangy taste was exactly what he needed to sustain his strength and quiet his hunger pangs. The strain of walking so far and the tension of plotting some kind of strategy had slowly taken its toll on him. So, he stress ate. Maybe John Henry needed to relieve some stress too.

He leaned over and handed another chunk of cheese to the monk. "Here, eat before we get any closer."

The monk accepted the snack, savoring the rich dairy treat. "Delicious, thank you," he said and paused for a moment before speaking again. "Look over there, do you see the unit in front of the west wing?"

"Yes, they've stopped there just before the wall," Bowen replied.

"Camping in front of the monk dormitories, which means we need to find another way inside the abbey." John Henry tugged on his robe. The breeze was starting to feel chillier than it had been during the day.

"Where do you think we should enter?" Bowen asked.

"There are several locations besides the obvious entry...through the front door of the church. One is through the north transept near the choir; the others are through openings to the dormitories. But," the monk rubbed his chin, "I think we'll have better luck entering inside the warming room."

John Henry headed toward the abbey wall with Bowen right behind him. They trekked along winding paths outlined with small trees and tall brush until they stopped at a clearing. With only a few feet from the stone wall, John Henry pointed to an area with crumbled bricks and several splintered planks.

"That way," he indicated.

Trotting to the area where fallen stones and wood pieces layered themselves on a mound, Bowen and John Henry stepped cautiously across the debris and hunkered down inside the property against the wall. Cold stones pierced through Bowen's tunic causing him to abruptly suck in his breath. Looking up to a window across from them, the two observed several monks walking by with lit candles in their hands. Bowen instinctively leaned over and extinguished the candle flame in his own lantern.

"It appears to be dinner time," John Henry stated. "We should wait here until all the monks have gathered in the dining room." He lowered the hood over his head to hide in the shadows completely.

A low hum and singing emanated from the dining area as the monks said their evening prayer and offered up songs of gratitude to their Creator. The familiar sounds were strangely comforting to the fox, and he relaxed long enough to enjoy each of them.

But outside, around the side of the wall, two soldiers scoured the perimeter for intruders: their footsteps muted by the table side rituals inside the dining room. Both carried swords, but one held a lantern near his face. He searched the area for anything out of place.

John Henry spotted the lantern first and said quietly, but firmly, to his companion, "Get up.... slowly."

Confused, Bowen stood up and looked in the same direction as the monk. Only a few feet away, the soldiers witnessed the movement and shouted at them, "You there! What are you doing?"

Bowen froze where he stood, his paws up. But the monk rolled away into the dark shadows.

"John Henry!" Bowen called out. "Where are you going?"

"Shhh!!" the monk hushed him.

The soldiers approached Bowen cautiously with their swords drawn. They patted him down, searching for weapons. Since the fox showed no threat to them, the soldiers sheathed their swords and started interrogating him.

"What are you doing here?"

"It is the house of God, is it not?" Bowen swallowed hard. "I've come to pray."

The first soldier, thin and bony, replied, "Hmmm, why are you hiding in this spot? Why not enter through the front door of the church?"

"Sir, I saw your soldiers near that door and was afraid."

The second soldier, much thicker than the first, laughed at Bowen. "Yeah, you should be scared!"

The first soldier whacked the other on his shoulder, silencing him quickly. But his eye caught sight of Bowen's bag. "Whatcha got in there?" he asked with a sinister smile. "Boss is searching for a traitor carrying a bag. One that looks like yours. Are you the traitor?!"

Bowen took a step back.

"Ah ah ah ah!!!! Stop right there and let's have a look," the skinny soldier commanded.

With his arm wrapped around the messenger bag, Bowen shook his head. There was no way these two were getting their paws on the contents of his bag; especially since he'd come so far.

The soldiers glared at each other, growling deep down in their throat and chest. As the two lunged at Bowen to seize his bag, the monk dove from his hiding spot, jumping directly onto the soldiers and crashing to the ground.

"Run!" John Henry yelled to the fox.

Bowen twisted around and scampered across the little creek, shuffling up to the small timber frame door. He swiftly turned his head and looked over his shoulder at the monk. In the dark, he could barely make out which one was John Henry as the monk rolled around on the ground with the soldiers. Pinned under a sweaty smelly soldier, John Henry searched the terrain with his paw and fumbled upon a piece of wood. Holding it securely between his paws, the monk swung the panel of wood, and struck the soldier across his head, knocking him to the ground. The second soldier popped his head up and swung squarely with his fist, making contact with John Henry's stomach. The monk doubled over, holding his arms close to his frame, and sunk down into a squatting position.

Seeing the monk struggle, Bowen scrambled back to the brawl and snatched a wooden plank on the way. Both paws held the plank above his head, and Bowen stood trembling and waiting.... but he didn't know what for. Then the hefty soldier saw his chance and charged Bowen. But the fox swung the plank, and hit the soldier directly on his cheek, knocking him out cold.

Bowen threw the wood piece down and ran over to help the monk up. He could hear the thin soldier groaning and rolling around on the ground.

"Hurry!" Bowen said as he assisted John Henry. "Let's go!!"

The monk grunted as he stood up and stumbled forward. As the two hurried toward the door, the soldiers shouted after them. But John Henry and Bowen scurried to the small door to the warming room and scooted through.

The stout soldier started to pursue the trespassers, but the thin soldier held him back, stopping him in his tracks. "We should report this," he stated.

"But they're getting away!"

"Relax!" the first soldier ordered. "Our soldiers are everywhere. Those two won't leave the abbey, I'm sure of it."

The two dashed back to their camp just outside the stone wall. Spewing orders to his soldiers, Reginald paced as he watched them scurry to fulfill his demands.

"Unload the wagon and set up on the other side of the wall," the leader commanded.

Rolf nodded solemnly and ordered several soldiers around him to remove the contents of the wagon. He was in no rush to see what was about to happen.

"Sir! Sir!" the thin soldier rushed up to Reginald while the shorter one dawdled behind him, leaning over and panting.

"What is it?!" Reginald barked.

"We saw him!" the first soldier reported excitedly. "The traitor you're searching for!"

"He's here?!" Reginald's wide eyes revealed his surprise. While he knew Bowen would eventually find the abbey, the leader didn't realize he'd be here so soon. "Where did you see him?"

The stout soldier held up his paw and said breathlessly, "He ran inside the abbey through a side door."

"Right, change of plans," the leader responded.

Reginald tightened his robe around him and spoke to his second in command, Lucien, "You! Take these three soldiers," he pointed to the ones standing near him, "AND Adler, and raid the abbey." He glared at Adler and commanded, "Find Bowen and bring him to me."

The soldiers stared at their leader, and then at Lucien, trying to process the orders they just received. They stood motionless; their feet felt like huge stones glued to the ground.

"Now!" the leader yelled.

Startled, the soldiers quickly grabbed their weapons and busied themselves so Reginald wouldn't reprimand them again.

"Sir?" Rolf asked as he overheard the orders. "Is this really necessary?"

"You do as I command!" Reginald shouted and shook his fist. "I'm in charge here! Now unload that cart!"

Rolf retreated to the wagon slowly. As he listened for more of the leader's outlandish requests, he pulled timber from the cart and laid it out near the wall as Reginald directed. He gathered stones and outlined the circular pile of wood the soldiers stacked in order to contain the flames.

Lucien motioned for the appointed soldiers to follow him; but Adler trailed behind. What would he do if they actually found Bowen? Could he hide him? Stuff him in an inner room perhaps?

The group made their way through a small entrance on the west side of the abbey. With footsteps echoing in the halls, the soldiers stepped as lightly as possible around bins of supplies stored there. Sacks of grain, boxes of vegetables and cheeses, and barrels of ale sat near stacks of aged wood and squares of cut stone; all stored in the aisles of this range.

Lucien motioned for the soldiers to follow him towards the church, avoiding the cloister so as not to be seen. As soon as the soldiers made it to the staircase near the church's nave, Adler ducked behind a large painting covered with a long cloth. Sitting in the shadows, he silently thanked the group for sneaking in through the storage area so he could hunker down and figure out a way to find Bowen before Reginald's soldiers did.

Where would he be hiding though? Knowing Bowen, he came to the abbey to retrieve something of significance. And it wouldn't be inside the church itself. Adler looked around nervously to make sure he was alone.

The library! If he could make it across the garden without being seen, then he might find Bowen there. But before he could stand up, Adler heard a rally cry and thunderous footsteps overhead. The rest of the unit had breached the abbey, including Reginald, himself, in the lead.

Chapter 29

Tegan, Beckett, and Kenna hid in the shadow of an apple tree near the west side of the stone wall. With several soldiers monitoring the entrance to both the church and the west range, the travelers decided to find another way inside the monastery unseen.

As they crept past the west dormitories, a cacophony of shouting emanated from the second story above them. Tegan watched as soldiers pushed and waved their arms around wildly. Then the sound decreased as it moved deeper into the structure.

The group ducked down and headed north around the outer side of the church.

"Let's get closer," Beckett suggested, pointing to a damaged spot in the wall. Stones lay scattered over the ground as a gaping hole the size of a wagon exposed the north wall of the church.

The travelers took turns darting over the wreckage and huddled close to the church's north face. Running lengthwise down the structure, Tegan stopped abruptly at the transept entrance.

"Through here!" she instructed.

Tegan tugged on the iron latch attached to the thick wooden door, struggling to open it.

"It's locked!" she announced. Pulling out her sword, Tegan used the handle as a hammer and pounded the inner section of the door trying to dislodge it from the frame.

Kenna ran to Tegan and shook her arm. "I'm sure there's another way," she said. "Let's keep going."

The little fox led the group as they circled around the north face of the church and walked alongside the east sections including the presbytery and the altars. Most of the stained-glass windows remained intact on this side, but as they trekked on, the rest of the living quarters had obviously seen conflict evidenced by visible damage.

"Where are we now?" Beckett whispered.

The group squeezed into a recess on the east side of the monastery.

"I believe we're standing next to the chapter house," Tegan replied. She leaned out of the makeshift hideaway and surveyed the length of the east range wall. "It looks like there's a better chance to get inside the abbey down near the river."

Out of the corner of her eye, Tegan noticed a soldier turn the north corner of the church, where they had just been. She jumped back into the recession and held her finger to her mouth to shush the others. Beckett and Kenna backed against the shadowed wall in silence, waiting for the soldier to pass. Tegan held her breath.

The sound of whistling closed in on them; a haunting noise flying low in a hollow breeze. Instead of marching past the group, the soldier hesitated just outside the recess to drink water from his leather skin bottle. Both Beckett and Tegan held their swords firmly in their paws while Kenna pulled a dagger from her belt; anxious but prepared to fight.

As the soldier secured his bottle, he paused and turned to face the structure's recess. "Is anyone in there?" he called into the shadowed recession.

Silence. Tegan hoped he would lose interest and move on. But he must've seen or heard something because he persisted. "Come out, I say!"

Tegan realized the soldier wouldn't leave until he had his answer. She stepped out of the shadow and into the waning light of dusk, sword low and nonthreatening. With her hood covering her head and the gleam of her sword blade, the intimidated soldier stepped back in awe of the sight he beheld.

"Who are you?" he asked timidly, raising his sword. "Come out now!"

Tegan hesitated, her heart racing. She breathed deeply and stepped forward. "I am Tegan from the Wells family." She uncovered her head and glared at the soldier.

He lowered his sword a bit, "What are you doing here?"

"We seek a special flag," she answered.

"Yeah!" Kenna shouted and stepped out beside Tegan. The soldier instantly raised his sword in defense. "We want the flag to find my father!" she stomped her right foot and threatened the soldier with a dagger.

Beckett slipped out and stood behind Kenna.

"There's three of you?!" the soldier squawked. "Are there any more back there?"

"No, sir," Beckett responded calmly. "We mean you no harm. We are here to see the abbot and ask for the flag. Then we'll be on our way."

"You will see Reginald first!" the soldier waved his sword at the group, motioning for them to move away from the recess and down toward the river.

Tegan sheathed her sword and held her paws up. Kenna and Beckett followed behind her. The three friends marched single file along the east wall, clearing the chapter house, as the soldier followed closely behind them with his sword drawn. Once they reached the river, Tegan hesitated, noticing a disturbance in the water.

"What is it?" Beckett asked, searching the water for a clue.

"I thought I saw—"

"Keep moving!" the soldier shouted and pushed Beckett with his sword tip.

Beckett winced as the tip punctured through his tunic and into his skin. Shoving both Beckett and Tegan away from the water and toward the wall, the soldier was the only one with his back facing the river.

But somewhere in the depths of that river, a creature breached the water line. Tegan caught a glimpse of the moonlight reflecting off the creature's monstrous eyes. She gasped, clenching Beckett's arm. In a matter of seconds, the creature waded onto the riverbank with a webbed foot and shot out a long, pinkish tongue, grabbing the soldier. He squealed and dropped his sword while Beckett, Tegan, and Kenna witnessed the scene in horror. They couldn't look away. The creature retracted its tongue with the soldier still attached and catapulted him across the river and into the woods somewhere.

With their arms interlinked, the friends took several steps back in unity. What did we just see? The creature shook its head and emerged completely from the river.

"Don't be afraid," it said.

In front of them stood a giant frog, although it was hard to tell just how big it was in the dark.

"Who...who are you?" Kenna asked. She was the only one that could form a sentence under the circumstances.

"Rana. I travelled here with a few of my clan members," she motioned to the river. Several heads with giant eyes peeked out along the water line.

"Thanks for helping us," Tegan said, still dumbfounded. Gathering her composure, she asked, "Wait...travelled? Where are you from? Why are you here?"

"We've been asked to follow Bowen Whitethorne; to watch over him," she replied. "We are keeping a careful eye on him while he's inside."

"My father is here?!!" Kenna exclaimed excitedly. She whipped around and scoured the wall for entry. "Up there! We can climb in through the windows." Kenna grabbed hold of the mismatched stones jutting out of the crumbled debris and climbed up with lightning speed.

"What's up there?" Beckett asked.

Kenna reached the window area and looked inside. "Toilets," she replied.

"Eww," Tegan mumbled under her breath and stepped up on the first stone.

Returning to the river side, Rana slowly waded back into the water, calling out over her shoulder, "Use caution in there!"

Tegan and Beckett made their way up the wall and into the toilet room. Unwilling to hide out in the smelly chamber, the two hurried to the door which exited into the east dormitory. Rows of modest beds and clean linens lined the room, a few candles placed by the bedsides remained unlit. Soon, the monks would retire here to sleep...except tonight. Tonight would be different.

Kenna was nowhere in sight—she had disappeared, searching for her father no doubt. So now the plan had to be: get her, get the flag, and get out. Tegan and Beckett drew their swords and slipped out single file through the door and down the steps to the first floor. Voices shouting from the other side of the abbey rang in their ears. To find Kenna, they needed to locate her father. Where would he be? Tegan couldn't imagine Bowen hiding out in the middle of this noisy chaos, (although Kenna wouldn't stop at a little skirmish), so they needed to investigate the quiet spaces.

Tiptoeing from the stairs to the garden, Tegan and Beckett stayed low. Although the sun already set, the moonlight overhead could still give away their position. Remaining close to the outer parts of the garden, the two hurried toward the church, stopping briefly near the library.

Beckett heard something from behind the library's closed door. "Did you hear that?" he asked his friend. Tegan shook her head.

They huddled close in silence, listening for another sound. Then a noise similar to moving a chair across the stone floor emanated from behind the door.

"Someone's in there," Beckett whispered.

Tegan nodded. "Ready to find out who?" She drew her sword.

Beckett smiled.

Lucien's group burst through the doors and into the church's nave. As they marched into the choir area, Father Ennis withdrew from the presbytery and stepped back to the high altar. He held his paws up, indicating he was not a threat to them. Two of Lucien's soldiers charged the abbot and pointed their swords at him, daring the abbot to run.

"Where are you hiding him?" Lucien asked as he motioned for the soldiers to lower their weapons.

"Who are you looking for?" Father Ennis asked.

"Bowen Whitethorne! We know he's here!"

"Sir, if I may," the abbot spoke calmly. "Bowen visited this very abbey a number of days ago. But he has not returned since."

Lucien studied his face and noted his reaction. "Hmm, that may be true. But we know he's returning to this abbey. Has he sent any messages?"

"No, I haven't received any kind of communication."

"Mind if we look around?" Lucien laughed and waved his sword over his head.

Just then, Reginald rushed in and knocked down one of the soldiers standing in front of the abbot. "Out of my way, you idiot!" he snarled. Taking his cue, Lucien backed down and let Reginald assume the spotlight.

"Where is the magic flag?!" Reginald hissed at the abbot.

Father Ennis, bewildered by the question, asked, "What are you talking about?" Several soldiers behind Lucien giggled and mocked him repeating, "magic flag, magic flag!"

But Reginald was in his own world, his own time frame. He clarified, "The Flag of Firinn! Where is it?"

The giggling stopped at the name of this flag, for everyone knew of its fairy origin and unsurpassed powers. In the quiet, Father Ennis shifted his weight and replied, "It is not here."

Reginald, in the heat of the moment, grabbed the abbot by the neck and began choking him. "Where is it?!! Where is it!!!"

Father Ennis panicked and swiped at the fox's bony arms frantically trying to free himself. He kicked and flailed, wiggling around to loosen the fox's grip. Smirking with power, adrenaline rushing to his head, Reginald laughed maniacally.

"Sir! Sir!! Stop!!" Lucien shouted, horrified at what was happening before his eyes. "You'll kill him!"

Reginald whipped his head around and snapped at the soldier. "Why should I stop?! You want me to show mercy?" He asked with his hand still wrapped around the abbot's neck.

"Sir! He's a holy man!" Lucien swallowed hard and tried to calm his voice. "The abbot is surely telling the truth." Desperation sounded so vile in his own ears. "Do you want cursed blood on your hands?"

Reginald faced the abbot again, who, by now, was fighting for his life. He grinned and finally released the abbot, watching as Father Ennis crumpled to the floor, gasping for air.

"You will tell me, abbot," Reginald wagged his finger in the holy man's face. "Lock him up! He'll talk soon enough."

Lucien nodded and a soldier seized Father Ennis by the arm, helping him stand.

"Where shall we take him?" the soldier asked.

Lucien looked around and noticed a set of stairs near the transept. "I believe those go down to the crypt under the main altar. Take him there. He'll be safe until we're done here."

The soldier nodded and marched the abbot to the staircase and down the stairs until they were standing on the crypt floor. Ancient statues, concrete tombs, prayer rooms, and an area just for ancient relic storage covered the entire floorplan. The soldier spotted an area behind a baptismal font that had been fenced off from the rest of the vaults. It was small with a wide concrete bench opposite an ornate tomb marker, covered with colorful swirls and knots.

"This will do," the soldier said and forced the iron gate open. The bars were narrow enough so no one could slip through them, and the iron bar tops were pointed like arrows, making it nearly impossible to escape. "We will release you once Reginald has what he came for," the soldier said, revealing a tiny smile to comfort the holy man. He hoped he wouldn't be held liable though. Father Ennis only stared at him through the iron gate and grunted.

The soldier took an iron spike from another soldier's bag and hammered it through the gate lock, jamming it to make it completely inaccessible. He handed the abbot a small lantern for light and said, "It's the least I can do," and left.

The abbot sat in the dark with only a dull glow of light and prayed for a miracle.

CHAPTER 30

J ohn Henry and Bowen stumbled through the warming room and into the dining area next door. The explosive entrance interrupted a pleasant dinner and conversation, but the monks were in danger.

"Brothers!" John Henry called out. "Brothers, listen to me!" The monks quieted down and turned their attention to the one speaking. "You're in danger! There's a group of soldiers outside the abbey intent on seizing, uh," the monk searched for words other than the Flag of Firinn, "uh, a relic." Bowen nodded emphatically. "Those of you previously trained with weapons, go defend our walls! The rest of you, take cover in the barn or stables outside."

All the monks stood up at the same time, fleeing this way and that. In the chaos and clatter, Bowen turned to John Henry and said, "I left something important in the library. I need to retrieve it."

John Henry nodded and produced the candle he kept hidden under his garment, saying, "Let's see where this leads us."

The flame burned low, an indication that they were far from the flag. But as they walked along the cloister to the library, and nearer to the church, the flame flickered and jumped.

"We may be on to something here," John Henry nodded to the candle.

The sound of soldiers shouting to one another echoed across the garden; their footsteps pounded on the stone walkway.

"Search every room!" Reginald called out. "The flag is here somewhere!"

John Henry watched as soldiers ducked in and out of rooms along the cloister, ransacking and pillaging valuable items, inevitably making their way to the library and the chapter house.

"Quick!" Bowen exclaimed and darted into the library. He only had a few minutes before the soldiers caught up and he wasn't taking any chances. He needed those documents he stashed here the first day he arrived.

Tall shelves lined with ancient books and scrolls, most attached with chains, overflowed onto the floor. Searching for anything familiar, Bowen upended boxes with files and thumbed through papers lying on a writing table. *Where was it?!* He squinted as he thought; John Henry stood near the door as lookout.

"They're coming!" the monk warned.

Frantic, Bowen turned his attention to the table and the tall stack of books. As he moved the books to search in between each one, he noticed a small wooden door, like a cabinet, hidden behind the stack and decorated with a red cardinal. Pulling the little wooden knob, the tiny door opened to reveal an alcove in the stone. Bowen impulsively thrust his paw inside and felt something smooth. Yanking the item out, he sighed with relief, "THIS is what I've been looking for!" He held in his paw a large brown envelope crammed with the incriminating papers he carried from Chipping Farms. Stuffing the bundle into his messenger bag, Bowen leapt for the door.

John Henry peeked out of the exit just as Reginald and two soldiers marched by, slipping into the chapter house. The monk opened the door wider and said, "Let's go, I'll cover you."

They slipped out onto the walkway, and John Henry positioned his robe around Bowen to cover any view of him. As they stepped inside the church, a few monks armed with swords stood guard over the front entrance and the altars where a few relics sat on display. John Henry strolled up to the high altar as the candle burned a deep red, signaling the close proximity of the flag. But neither of them spotted the object in the room.

"Maybe it's in the crypt," the monk suggested.

"Where's that?" Bowen asked.

"Just below us."

The two trotted off to the stairs and descended into the crypt below; the candle continued burning a definite red flame. Bowen couldn't see a thing in the darkness as his eyes had not yet adjusted, but the air was cool and the noise level was low. John Henry held his candle to navigate the best he could in the dark, at least until his own eyes safely adjusted. Surely the flag was here somewhere, and the candle would show him the location.

Inching a few steps forward caused the candle's red flame to jump higher. They stood close to the right place now! Bowen followed carefully behind the monk and detected a lantern across the room. The light was dim, but it was enough to grab their attention.

"Hello?" A voice echoed out from the dark.

Bowen and John Henry froze, completely terrified. Both firmly believed they heard the voice of a ghost.

"Just a monk," Beckett said as he observed movement from the library door.

"Just a monk with someone else," Tegan added. "*And* a strange candle."

"In any case," Beckett replied, "not a threat to us, thankfully."

Tegan and Beckett hid in the garden waiting for the chance to move. Kenna was here somewhere and they had to find her before the soldiers did.

"Follow that monk," Tegan suggested. "He looks like he knows something."

The two left their hiding place and headed in the same direction as John Henry and his weird candle. But before they reached the church entrance, Tegan and Beckett heard a voice behind them. They turned to see who it was.

"Stop where you are!" It was Reginald.

The leader and a handful of his soldiers stood opposite the two travelers. Tegan and Beckett drew their swords, but Reginald laughed at them.

"What do you want?" Tegan shouted, her sword pointed directly at Reginald.

"Ah, the same thing as you, lass," the leader snarled, "that flag."

"We only want to find our friend," Beckett offered. "We are no threat to you."

"Ha! I know better than that!" the leader growled. "Considering how our last meeting ended, I'll be taking both of you with me!" Reginald turned to his soldiers and ordered, "Get them!"

Two fox soldiers lunged toward the sombels, but Tegan swiped at them with her sword. Jumping backwards, the soldiers tried again, pressing forward with swords slicing through the heavy night air. Without much light, the soldiers fumbled with their weapons, employing all their strength in face-to-face combat.

Beckett managed to fight off one soldier, wounding him with his sword in the left shoulder. He then shoved the soldier back into Reginald and watched as they both hit the ground together. The second soldier didn't waste any time and pounced on Tegan, knocking the sword out of her grasp. As the two rolled around swinging paws at each other, Beckett scrambled to her side. He managed to get close enough to shove his foot squarely on the soldier's rear end and knock him over. While the soldier looked around confused, Tegan scrounged for her sword, finding it only an arm's length away. Beckett helped her back on her feet while he watched Reginald and the other soldiers struggle to stand up.

"Don't come any closer!" Tegan threatened as she pointed her sword at Reginald.

"Pathetic. Finish them!" Reginald shouted at his soldiers.

When the soldiers moved forward, Tegan closed her eyes and growled, concentrating on defending herself and her friend. A small transparent dome appeared from the green moonstone in the hilt of the sword and blossomed into an umbrella-like shield. She opened her eyes while Beckett stepped into the protective dome. Both fox soldiers ran into the shield and bounced off, like it was a giant bouncing ball. Confused, they stood dumbfounded, staring at the glowing stone and unable to process what they were witnessing.

Tegan slowly backed away from Reginald and his soldiers, keeping her eye on them in case they charged again. One soldier stepped forward, but Reginald stopped him and said, "Let them go. They'll find the flag for us. Just follow them from a distance."

Tegan felt far enough away to turn and run toward the church, sword in her paws and the shield withdrawn. She smiled with satisfaction; the moonstone simply responded to her emotional state.

Inside the doorway, several monks stood at attention with their weapons. However, Tegan and Beckett's theatrical entrance startled them. Each presented their sword at the sight of the intruders and demanded an explanation.

"What are you doing here?" A monk asked.

Tegan and Beckett put their own swords away and lifted their paws to demonstrate their goodwill.

"We're on your side," Beckett stated. "We come in peace. We're trying to help."

"Yes, we're looking for a monk holding a strange candle," Tegan called out to the monk guarding the door. "Did he come through here?"

The monk nodded and said, "Down the stairs, in the crypt."

"Seriously?!" Beckett asked, throwing his paws in in air. "A crypt? In the dark?" He glanced around and snatched one of the lanterns from the choir area. "Just going to borrow this." He said to no one in particular.

Tegan joined him and they descended the stairs together in silence. As soon as they reached the bottom floor, they overheard voices on the far side of the room.

Tegan stopped. "Either that sound is my imagination or we're hearing ghosts."

"No," Beckett replied. He tiptoed further into the crypt to locate the origin of the voices. "I hear it too."

Adler kept quiet in his hiding spot beside the covered painting. From the shouts above him and random footsteps behind him, the fox couldn't tell which was worse. But without hesitation, he figured he'd face the unknown footsteps rather than the chaos upstairs.

Looking up and down the room, Adler stepped out and dashed toward the kitchen and dining room. A group of monks racing to evacuate the abbey rushed past him in the stairwell. Adler stepped back into the shadows and let the monks through, their robes kicking up a noticeable breeze as they sprinted by. He waited a few minutes until they disappeared and then darted out again. But this time, Adler ran smack into another fox—a soldier! They collided and fell on the ground simultaneously. The other fox scrambled to his feet and stood where lantern light revealed his identity. It was Rolf.

"What are you doing here?!" Rolf asked incredulously. He leaned over and helped Adler up with a noticeable groan.

"I should ask you the same thing!" Adler replied.

"Aye, I'm helping these poor monks get out," Rolf answered a bit sheepishly. "I can't watch Reginald's soldiers destroy anything else in here." He shook his head.

"Well, I'm heading to the library...searching for Bowen Whitethorne," Adler explained. "I need to find him before Reginald does."

"You're in luck! I saw him and another monk in the church on my way here."

"Really? He wasn't in the library?" Adler wondered.

"No. And they appeared to be searching for something."

"I'm going to the church then," Adler said. "Where are your soldiers?"

"Reginald recruited a few into Lucien's group, but the rest have mostly assembled in the east range waiting for orders," Rolf replied.

"And Reginald himself?"

"The last I saw, he ordered a few soldiers to search the chapter house while Lucien and his troops rummaged through the west range," Rolf said. "All of them seeking the same thing."

"The Flag of Firinn," Adler finished his statement.

"Adler?"

"Yes."

"Do you really think the flag is here? In this abbey?"

"I do," Adler answered. "Why else would Reginald be so intent on finding it in person?"

"Hmm."

"Just make sure your soldiers are ready when I give the order," Adler emphasized.

"Understood. And what about Lucien's group?"

"Maybe we can convince them to join us," Adler replied. "When the time is right."

"Of course," Rolf said. "We can always pray for a miracle."

CHAPTER 31

"Hello?" the voice echoed again. "Who's there?"

It sounded familiar to John Henry. He stepped closer to the lantern light and let out a sigh of relief. "It's Father Ennis!" he called out.

Bowen walked up to the vault and caught a glimpse of the abbot in the lantern's shadows. "How long have you been in here?" he asked.

"Long enough," the abbot replied.

Using the lantern light as best he could, Bowen studied the lock holding the gate closed. He pulled at the spike driven through the lock without success. As he fiddled with the intertwined metal, John Henry spoke to the abbot.

"Do you have the candle?" the abbot asked.

"Yes." The monk presented the candle to Father Ennis. "But you haven't disclosed the real purpose of the candle. What—"

Another sound of footsteps and whispers entered the crypt. The abbot, John Henry, and Bowen fell silent. But as the footsteps crept closer, Father Ennis finally asked the shadows, "Who is it? Who's there?"

The footsteps stopped and the sound of someone clearing their throat rang out, "I'm Tegan...of the Wells clan." The soft voice echoed through the basement air.

"Tegan?" Bowen called out. "As in, my Kenna's Tegan?"

"Yes!" Tegan cried out. "I am!" Both Tegan and Beckett skipped to the vault where the lantern light barely glowed. She held her lantern light up to view the faces of Bowen, John Henry, and Father Ennis.

As soon as quick introductions were made, Bowen asked, "Where's my daughter?"

"Kenna is here...somewhere," Beckett replied. "She disappeared when we crawled in through a window. No doubt she's looking for you."

Tegan noticed the monk's candle burning a red flame. She held her paw close to it and the flame jumped, tickling her fingers. "Whoa, what is this?"

"We were just talking to the abbot about this candle," John Henry said. "Father Ennis," he looked at him through the iron bars, "what are you planning to do with this candle?"

"It must find the Flag of Firinn," the abbot responded.

"You're searching for it too?" Tegan asked.

Bowen nodded.

"What will we do once we have the flag?" John Henry asked.

"Ruin Reginald's life!" Beckett hissed.

"Listen, I'm no stranger to the conflicts in the north," the abbot stated gravely. "And hearing the news of Reginald's raiding parties has sickened me to the core. It's time to confront him and reveal the lies he holds on to so vehemently." Father Ennis straightened his tunic and cleared his throat in an effort to suppress his emotions. "We've got to act quickly though. Can you get me out of here?"

Beckett jammed his sword blade into the busted lock and pounded on it with his fist. But nothing happened. The metal spike was jammed in too tight.

"Here, let me try," Tegan offered. Beckett backed up with his sword still lodged in the lock. She raised her sword over her head and swung, the green moonstone flickered in the dark. *Crack!* The metal splintered and Beckett tugged at it furiously.

"One more time," Beckett suggested.

Tegan swung her sword again, hitting the lock square on. This time the gemstone flashed boldly and the lock split in half; the metal pieces fell off and clanged noisily on the stone floor.

Beckett pulled on the gate and opened it, allowing the abbot to squeeze through safely.

"Quick now, find the flag!" Father Ennis said to John Henry. "I'll go somewhere to hide. Bowen, come with me." Then the two disappeared into the shadows.

Tegan and Beckett followed John Henry as he tiptoed around the crypt. Exploring every nook and cranny, the monk held the candle in front of him while he studied the flame's reaction. Near the walls, the flame steadied itself as Tegan caught glimpses of ancient prayers and religious icons chiseled into the stone fortification. Holding the lantern low to keep from stumbling in the dark, the group crossed over a small worship area in the center of the crypt. On the far side of the room, Tegan recognized a religious statue with a small collection of musical instruments abandoned at its base.

As they approached a stone podium displaying an urn, the candle's flame glowed a bright red, causing John Henry to stop in his tracks. "What is this?" he asked.

Tegan held her breath as she watched the fire radiate in all directions.

"It's here somewhere, look around!" the monk called out.

Beckett and Tegan searched behind the podium and the surrounding area. No sight of the flag. John Henry placed the candle on top of the podium to free his hands...the flame burning a consistent blaze of red. Beckett dusted off the inscription on the podium reading the name, "Ruarcc Dearg. Who's that?"

"It's Ruarcc, the red dragon," the monk replied. "A legend in his own time."

Beckett leaned on the podium and inadvertantly shoved the urn with the dragon's ashes aside. Tegan's reflexes stopped it from dropping to the floor, but now the empty space revealed an opening in the stone podium. Beckett motioned to Tegan for the lantern.

"What is this?" Beckett asked out loud.

Tegan tilted the lantern so the light illuminated the crevice. All three seekers gazed into the opening to see what was there. Cautiously probing the gap with his paw, Beckett felt something soft. Gripping tighter, he realized the soft item surrounded a pole of some kind. His heart jumped. With both paws, Beckett dove in and produced a weathered wooden pole with an ancient silk material wrapped and secured around it. Even in the shadows, they could make out its intricate weaving and beautiful blue tint.

"We found it!" Tegan squealed. "We actually found it!!"

Beckett and John Henry cheered in unison.

"May I present to you, my friends," John Henry said as he smiled, "the famous Flag of Firinn!"

Bowen and Father Ennis ran across the nave of the church and into the recesses of the narthex, hiding near a welcome table draped with a white cloth. The abbot peeked out of the door and to his relief, no soldiers remained on duty there.

To the left, a bonfire raged; smoke billowing high into the clouds. A few soldiers sat on the far side flinging wood pieces into the flames. The fire itself was the ideal distraction the abbot needed to flee without being seen.

"There are caves not far from here," the abbot whispered. "They have provisions for a few days rest. We can escape while the soldiers are busy tending to the flames."

Bowen relaxed his furrowed eyebrows. He couldn't run away now, not when his daughter was so close. He rested his paw on the abbot's shoulder and said, "Go, Father, and be safe. Take one of your armed monks and flee now." He bowed slightly and then lifted his head. "I must stay."

"Ah, Kenna," the abbot smiled and nodded. He understood completely. "In that case, I wish you well."

Father Ennis instructed the monk nearest the entrance to escort him while Bowen walked back into the church. *Where are you, my dear Kenna?* Scurrying out of the nave toward the west stairs, Bowen rushed into the garden, covered by the night. Tiptoeing through the vegetables and sprouting herbs, he crossed to the other side and noticed the door to the library stood ajar. Wondering if his daughter could be inside, he set out to search the room.

But as he approached the door, the hair on the back of his neck stood up. Bowen hesitated and slowly turned around. Afraid of what might be standing there, he held his breath, imagining the worst.

"Father?" A female voice squeaked.

Bowen's mouth dropped as he stared at a shadowy vision of Kenna.

"Kenna?!" he shrieked.

But something was off. Why didn't she run to him?

He blinked hard a few times and noticed movement behind her.

"Kenna?" Bowen asked again.

Then he realized why she acted so solemnly. Out from behind his daughter strutted a very pompous Reginald. She had been captured by Lucien's soldiers.

Rolf burst through the east range dormitory, out of breath, shouting, "Orders have come through!" He panted, swallowing hard to regain control of his breathing. "Half of you report to the west range. The other half," he signaled to the soldiers individually, "we have a hostage situation near the chapter house. Go! Go! Go!" He shouted, pointing to the exit.

The soldiers streamed out of the east range door with glowing lanterns like water flowing through a downturned pipe, each scurrying to their own assignments. With ten soldiers guarding the area closest to the bonfire, Adler anticipated something enormous. The other soldiers had been assigned to free the hostage, which wouldn't be a simple task either.

Rolf chose to monitor the fire and headed to the west range. He sensed doom all around him and his patience finally ran out.

"Where to now?" Beckett asked the monk.

John Henry fumbled with securing the flag under his arm. So he removed the silk material from around the pole and folded it up for easier transport. Tossing the wooden pole on the ground, the monk shoved the folded flag under his arm and instructed the others, "Find the closest staircase. We can unfold this flag on the top floor and expose Reginald for what he really is!"

The three rushed to the south transept and exited into the cloister. With the stairs in sight, they paused to listen to footsteps descending from the staircase beside them. One by one, the fox soldiers assembled at the bottom of the stairway. Tegan and Beckett halted in confusion, but John Henry lowered his head and pushed through the crowd, ascending the stairs one by one. Unable to escape, Tegan and Beckett drew their swords, blood flow quickening in their ears.

One of the soldiers held his paw up and announced, "Don't be afraid. We're merely searching for the hostage."

John Henry stopped halfway up the staircase and turned around to listen.

"Hostage?" Tegan asked, lowering her sword briefly.

"Yes, we were instructed to free the hostage," the soldier replied. He locked eyes with Tegan and asked, "Do you know where the captive is?"

"You're...helping us?" That's all she could think to say. "But aren't you one of *Reginald's* soldiers?"

The soldier stepped close to the sombel and said, "We're on the side of truth." He winked at her and waved to the other fighters to spread out and find the hostage. But a sound echoed from the cloister and footsteps approached.

"Why yes, this soldier is one of Reginald's," a voice rang out as a figure appeared. It was Lucien. "I see you've met Osric." He walked up to the soldier and said, "I'm confused. Why would one of Reginald's soldiers want to free his hostage?"

"Because it's the right thing to do," Osric replied. His soldiers lined up behind him in support of his position.

"Is that right?" Lucien turned to ask his unit this rhetorical question.

But as soon as the question presented itself, Osric leaned over and pushed Lucien as hard as he could. Lucien stumbled back and fell on one of his officers. Enraged, he stood up with his fists ready to swing at anyone in his way. Lucien's soldiers rallied behind him, waiting for an order to attack.

Tegan and Beckett huddled behind Osric while Osric's followers gathered around him. Holding swords of their own, Osric's fighters surged forward and swung their weapons with force. The soldiers under Lucien's command responded with their own intensity, slashing with knives and swords, but ultimately throwing punches and wrestling their opponents to the ground. Tegan and Beckett escaped the brawl and proceeded to the staircase to meet up with John Henry. With any luck, they could still make it to the top floor and unfurl the flag.

Beckett raced up the staircase first and stopped midway to wait for his friend. As Tegan started up the stairs, something caught hold of her leg. She quickly looked around to see what was restraining her, but the grip tightened...and then it pulled! Tegan lost her balance, dropped her sword, and tumbled down the stairs. Hitting the floor, she scrambled for her sword and abruptly sat up. *What just happened?!* She blinked a few times and tried to focus her eyes in the shadows.

"Tegan!" a voice called out. "Are you alright?" Beckett swooped down to help his friend.

As he leaned over to help Tegan up, they both noticed Kenna walking towards them... and then Bowen. But their hearts sank when Tegan and Beckett recognized Reginald strolling behind their friend and her father.

"Oh good," Reginald clapped his paws together and smiled deviously. "Everyone is here!"

CHAPTER 32

On hearing Reginald's voice, John Henry ceased ascending the stairs and paused to listen to the argument below. He needed help unfurling the flag, but that 'help' was being detained by a dictator at the moment. Hiding behind the curve of the staircase, he eavesdropped as best he could.

Kenna, on the other hand, had a lot to say. She fussed with the scratchy rope tied around her wrists and sounded off to anyone that would listen. "You can't do this!" she told them. "You'll be sorry!" and "Let us go!"

Quiet and dejected, Bowen trekked behind her, unsure of what would happen to them both. He had failed. And what could her friends do? No use counting them to free his daughter *or* himself. The odds were simply not in their favor.

Reginald pushed through his group of soldiers to face Osric one on one. Since the leader gathered more soldiers than Osric had, Reginald couldn't help but feel victorious already. The flag was as good as destroyed. He just needed to get his paws on it, and that shouldn't be a problem. He'd use Bowen and the girl as his leverage.

"Osric, you know the consequences of turning traitor, right?" Reginald asked rhetorically.

The soldier endured the leader's antics stone-faced.

Reginald circled around him and stopped abruptly, almost tripping over Tegan, who watched the commotion from behind Osric. "Well, well, who do we have here?" the leader asked and then turned to look at his soldiers.

Tegan thrust her sword in the defensive position, but Reginald just flicked the blade with his digit. Beckett slid next to her with his sword drawn as well.

"Now, now," Reginald pretended to scold and wagged his finger at the two sombels. "We are not going to fight."

"You will give us our friend!" Tegan growled.

"Impudent creature!" Reginald recoiled in disgust. "How dare you tell me what to do!"

Osric's soldiers crowded around the sombels to show their united support.

"Give us the friend, Reginald, and back away," Osric advised. "You're outnumbered here."

Reginald laughed raucously, "Am I? Am I outnumbered?" He turned around surveying his unit of soldiers behind him. "Hardly!" Then he got in Osric's face and pointed at his snout, speaking between clenched teeth, "Even if that were so, *you* are out of place and will be hanged for this!" Straightening his posture, Reginald stepped menacingly toward Tegan and commanded, "Give me the flag!"

Beckett squeezed in between the fox and his friend and shouted, "We don't have the flag!"

"He's right," Tegan nodded confidently. "It's not in our paws."

"Sir," one of Reginald's soldiers nudged him and pointed up the stairs where the monk was listening.

John Henry realized he'd been seen and froze behind the staircase. No way he could outrun them now.

Reginald sauntered over to Kenna, snatching a dagger from another of his soldiers. Clutching her by the tunic, he pointed the dagger at her neck and shouted, "You up there! Do you see this?" He turned Kenna around to face the stairs while she kicked with her feet. "If I do not get the flag, your friend will be the first to suffer!"

"No!!!" Tegan and Bowen squealed.

Kenna swung both paws trying to make contact, but she was entirely too short for Reginald to be concerned. Two soldiers climbed the stairs cautiously and threatened the monk with their swords. Hesitating, John Henry finally stepped out from behind the structure and took his time descending the stairs.

"Please don't hurt them," the monk said as he caught Kenna's eye.

John Henry meant what he said. Keeping the flag wasn't worth losing any lives so he decided to hand it over. Once he landed on the base of the stairs, Reginald dropped Kenna and snatched the flag from the monk's paws.

Kenna rocked on the floor in despair, the moonlight flooding over her tiny frame. Turning her face up, she sobbed, "You shouldn't have done that!! You shouldn't have given him the flag. It was our only hope!!" She crumpled into a ball.

Reginald's lip curled at her response. "Burn it!" he shouted to his soldier.

"What?!" Tegan shrieked.

"Out of my way!" Reginald and his soldiers forced their way past Osric and his unit as Osric still reeled from the confrontation.

Tegan and Beckett scooted around and found Kenna curled up on the floor with her father. Bowen stroked her fur and talked to her softly.

"Is she alright?" Beckett asked Bowen.

Her father nodded. "She will be."

But Tegan noticed something. She knelt close and Kenna lifted her head slightly. Scanning to see if any of Reginald's unit remained, she whispered, "Are they gone?"

"Yes," Tegan replied. "Only Osric and his soldiers remain."

In fact, Osric gathered his group into the corner of the room, out of sight, and immediately proposed new orders.

Kenna rubbed her eyes and dried them with the sleeve of her tunic. "Good," she whispered and sat up cautiously, motioning for her friends to draw near. "I have a plan," she whispered, "but I need your help."

"Are you feeling alright?" Tegan asked.

"Nonsense, I'm fine," Kenna wiped another tear from her eye. "Well," she paused. "I *am* heartbroken over Reginald stealing the flag. But I believe we have a chance to get it back."

Bowen looked perplexed, "How do you suppose we do that?"

"Yeah, what do you have in mind?" Beckett asked suspiciously.

Kenna managed to smile slightly and said, "Don't worry. While I was gone, I made a new friend."

Outside the gate in front of the monastery, Reginald ordered soldiers to stoke the bonfire blazing in the dark of night. At least ten soldiers worked on the flames by adding loads of dry timber to the already overwhelming pillar of fire. With flames crackling and popping, the smell of burning wood and ash wafted around the stone gate and into the entrance of the abbey. Tegan's whiskers tingled and she rubbed her nose with the back of her paw. Kenna motioned for Tegan and Beckett to follow her through the garden and out to the west range wall. They chose a spot near a partial, derelict barrier so they could observe the fire through the crumbled stones without being seen.

Reginald paced around the base of the bonfire barking at soldiers in his unit. From what Reginald knew about local legends, the fire needed to be a certain temperature to destroy the magical flag. And it was almost there. While he impatiently waited, the leader took out his frustration on any one in his way. He knew the sun would be up in a few hours, so he needed to destroy the flag as soon as possible.

"More timber!" he yelled at a soldier. The fox scrambled to find dried wood in the cart and threw a few logs into the flames to appease him.

The leader stomped over to the soldier holding the folded flag and shouted at him. Kenna watched closely as she tried reading Reginald's lips as he gave orders. But to no avail, she had nothing.

"I'm not sure what's going on but we have to stop him," Kenna announced and sprang up on her two petite legs. As the little fox readied her weapon, she faced Tegan and Beckett and instructed, "Go out there and cause some kind of distraction. I'll be back in a bit."

Tegan and Beckett looked at her with skepticism. "A distraction?" Beckett asked. "You don't want us to accompany you?"

Kenna shook her head. "Trust me, I got this," she replied and sprinted out from the behind the wall and into the shadows of the fire.

"Well, what kind of mayhem would you like to cause tonight?" Tegan joked.

"Ha!" Beckett chuckled. "You know me too well, my friend."

Beckett stepped out first and crept along the wall, Tegan right behind him guarding his back. The light from the fire illuminated the monastery and most of the camp where the soldiers had gathered for orders. Many sat and sharpened their swords or talked while eating cheese and bread, waiting for something...anything...interesting to happen. A pair of soldiers in front of Beckett played a game with dice; completely indifferent to what was about to happen.

Beckett and Tegan crawled toward the soldiers and held their breath. What could they possibly do to distract Reginald and his unit except walk out and say hello? Whatever they decided to do would be a suicide mission. And this time, they wouldn't get off so easily.

Should they trust Kenna like she asked? Was it the right thing to do? Tegan hoped so. But as the night wore on, she grew weary and forced herself to focus her thoughts. Beckett had been up for far too long as well. But even with the lack of sleep, both Tegan and Beckett knew they needed to do something to assist their friend.

Tegan stood up and approached a couple of soldiers in the middle of their game; Beckett followed clumsily behind her. "Whatcha doing?" she asked them coyly.

Startled, the soldiers threw up their cards and scrambled for their swords.

"Nope," Beckett said as he pushed his weapon into the back of the soldier closest to him.

Tegan walked further toward Reginald and the bonfire. When the soldiers realized an intruder was among them, they quickly assembled around their leader. Most were merely intrigued by the sombel. With her heart racing, Tegan's eyes darted right and then left, searching for Kenna. *Where was she? How long should I keep this up?* She pretended to be brave, but really, Tegan was petrified.

"Reginald!" Tegan called out in a squeaky voice. "You have one last chance to hand over that flag!" She hoped Reginald didn't see her paws trembling.

"Or what?!" he laughed. The soldiers near him chuckled to appease their leader.

She hesitated, collecting her thoughts for a pithy response. "Or—"

"Or we'll get it ourselves!" A strong, male voice echoed from behind the sombel.

It was Adler!!

Soldiers ran out from the west range dormitory with Adler in the lead. Twenty soldiers in all rushed to back Tegan as she faced off with Reginald.

Panic-stricken, Reginald ordered, "Burn the flag! Burn it now!!!"

And in a race to toss the flag into the fire before Adler and his group caught up with Reginald, the soldier heaved the folded flag over his shoulders and directly toward the flames.

Reginald was as giddy as could be. He stomped his feet and clapped his hands in triumph as he watched the flag go air born. Tegan and Beckett both dropped their swords in disbelief while Adler raised his paw to slow his soldiers from running over the leader.

What... just...happened?

Then, bonfire flames illuminated movement from an area behind the fire. And just before the Flag of Firinn met its demise in the massive blaze, a giant frog appeared on land. Its long pink tongue shot out of its mouth and snatched the flag from landing in the fire, reeling it in like a fishing line.

Everyone watched in disbelief as the frog hopped closer to the flame. The light from the blaze revealed the hero that rescued the flag. And a familiar figure sat on the frog's back, waving at the crowd of soldiers. Tegan smiled because she recognized that figure.

CHAPTER 33

"Kenna!" Tegan shouted and raised her sword. Beckett whooped and hollered in excitement, raising his paws in joyful relief.

Adler and his soldiers cheered; but Reginald screamed in anger. Full of rage, Reginald growled, gritted his teeth, and plunged himself at Tegan. But Adler tackled him before he could jump on the sombel. Pinned to the ground, Reginald wrestled his bodyguard until he finally shook Adler off. He stood up to search for the flag. Desperation completely drove Reginald now and he raced to get his paws on the flag again.

Kenna slid off the frog's back and retrieved the flag from its tongue. Tegan and Beckett rushed to their friend and helped her unfurl it, fold by fold, without letting the flag touch the ground. Kenna and Beckett held one corner high and Tegan hoisted the other corner: the Flag of Firinn finally displayed in all its beauty.

"NOOOOOOOOOOO!!!" Reginald screamed, shaking his fists in the air.

But it was too late.

The brilliant blue flag with a white cross gently flapped in the night's breeze, bursting with color as if it were on fire itself. A bold shaft of light shot straight up into the dark sky, illuminating everything around them. Another stream of light sought Reginald; the urge for truth manifesting in the fibers of the flag that unleashed itself onto the unsuspecting leader.

Reginald stood with that beam of light shining directly on him like a tangible moral spotlight. He covered his eyes with his right arm and waved his other in anguish, eager to stop the blinding brilliance.

Soldiers from both sides of the regime watched in horror as their leader shrieked and wailed in front of them. Reginald's body contorted gruesomely as it shifted its form from a fox to a wolf. Now with longer fur and walking on four legs, Reginald's new ghastly state caused the crowd to shudder. Even Tegan and Beckett were repulsed by the conversion.

But it wasn't over. Reginald changed forms again, this time into a troll with a crooked spine and gnarly teeth. Fragments of hair and knotted fingers frightened the soldiers so much that they gasped at the sight of him. There were other manifestations too: a fairy, a hound, a goblin, and a host of land creatures--each metamorphosis more traumatizing than before. Stunned by the freak show, the soldiers couldn't look away. That is, until someone noticed Bowen waving his arms and standing on the back of the heroic frog.

"Soldiers!" Bowen called out. "Allow me a few minutes of your time." Eyes and ears gravitated from a beastly Reginald writhing on the ground to the pleasant sound of Bowen's voice. The soldiers yearned for an explanation of what they were witnessing and assumed Bowen held the answer, so they tuned in willingly.

"I am Bowen Whitethorne, as most of you know, and I worked for Edwin before this buffoon overthrew him." He pointed to Reginald still wiggling around on the ground like he was enduring electrocution. "I spent the past few weeks collecting evidence that proves this creature before you is NOT who he says he is. As witnessed by the majestic Flag of Firinn, a truth revealing flag, Reginald is not a fox. As you can see, he is a shapeshifter, a wolf shapeshifter at that. I have the ancestral documents here to prove it...cursed from birth into this monster. So let me ask you a question. If Reginald is lying about his identity, what else is he dishonest about? Hmmm?"

Kenna stood near her father and chimed in, "Look!" She pointed to Reginald twisting around on the ground. "You are the eyewitness to many forms of your so-called leader! He's not even a fox! Why do you support this monster?!"

Some soldiers clapped in response while Adler's group cheered, including Rolf and his unit. Bowen continued, "Exactly! Why do you support a creature that does not have your best interest at heart? Someone who lies to obtain your service but serves only himself? Here is the proof," he presented a notebook and piles of papers in which he held above his head for everyone to see.

"Come have a look! Reginald raided the lands to the north strictly for greed, taking all that he wanted, lands inhabited by the Branwell clan of foxes, Reginald's own cousins (he falsely proclaimed)! Yet he told you that these raids were to secure land for a better economy and unrestricted trade. Absolute nonsense!" Bowen shook his head. "Edwin sought a better life for his villagers...for you...so he tasked me to purchase land *legally* that would guarantee strong economic trades with tribes farther north. However, Reginald assigned someone to sabotage those legitimate plans!"

Boos rang out from the audience. Pausing for effect, Bowen pointed to a particular paper and said, "This...this is the agreement from the land agent that never reached my office. I never received it. But guess where I found it? In Reginald's desk AFTER I sent multiple correspondence letters requesting a reply." He nodded to the crowd and then put the papers down. "Let's be honest. Reginald forces your loved ones to serve him, against their better judgment. He treats us like personal slaves when the whole time, Reginald is a fake!"

Reginald remained in a wolf state positioned on his side, twitching as the flag's truth-revealing light continued to illuminate him.

"So, the question is," Bowen offered. "Will you continue to be exploited by this creature? Or will you stand with us...with Adler and his soldiers...to secure Edwin's return to the throne? Will you abandon the bondage of Reginald's reign and uphold this request for his imprisonment?"

Lucien, who had been guarding Reginald, motioned to his soldiers to back away from the leader. As the crowd clapped boisterously in unison, Lucien's group gradually joined in. It now appeared the audience was in total agreement. The crowd cheered and shouted in celebration.

Satisfied with the outcome, Bowen jumped to the ground and hugged Kenna with all his might. He was so proud of her!

"How did you make this happen?" he asked his daughter.

"I searched for you, father, but I couldn't find you," Kenna's eyes glistened. "And when I thought I couldn't go on, Rana found me." She patted the frog on the nose. "She knew you were my father and offered to help me. She says you saved her life once."

Bowen looked into Rana's giant eyes, "I guess I did."

"We do not forget sacrifices like that, my friend," Rana replied.

Bowen smiled, "Looks like we're even now."

Rana chuckled. "I'll keep an eye on you though. You'll see." She hopped away with two other frogs and disappeared into the shadows.

Beckett and Tegan folded the flag back into an easy-to-carry item. Once tucked away, the bold shaft of light retracted from the sky and returned from Reginald's body. The Flag of Firinn had once again revealed the truths lurking in the darkness. Now, the only source of illumination was the weakening bonfire thirsting for fuel.

"Arrest him!" Adler's voice resonated above the chaos.

Soldiers, eager to please Adler, filed in unison and approached Reginald in his wolf form. While they wrangled the creature into shackles, Adler observed with disbelief. He never thought he'd be here to witness such a monumental event.

"Sir," Lucien sidled up next to him. "I...I'm not sure what to say...but--"

"Lucien, you're a capable soldier. You followed orders and I respect that," Adler said and stuck out his paw.

Lucien smiled and shook it gladly. They were now square.

Adler watched Lucien join the other soldiers as they marched Reginald to the empty wagon and secured him to the structure with tight rope. Four soldiers hopped in the cart with him while the others surrounded the wagon for additional security.

But there was one more issue Adler had to resolve. And that involved Bin.

Approaching the group of soldiers surrounding the wagon, Adler spotted Bin knotting a rope to the cart's infrastructure. He tapped Bin on the shoulder and said, "Come with me."

Bin followed Adler a few steps away from the cart, uncertain of Adler's motive.

"Do you remember the evening I fell sick?" Adler asked.

Bin fumbled with his tunic; his eyes focused on the ground. "Yes," he replied.

"Turns out, I was poisoned. Do you know anything about that?"

"No, of course not!" Bin snapped. "Why would I know anything about a poisoning?"

"Because you were seen in my house while I was working...the same day I got sick."

Bin didn't speak, his lips clamped shut.

Adler continued, "I have a reliable source that says you entered my house after I left for work that day. That same source said you exited only after a few minutes inside. Is that true?"

"I...I...," Bin couldn't think of what to say. But Adler's eyes stared deep into his soul until he finally relented. "Yes, alright! I put something in the water pitcher you drank from. I didn't want to. But Reginald said if I didn't, he'd do something horrible to my family!" He dropped to the ground. "I'm sorry! I'm sorry!"

"I see," Adler stepped away from the cowering Bin. Instead, he turned his attention to the soldiers behind him and ordered, "Take Reginald away! Now!"

With the demise of Reginald, Adler's robust frame finally relaxed. His shoulders no longer felt tense and sore and the shadows darkening his mind evaporated instantly. He even felt a tiny spark of joy for the first time in months. Joy that maybe things could go back to the way they were. But even if they didn't, maybe, just maybe, he could nurture hope for a fulfilling future for his village...and for himself.

Out of the corner of his eye, Adler spotted Tegan and Beckett embracing Kenna. The three friends danced around each other gleefully, unaware of the freedom they just restored to a weary community constrained with tyranny. Beckett picked up Kenna and twirled her around in his arms while she giggled uncontrollably. Bowen and Kenna danced playfully; Bowen bowed and Tegan curtsied. Then Beckett, Tegan, and Kenna held paws and danced a little reel together. Bowen clapped out the beat.

Smiling to himself, Adler shook his head; his heart was full. He sprinted towards the happy group and did something else he never thought he'd do. He joined in and danced.

The End

EPILOGUE

All the adrenaline from the celebrations allowed Tegan, Beckett, Kenna, and Bowen to hike back to Chipping Farms without stopping once. As the sun crept over the horizon and dawn came out to play, the group caught sight of Chipping Farms. And though this was Kenna's home, Tegan and Beckett were more than pleased to hang out a few days before returning to their own village of Haven.

Adler asked Rolf to gather the soldiers and head home to rest. Adler, himself, was exhausted but looked forward to seeing Edwin's face when he returned to his post. More than anything though, he wished to see Edwin resume his leadership in his little community.

Word spread faster than the travelers could walk. Shop owners and townsfolk lined the main street cheering for their heroes as they returned to the village. Kenna had never felt such joy and reveled in the happiness of the moment. Tegan and Beckett strolled beside her elated.

Adler arrived in Chipping Farms before the soldiers did since they had a prisoner in tow. At first, he thought he was hallucinating. But as he focused his eyes, Adler noticed a figure outside the Boar's Nest pub that was drawing quite the crowd. *What local celebrity is this?* The closer he walked, the more he realized who it was.

"Edwin?!" Adler shouted.

Edwin looked over the crowd of folks gathering around him and waved. Somehow, the rumor of Reginald's defeat reached the inhabitants of Chipping Farms, and someone freed their former leader.

"Come with me," Edwin said to Adler as he pushed his way through the crowd. "I want to address the townsfolk." Edwin made his way to a pavilion near a makeshift stage to shade himself from the midday sun.

"Friends!" Edwin called out. Holding up his paws, he waited until everyone's attention focused on him. "I would like to recognize a few individuals and thank them for their courageous assistance in the capture of a dreadful villain."

Edwin motioned to Tegan, Beckett, and Kenna in the audience to join him. As they made their way to the pavilion, he continued speaking, "I governed this town for over thirty years..." the audience cheered, "...until a vile creature by the name of Reginald came to wreak havoc in our village." The townsfolk booed and groaned at the mention of Reginald's name. Edwin let a few minutes pass before silencing the crowd again. "In our darkest hour, these three friends...Tegan," she bowed slightly, "Beckett..." he raised his sword, "and our very own, Kenna," she jumped up and down, "risked their lives to bring justice and freedom to ours.

Let's show them our appreciation!" The audience roared with clapping and shouting.

"I would also like to address a question that everyone is asking, which is, will I assume the throne again?" Edwin paused and fell silent. Taking a deep breath, he said gently, "No. No, I will not." Everyone gasped at the same time, confused by Edwin's admission.

Hearing this statement, Adler forced his way through the crowd to stand near Edwin. "Sir, are you sure?" Adler asked him, bewildered by his remark. "We fought so you could govern again."

Patting Adler on the shoulder, Edwin smiled and turned to the audience with Adler beside him. "While I was imprisoned, I had lots of time to think about the future of this community. And I believe this town needs a fresh start with new direction. That's why I wish to nominate someone very special for the position."

The audience fell into silence.

Edwin cleared his throat, "Adler, would you be willing to pick up where I left off?"

"Wha...what do you mean?" he stammered. "Me?!"

"Yes, I believe you're the fresh start we need," Edwin replied. "What do you say?"

Adler couldn't speak.

"Friends of Chipping Farms," Edwin turned to his audience. "What do you say?"

The town erupted in cheering and clapping as loud as they could.

"There, you see?" Edwin laughed a little. "You will make a great leader, Adler. Have faith in your intuition."

At this point, all Adler could do was nod his head. Overwhelmed with emotion, he hugged Edwin as tight as he could and said, "Thank you, sir, I will make you *and* these folks proud, I promise!"

Edwin smiled. Yes, indeed he would.

Afterword

For more information on the Chronicles of Fellnore adventures, please visit jenniferwhiddon.com.